THE
Miner's
LADY

Books by Tracie Peterson

www.traciepeterson.com

House of Secrets
A Slender Thread
Where My Heart Belongs

LAND OF SHINING WATER
The Icecutter's Daughter
The Quarryman's Bride
The Miner's Lady

LAND OF THE LONE STAR
Chasing the Sun
Touching the Sky
Taming the Wind

BRIDAL VEIL ISLAND★
To Have and To Hold
To Love and Cherish
To Honor and Trust

SONG OF ALASKA
Dawn's Prelude
Morning's Refrain
Twilight's Serenade

STRIKING A MATCH
Embers of Love
Hearts Aglow
Hope Rekindled

ALASKAN QUEST
Summer of the Midnight Sun
Under the Northern Lights
Whispers of Winter
Alaskan Quest (3 in 1)

BRIDES OF GALLATÍN COUNTY
A Promise to Believe In
A Love to Last Forever
A Dream to Call My Own

THE BROADMOOR LEGACY★
A Daughter's Inheritance
An Unexpected Love
A Surrendered Heart

BELLS OF LOWELL★
Daughter of the Loom
A Fragile Design
These Tangled Threads

LIGHTS OF LOWELL★
A Tapestry of Hope
A Love Woven True
The Pattern of Her Heart

DESERT ROSES
Shadows of the Canyon
Across the Years
Beneath a Harvest Sky

HEIRS OF MONTANA
Land of My Heart
The Coming Storm
To Dream Anew
The Hope Within

LADIES OF LIBERTY
A Lady of High Regard
A Lady of Hidden Intent
A Lady of Secret Devotion

RIBBONS OF STEEL★★
Distant Dreams
A Hope Beyond
A Promise for Tomorrow

RIBBONS WEST★★
Westward the Dream
Separate Roads
Ties That Bind

WESTWARD CHRONICLES
A Shelter of Hope
Hidden in a Whisper
A Veiled Reflection

YUKON QUEST
Treasures of the North
Ashes and Ice
Rivers of Gold

★*with Judith Miller* ★★*with Judith Pella*

THE
Miner's
LADY

TRACIE
PETERSON

WITHDRAWN

BETHANYHOUSE
a division of Baker Publishing Group
Minneapolis, Minnesota

© 2013 by Tracie Peterson

Published by Bethany House Publishers
11400 Hampshire Avenue South
Bloomington, Minnesota 55438
www.bethanyhouse.com

Bethany House Publishers is a division of
Baker Publishing Group, Grand Rapids, Michigan

Printed in the United States of America

Library of Congress Cataloging-in-Publication Data
Peterson, Tracie.
    The miner's lady / Tracie Peterson.
       pages cm. — (Land of Shining Water)
    Summary: "When Chantel's sister falls in love with a sworn enemy in their 1890s iron-mining community, will Chantel's attempts to aid the couple result in a romance of her own?"—Provided by publisher.
      ISBN 978-0-7642-1146-1 (cloth : alk. paper)
      ISBN 978-0-7642-0621-4 (pbk.)
      ISBN 978-0-7642-1147-8 (large-print pbk.)
    1. Families—Minnesota—Fiction. 2. Minnesota—History—19th century—Fiction. I. Title.
PS3566.E7717M56 2013
813'.54—dc23   2013016389

Scripture quotations are from the King James Version of the Bible.

Cover design by Brand Navigation

13 14 15 16 17 18 19   7 6 5 4 3 2 1

To Chantel Karch

You are an awesome young woman.
Always look to Jesus!

Chapter 1

"A Calarco?" Chantelly Panetta looked at her sister in disbelief. "You want to marry a Calarco?"

Seventeen-year-old Isabella shook her head. "Not just any Calarco. Orlando Calarco. We're in love, Chantel. I can't tell my heart not to love him. You haven't been here this last year, so you don't know him like I do."

"I may have been gone, but I do know that the Calarcos and Panettas have been at odds for over fifty years."

Isabella flipped long honey-brown hair over her shoulder. "The feud means nothing to Orlando and me."

Scrutinizing her younger sister's womanly figure and full lips, Chantel shook her head. Isabella looked years beyond her seventeen. She seemed just a child when Chantel had left, but now she spoke of marriage and love.

"Have you told Mama or Papa?"

"No, of course not." Isabella threw herself

across the bed. "I wanted to wait until you returned from Italy."

Chantel sat on the edge of her sister's bed and carefully considered her words. "You know they'll never approve."

Isabella reared up like a cat about to attack its prey. "They'll have to. Orlando and I plan to marry. This feud is ridiculous, and I don't care if I'm disowned. I love him."

"But how did this happen?" Chantel questioned. "Surely Marco and Alfredo would never allow you to be alone with a Calarco."

"Our brothers can't be everywhere. They went with Papa to the iron mine every day to work, and sometimes I slipped away—alone— to meet Orlando there."

"You went to the mine?" Chantel realized she was nearly shouting, and hurried to lower her voice. "You can't be serious. You know we're not supposed to go unless we're with other women—it's dangerous there. The men have no reason to treat you like a lady if you show up at the mines. Only a loose woman would do that."

"You know full well there are exceptions, even in our family. I seem to remember more than once when we delivered food to our men- folk. Anyway, it's not like I made a public spectacle," Isabella said, easing into a sitting position. "I kept myself hidden and disguised.

Only Orlando saw me. Even his brother and father have no idea."

The very thought of her sister risking her innocence, even her life, to visit a man she knew her parents would never approve of, gave Chantel a shiver. If spending the last year in Italy visiting their grandparents had taught Chantel anything, it was just how possessive family could be. In the old country young ladies didn't so much as speak to a man without their father's permission.

"Stop frowning like that," Isabella declared. "It's not the end of the world. You'll see. Orlando and I figure this is exactly what's needed to put an end to the feud."

Chantel wished she could be as sure as her sister. "You know that this problem between the families won't go away easily. It's more likely that your marriage would only cause further division."

"Nonsense." Isabella twisted a long strand of hair between her fingers. "If we're married and produce children, they will belong to both the Calarco and the Panetta families. Think of it, Chantel. It's really an answer to Mama's prayers."

Their mother had long wished for an end to the ongoing feud. As Chantel understood it, the entire affair had occurred in Italy and was over some dispute that no one would speak about. Frankly, Chantel wondered if anyone even knew for sure what had started the matter. She did know that it ended in the killing of a mule, which threatened the livelihood of the Calarco family. Mama said the mule's death was an accident, but that because there was already bad blood between the two families, it could not be forgiven or seen as anything but a purposeful attack. Chantel had tried to get her Nonna Panetta to speak on the matter, but her grandmother was even more closemouthed about it than Mama.

With a sigh, Chantel forced a smile. "Well, it's good to see you again, nevertheless. I can't say the same for this filthy, depressing town. The past year in Italy has only made me realize just how awful this place truly is."

"It's a mining town. You know what Mama says about them." Isabella scooted to the edge of the bed.

"It's the last stop before the gates of hell," the girls said in unison and laughed.

Chantel looked around the room she'd shared with her sister since the family had moved to Ely three years earlier. Her father's years of iron mining work had taken them from back east to Michigan, and now to Minnesota. They had lived for a short time in Duluth near their mother's sister Marilla. But even that larger town failed to shine in light of Chantel's memories of the Italian countryside.

"So was your trip as wonderful as your letters implied?" Isabella questioned. "I'd always looked forward to going there myself, but now I suppose I won't have the opportunity. At least not for a time."

Their parents had a tradition of sending each of their children to stay with their grandparents in Italy. Upon turning twenty-one, the siblings, if unmarried, would leave home for a year to learn about the old country and their ancestors. Marco and Alfredo had each had their turn, and now Chantel had experienced the same.

"It is truly unlike anything I could have anticipated," she said. "Nonna and Nonno have such a beautiful home," Chantel continued. "And the scenery is incredible. You can see the vineyards and orchards for miles and miles. And Nonna and I had great fun tatting and making bobbin lace. I brought a crateful home with me and made more on the ship."

"You wrote about the family dinners," Isabella interjected with a wistful look on her face. "They sounded so wonderful. All those people and the music and dancing."

"They were," Chantel admitted. "Every Sunday relatives would come from all over, and we would feast. Nonna's tables would practically bow from the weight of the food. Oh, and such food! You think Mama is a good cook; well, let me tell you there's nothing quite so wonderful as Nonna's dishes made with fresh ingredients." She put her thumb and middle finger to her lips and kissed. "With all that good food, it was hard to wait for the prayer. Nonno would practically preach a sermon when he stood to bless the food. It was amazing. His faith in God is so strong."

"Yet he allows for this stupid feud between families. And all because some mule was accidentally killed," Isabella muttered. "I don't understand how that's godly."

Chantel shook her head. "No, I don't suppose it is. Forgiveness is something that people in the old country seem reluctant to give, and I don't know why it should follow us here. Old traditions die hard, I suppose, but America is a land for new traditions and opportunities. It seems to me that such grudges should be set aside."

Just then their mother burst into the room carrying a huge stack of clean linens. *"Buon giorno."*

"Good morning, Mama." Chantel crossed the room to help her mother with the laundry.

"It's so good to have you home," their mother said, beaming from ear to ear. She rattled away in rapid-fire Italian, proclaiming how much she'd missed Chantel and how empty the house seemed without her, before slowing down to return again to English. "Your papa is so happy you have returned."

Chantel placed the linens atop an empty chair. "I'm glad to see you all again, but I cannot say I'm happy to be in Ely."

"E-lee is no so beautiful as Italy," her mother declared. Although she was half French, her accent was decidedly Italian.

"No, it's not," Chantel agreed.

The mining town sported twenty-six saloons, compared to only five churches. There were a variety of other businesses: general stores, banks, doctors and lawyers, jewelers and dressmakers. But it was what happened in the backrooms and upper floors of the saloons and brothels that was most distressing. Prostitution, gambling, and all manner of vice went on, and there were almost daily reports of someone having been killed in a fight or of drinking themselves into such a stupor that they fell on the railroad tracks to be run over by the morning freight. The latter was so common, in fact, that the marshal had taken to checking the tracks before the train was due in. Of course, it was rumored that many of the bodies discovered on the tracks had been placed there purposefully to disguise murders.

Mother bustled around the room, tidying things as she went. "And did you find a special boy?" Mother asked. "An *Italiano* boy?"

There had been a bevy of nice-looking young men who paid court to Chantel, but none that drew more than momentary interest. Chantel knew her mother had hoped that romance would blossom and that perhaps her daughter would return to America a married woman bringing yet another Italian to settle the country.

"No, no one special, Mama."

"Oh, it's too bad. You're such a pretty girl. You need to find a good husband." Mama stopped cleaning and looked at her daughters. "But God will provide. *Non è forse così?*"

"Yes, it is so, Mama." *Just don't go trying to do God's work for Him.* Chantel could tell by the look on her mother's face that the idea had crossed her mind.

Isabella forced herself up off the bed. "I'm going to take Chantel to the new dressmaker's shop, Mama. I want to introduce her to the Miller sisters."

"*Sì*, and show her the new meat market," their mother suggested. "Such good meats to be had there. They make a wonderful sausage."

Mama loved her sausage. Chantel smiled and moved toward the door. "Let me get my walking shoes on."

"Better to wear boots," Mama countered. "The rains, they make the streets like-a mud pit."

The girls nodded in unison and went to the mud porch to retrieve their boots. Chantel took up a woolen shawl and wrapped it around her head and shoulders. The damp October air chilled her to the bone as they began the walk. For several blocks Chantel said nothing.

It looked a little better than it did last year. At least they'd removed a good many tree stumps. Many of the trees that had been cut down for mining use had once littered the area with stumps. But now in their place new buildings were erected. It was a vast improvement.

"It's colder than I expected."

Isabella shrugged, doing up the buttons on her brown wool coat. "It is nearly November. In another week or two we'll be ice skating on the lake."

Chantel nodded. "I suppose it's to be expected, but even so, I shall miss the summer warmth of Italy."

"Winter must come. It can't stay summer forever," her sister replied. "Summer here is quite lovely, as you must remember."

She did. Summer picnics at Lake Shagawa and picking blueberries on some of the small lake islands.

"You've missed a great deal around here."

Isabella waved her hand toward the town's buildings. "The Reverend Freeman left his position at the Presbyterian Church to resume his studies in Chicago. Oh, and we have a brand-new church building for St. Anthony's. Soon we'll be holding services there instead of the boardinghouse. Father Buh raised the money and oversaw the building. It's going to be quite wonderful."

Chantel considered many of the new structures. "It's almost like the town grew up overnight."

Isabella continued. "We have a new drugstore and a new hotel. The Oliver Hotel is quite modern and is said to be just the thing to bring in tourists for fishing and hunting."

"I'm impressed, I must admit," Chantel declared. "I even heard some men talking on the train about ice fishing this winter. Of course there were also a fair number of men who were coming to find work."

"Papa says that with the new iron mines being established, we'll soon have hundreds more people. Maybe thousands."

"As if the Chandler Mine wasn't enough of a destruction to this land."

Isabella didn't seem to hear. "Oh, remember Sara Norman? Well, she married Mr. Ellefesen. You know he's a member of the Ely Fire Department, so the other firemen went together and gave them a sofa and armchair. Mama said it came all the way from Chicago."

"No doubt that cost a pretty penny," Chantel replied. She looked around the town, trying to imagine spending the rest of her life here. She doubted that she could be happy even with a new sofa and armchair from Chicago. The dirt and noise, damp cold and unpainted buildings made her long for Italy. As homesick as she'd been at times while abroad, Chantel suddenly felt completely displaced.

"You should have been here for the Firemen's Ball," Isabella continued, not noticing her sister's mood. "The entire department ordered special suits and looked quite grand. They wore black pants, red flannel shirts with blue collar, cuffs, and breastplate. Whiteside Hall has never held such a spectacular affair. We all dressed in our finest and went to celebrate."

"Celebrate what?" Chantel asked.

Isabella threw her a look of amusement. "Something different. We were just happy to have a diversion. We danced and ate and made merry."

Chantel could well understand that. As they crossed Chapman Street, Chantel felt her boots sink in the muddy ruts of the road. She hurried to regain solid footing on the boardwalk, carrying what felt like five pounds of muck on each foot. Wiping her boots against the edge of the walk, she shook her head.

Isabella was unfazed. "See over there? We've been told that a fruit and candy store will open there in January. I, for one, am quite excited."

Chantel smiled, knowing her sister's penchant for sweets. "Nonna taught me to make some wonderful family recipes, including some candy that Mama used to make when she was a little girl." To her surprise Isabella gave her an impromptu hug.

"It's so good to have you home. I missed you so much."

Chantel returned the embrace. "I'm glad to be home." It wasn't exactly a lie, but neither was it the truth.

Chapter 2

"It's got to stop," Dante Calarco told his younger brother Orlando. "You can't go on sneaking around to meet that Panetta tramp."

"She's no tramp!" Orlando shot up to stand nose to nose with his brother. "I love her and intend for her to be my wife."

Dante rolled his eyes heavenward. "You're nineteen and have no business even thinking about marriage. You've only been working the mine for the last year. You have nothing to your name and certainly cannot afford a wife. Not only that, but you know our father will never allow you to marry a Panetta. And for good reason."

"Reason, good or otherwise, never has figured into this ridiculous feud." Orlando pushed back thick black hair and reclaimed his seat at the dining room table. "Am I the only one bothered by the fact that our families are at odds over a stupid mule? I mean, think about it. Two families hate each other because a mule accidentally got killed."

"Our grandfather apparently didn't believe

it to be an accident. Besides, you know as well as I do there were already problems between the two families."

"But I don't have any problem with the Panettas, and I don't see why I should."

Dante wanted very much to get his brother to acknowledge the truth. "It matters little whether or not you agree with the two families being at odds. The fact is, Father believes in loyalty to our family."

"What about loyalty to his sons? What about learning to live in peace like the Good Book says? What about that?"

Dante had never been much for religious nonsense. He believed in God. He even believed that He had a Son named Jesus who died on the cross in some sort of sacrifice for all of mankind. What he didn't believe in was the nonsense that took place in the church. As far as he'd ever been able to tell, church was useful for one thing and one thing only: heaping guilt upon the weak-minded.

"I'm not going to argue with you about religion. I'm not even going to challenge you on the whole concept of trying to be at peace in a world filled with warring people." Dante took the seat opposite his brother while their grandmother scurried around to put supper on the table. "But you know how our father feels regarding family. Family is everything.

For you to sneak around with her is like putting a knife in his back."

"That has never been my intention." Orlando met Dante's gaze. "You know that. I love my family, but I love Isabella, too."

"Ora ragazzi," said their Nonna Barbato in her native Italian. *"Il papá sarà qui presto."*

Dante squared his shoulders. She was right. Their father would be here any moment, and it wouldn't serve either of them well to have him question their discussion.

"I'm sorry, Orlando. I'm sorry that you love her, and I'm sorry that nothing can ever come of it."

Just then they could hear their father scraping his boots outside the back door. Both young men straightened in their chairs as if they were boys awaiting parental inspection. Nonna put the last of the food on the table and took her seat.

Vittorio Calarco rubbed his hands together and entered the kitchen. "The wind has a bite to it. Hopefully we'll get a hard freeze and that muck they call a road will harden up."

Dante couldn't help but smile. His father stood bootless in his dirty socks. He took orders from the mining captain and no one else . . . except his mother-in-law. Nonna Barbato insisted the men take their boots off before entering the house, and even Vittorio Calarco was obedient. Of course, Dante knew his father had been dependent upon the older woman since losing his wife in childbirth. Nonna had been newly widowed, and the trip to America to care for her daughter's newborn and eight-year-old sons gave her a new lease on life. Dante's father had struggled to find the money for such a trip, but with the help of family he had managed to bring Nonna to America only weeks after he'd buried Dante and Orlando's mother.

Their father took a seat at the table and reached for his bowl of *zuppa de zucca*, his favorite pumpkin soup. Nonna waggled a finger and admonished him. "First we pray," she said as she always did.

His father gave a nod. When Nonna said they would pray first, they prayed.

Nonna offered grace for the food, then poured her heart out in prayers for the family. She asked forgiveness for each of her men, pleading with God for their protection. Dante knew this never boded well with his father, but he found it somewhat comforting. Even if he wasn't given to praying himself, it was nice to know that someone else was offering up prayers on his behalf.

"Amen," said Nonna.

Dante and Orlando murmured the word in return, but their father only grunted and reached again for the soup.

Supper was always a time for Nonna to share the latest information from family or the ongoing affairs of neighbors. Dante's father would chime in on politics and matters of the town, while Dante and Orlando picked up the conversation when they had something to add. And always, it was in Italian. Nonna could speak English, though not well. She considered it a vulgar language. It was a rare occasion when Anna Teresa Barbato spoke what she called "that American garble."

Ely was a town of many nationalities, but the far east side was predominantly settled by Slavic-Austrians and Italians. Nonna knew every man, woman, and child in their neighborhood and thought it her duty to keep up on the details of their lives. Often the women washed clothes or sewed together, and while they did they told news from the old country or spoke of problems with their families. Nonna had become something of a matriarch among the women, and she held the position with the authority of a queen.

"The Dicellos have a new baby," Nonna announced. "A fat, healthy boy." She extended a rose-colored glass serving bowl to

Dante. "You should marry and have children, Dante. Goodness, but you are twenty-seven years old. Well past the time a man should settle down. You need children of your own to carry on the family name."

Orlando opened his mouth as if to comment on that, but Dante quickly silenced him. "Nonna, you always said that marriage was the hardest work a man and woman would ever do. Frankly, the mine exhausts me. I don't have the energy to marry."

She laughed and motioned to the bowl he'd just taken. "Eat up and you'll have energy aplenty. This is your favorite *agnolotti*."

Dante smiled and began to spoon himself a healthy portion of the ravioli. Each little pasta pocket was filled with tender roast beef and seasoned vegetables. His grandmother had such a way with the dish that he had to admit he'd rather eat extra helpings of this than have dessert.

The table talk continued with Nonna telling of her visit to the meat market with several other women. She spoke of new families moving to the area to accommodate the growing mine industry. At this Dante's father joined in.

"Papers have already been drawn up to make Ely an incorporated town," he told them. "Once this officially happens, we will see many more changes. There are plans to put in sewer and water lines, as well as better streets."

"That is good," Nonna said, nodding. She tore off a piece of bread from a large round loaf. "The streets here are terrible."

Dante paid only a token interest to the conversation. His mind was focused on Orlando's interest in Isabella Panetta. Dante had had suspicions for some time that his brother was sneaking off to meet with a young lady, but never could he have imagined it would be a Panetta.

The boy was insane. He had to know the relationship would never be allowed, and if Orlando insisted, their father would simply disown him. And then what? Would the two marry and move in with her family? The shame of it would cause their father no end of grief, and that in turn would trickle down to affect Dante and Nonna.

As he ate, Dante tried to reason how he might best deal with the situation. There was always the chance that Isabella's family didn't realize what was going on. Perhaps if Dante cornered one of her brothers at the mine, he could explain what was happening and get their help on the matter. Of course, it wasn't likely that a Panetta would give him the time of day, much less listen to him.

"They say the Pioneer Mine will deliver the same quality Bessemer ore that the Chandler has," Dante heard his father declare. "And there are other mines opening, as well. If they're all Bessemer quality, we'll be making the owners quite wealthy."

Bessemer ore held the richest iron content. The problem with some iron ore was a high percentage of phosphorus. Henry Bessemer, an English iron master, had created a way to burn away the impurities from iron to make steel. Because of this wondrous contribution, the finest ore had been named after him.

One benefit of the Chandler Mine and the rich Bessemer ore was that it didn't require a great deal of processing in order to make it useful. Not only that, but the vein of ore had endured a massive folding during its creation. This resulted in the ore breaking naturally into pieces very nearly the right size for the mills, which eliminated the need to run it through a crusher first. This, along with the fact that the ore was readily available and not at all laborious to mine—at least not in the early pit mining years—proved very valuable to the stockholders. It was said that the mine paid out $100,000 a month net profit. Of course, Dante found that hard to believe, but if the growth of the city and digging of new mines was any indication, it must be true.

"Dr. Shipman intends to see those terrible houses of ill repute closed," Nonna declared. "He makes a good village president, even if he isn't Italiano."

"He is a good man," Father replied, "but if they close down the brothels, how will they fund the town?" He gave a laugh. "It's only the fines brought in by the marshal that pay Ely's bills." It was a well-known fact that the marshal visited the brothels on a monthly basis to "arrest" the madams. They simply paid a large fine and returned to business. It served to give the pretense of law and order, make money for the town, and keep the miners happy.

"Bah!" Nonna said, waving him away with her hand. "We will be a better city without them."

"Well, if they have their way and incorporate the mines into the city limits," Father said, reaching for the bread, "they will have money enough. The state may receive a penny a ton on what is shipped out of the mines, but the city gets nothing. That will change soon enough if the incorporation goes through."

Dante tired of the politics and again found himself thinking about Orlando's situation. His brother had crossed a line that would not easily be forgotten if their father learned the truth. So the trick would be to find a way to get Orlando back on the right side before he could be found out.

I could just threaten him, Dante thought, then very nearly smiled. His brother was not easily intimidated. They had endured many a brawl in their younger days, and Orlando could put up quite a fight. He was strong and muscular like Dante, although he was shorter by two or three inches. If anything, that only served to give his brother an advantage in maneuvering around Dante's attacks.

I could bribe him to let her go. But Dante knew that wouldn't work, either. He knew his brother couldn't be bought off. Not when he fancied himself truly in love.

He was still lost in thought well after Nonna had served dessert. When his brother and father got up from the table, Dante continued to pick at the pear tart his grandmother had put in front of him.

"You no like?" she asked in English.

Dante, surprised by her change of language, glanced around the room. Seeing his father and brother gone, he shook his head. "I'm just worried about Orlando."

Nonna waggled a finger at him. "You worry too much." She switched back into Italian and began clearing the table. "Your brother will be fine."

Lowering his voice to a whisper, Dante replied, "Not if he keeps thinking with his heart instead of his head."

His grandmother straightened for a moment and shook her head. "Ah, Dante, the heart it cannot be controlled by anyone save God. It will choose whom it will choose. It's *amore*."

"It's dangerous," Dante said, getting to his feet. "And it's foolish."

At seven the next morning, Dante, Orlando, and their father were back to work at the mine. The shifts ran in ten-hour segments, two shifts a day, every day but Sunday. Vittorio Calarco and his sons were contract miners. They handled dynamite and nitroglycerin—blasting holes in the iron ore to sink shafts or create the horizontal drifts. This dangerous job allowed them additional pay, for it required steady hands and even stronger nerves. Vittorio Calarco preferred it this way. He answered only to the mine's captain, as they called the big boss, but paid nominal heed to the instructions of the shift foreman. Luckily Dante's father liked the man whom he called "Mr. Foreman" in a sort of mock salute to the position.

What Dante's father did not like was the fact that Panettas worked in the same mine. Dante fervently hoped that their enemies might transfer to another mine. At best they were often working in one of the other four shafts. But even with five separate areas to work, their paths would cross and words would be exchanged. The latter was usually only between the two patriarchs, while their sons silently observed, watching and waiting lest one man or the other decide to do more than talk.

As Father stood instructing Orlando, Dante couldn't help but study his brother. He seemed so carefree, so unconcerned with his deception. Would he truly risk being ostracized from the family for the love of a woman?

"Are you going to help us or just stand there?"

Dante met his father's stern expression. "Tell me what you want done."

"We will drill blasting points here and here," his father said, pointing. The iron deposits were removed in a stoping system that was well suited to the area's formations. Segments of ore were taken out parallel to the drift or horizontal shaft, creating a sort of stepped appearance at the top of the stope— the ever-expanding hollow created by the mining work. Underground iron miners always tried to let gravity work for them, using the overhand or upward method. This allowed the ore to fall to the bottom of the stope, and from there it would be scraped into chutes and loaded into the ore cars located below the floor of the work area. It was tedious work, often referred to as caving. Eventually all of the ore would be mined in that area, and the Calarcos would blast the surrounding rock to fill in the stope. The process went on and on in order to recover as much ore as possible.

Dante tried not to give much thought to the dangers they faced, though they were many. Walls of the stopes often collapsed without warning. Blasts could go off prematurely, although the Calarcos had not been victim of that due to their father's vigilant care in everything he did. Of course, just because they were careful didn't mean everyone else was. There were plenty of new muckers who had no idea of the risk.

Fires were always feared in the mines, but it was often accidents with the machinery or tram cars that caused injury and death. Dante had seen men lose fingers and feet because of being less than aware of their surroundings.

"This is no place to daydream," his father admonished.

A knot of fear and embarrassment sat in

his gut at his father's words. He knew better. "Sorry," Dante said.

Father handed him a twisted roll of fuse. "Sorry will get you blown up, son."

Dante met his brother's curious gaze. With a quick grin Orlando went back to work, mindless of what was truly bothering his older brother. They would simply have to settle this later, Dante determined, and pushed the problem to the back of his mind.

Chapter 3

"Mama, we're going to Cormack's store to pick up that thread you wanted to make lace," Isabella told their mother. "Do you need anything else?"

Chantel pulled on a wool coat she had just unpacked from the attic storage the night before. The fit was snug. The coat had been handed down to her long before her figure had filled out, and it was well past time to replace it with something new. Maybe she would sell some of her lace and order a new coat.

"We need more sugar," Mama said, looking to the ceiling as though there were a list written there. "And see if we can purchase more eggs from Stanley's boardinghouse. They have the best eggs."

"Sí, Mama." Isabella kissed her mother on the cheek. "And do you want me to put it on account or take money?"

Mama went to the cupboard and pulled down a tin marked *Tea*. Chantel knew her parents, like most immigrants, didn't trust the banks. They hid their money around the house rather than trust it to strangers. The older woman pulled out some change from the tin and handed it to Isabella. "Pay for the eggs and charge the sugar to our account. Tell Mr. Cormack to charge the silk thread, as well. Tell him we'll come tomorrow after your papa gets paid and settle the account."

With that, the girls exited the house. Chantel secured a wool bonnet atop her carefully pinned brown hair. The temperatures had dropped again.

"At least the roads are hard now," Isabella said, tying her own bonnet.

Chantel waited until they were a bit down the road to question her sister. "What are you up to, Isabella? You seemed very eager to run this errand."

Isabella threw Chantel a grin. "I am going to meet Orlando behind the store. Being how it's Friday, Orlando's father will have to remain at the mine for a meeting, but Orlando and Dante will leave their shift early. They always stop in town for their Nonna on their way home. I want you to come along in case I need you to keep Dante occupied so that Orlando can slip away to meet me."

Chantel frowned. She'd not seen the older Calarco son in some time. "What do you mean, 'keep him occupied'?"

"You know, talk to him. Goodness, Chantel,

you would think you'd never had a conversation with a young man."

"And if he won't speak to me?"

Isabella rolled her eyes. "I'm sure you can find a way to intrigue him. Irritate him, if all else fails."

She looked at Isabella in disbelief. "When did you become so conniving?"

Isabella laughed. "It's not conniving, it's just the way it is. Last time I had one of my friends stop Dante and ask him to help her carry a sack of potatoes. I do what I have to in order to meet my love."

"Well, if it keeps you away from the mines, I'm all for that."

"Most of the time Orlando can get away without arousing suspicion, but sometimes Dante seems to stick to him like glue. I've told Orlando it isn't a problem even if he can't meet me. I'll still show up. It's not like I have to walk very far."

Living in town had its advantages. It was simple enough to walk to the stores and acquire the needed merchandise. There was no need for a horse or carriage, both of which required more upkeep and expense than Chantel's parents wanted to spend. Most of the miners walked to work for the same reason, and only the wealthier store owners and officials had horses and buggies.

Today the town was bustling. Mining towns were always noisy places, with the constant hum and rumble of machinery, blasting, and loading. The mining day shift would end in another hour or two, and then the town would really get busy. The whistle would sound and the night shift workers would make their way to the mines. While they took over the tasks at hand, the day shift workers would make their way home through town, and those who still had money from last week's pay would frequent the local businesses to purchase food, liquor, and other pleasures. For a price, most anything could be had. Chantel had even seen a Finnish sauna. There were a large number of Finns living and working in Ely, and most Finnish households sported some form of a sauna. It seemed only right that someone should utilize their popularity and make a business of it.

Chantel knew their mother was less than enthusiastic to have her unmarried daughters on the town's streets when the miners were getting off work, so they had assured her they would make it back before the whistle blew to signal the end of the shift. Not only that, but the days were becoming shorter as winter approached, and already the skies were blending into evening twilight.

"There have been so many changes in the

past year," Chantel murmured. And the biggest change of all was Isabella's plans to marry. Chantel shook her head. Wasn't it just yesterday that her sister played with dolls?

They made their way to the general store and hurried inside to escape the brisk wind. "Well, if it isn't the Panetta sisters," the clerk declared. "I had heard you were back home, Miss Chantel." The older man smiled. "I suppose you'll be ordering more thread for tatting now."

Chantel returned the smile. "Indeed. Mama said she had some black silk thread ordered. She felt confident it would have come in by now."

"Yes, ma'am. I was going to have it delivered if she didn't send Miss Isabella over for it. I have it set aside in the back room. Was there anything else you were needing?"

Isabella touched her sister's coat sleeve. "I'm going to slip out back. I won't be long. If Dante shows up in here, be sure and keep him busy. Don't forget the sugar."

She had no chance to protest, so Chantel merely looked back at the clerk. "Mama wanted some sugar. She asked that you put that and the thread on our account. She'll settle up tomorrow after Papa is paid." Chantel thought of her coat. "Oh and I need to get a new coat. Do you have any in stock right now?"

"I do. There are several nice ladies' coats near the front of the store." He pointed to the display window. "I also have some new things we just got in. Christmas will soon be here, and we have some lovely items for gifts."

Chantel nodded and made her way to the front. She looked over some embroidered gloves, several lovely enamel brooches, and a few cameos before she heard the store door open.

She turned and recognized Orlando Calarco, but he didn't even seem to notice her. Instead, he hurried toward the back of the store, disappearing out the same way Isabella had gone. Chantel stood transfixed for a moment, then turned her attention back to a selection of items for men. She tried hard to ignore what was taking place out back. Focusing on Christmas and her brothers instead, Chantel decided the heavy leather gloves and warm woolen caps might well be something her brothers would need. She had brought each family member a Christmas present from Italy, but something practical might well be appreciated, as well. She'd speak to Mama about it and see what she and Papa had planned.

She looked the coats over and found a dark burgundy wool that suited her well. It was trimmed in black and looked to be just her size. She would have the clerk hold it for her. Taking it to the counter, she checked the price and winced. It was nearly nine dollars. She would have to sell a good amount of her tatting to help offset the cost.

"Here you are," the clerk said, returning with her sugar and thread.

Chantel handed him the coat. "I wonder if you would hold this for me. I need to sell some tatting and make certain Papa approves the purchase of this expensive an item." She smiled. "I know he will, but it's always best to ask."

The clerk smiled. "I will trust you for it. It's too cold to be without a good coat, and I see that one is getting quite worn. You take it now, and I will put it on a separate account for you. When you get your tatting money, you can pay me."

Chantel thanked him and waited while he folded it neatly into a box and tied it off with string. When he brought it back to the counter, he placed the box beside the sugar and thread. "So how was your trip abroad? Was it good?"

"It was wonderful. I very much enjoyed spending the year with my Nonna and Nonno in Italy. They have a lovely house up on a hill that looks down over the little town where we walked to the market and church. It was quite beautiful."

"And warm?"

"In the summer, it was paradise. Winter was . . . well . . . winter. We had a bit of snow, but not a great deal. When the weather was nice, however, we were outside as much as possible. I found it very hard to leave."

"You aren't sorry to have returned to Ely, are you?" he asked with a hint of admonition in his tone. "You know, we have some very nice things to offer here, as well. Lake Shagawa was the scene of some good times this summer, and the ice is very nearly thick enough to begin winter skating. And you might want to know there's a new ladies' snowshoe club that formed just last winter. The young ladies plan outings together and go for winter walks."

Chantel picked up the sugar and thread and smiled. "I'm not much for the cold. I prefer a hot, sunny day, myself."

Just then three women entered the store, chattering up a storm about some problem they were seeking to resolve. Chantel grabbed the coat box and took the opportunity to slip out as the clerk welcomed the ladies and found himself drawn into the fracas. She had all but forgotten her assigned task, however, when she walked straight into Dante Calarco.

"Pardon me. I'm so sorry," she said, glancing up to meet his surprised expression. For a moment his features were welcoming, but just as quickly they changed as he recognized her.

"Miss Panetta," he said. The words sounded forced.

"Mr. Calarco." She eyed him with a false sense of confidence.

His dark eyes seemed to scrutinize her face as if looking for some flaw. Chantel felt her poise begin to slip. She knew she would have to take charge of the situation. She held her position in front of the store's entryway.

"I've just returned from Italy." She knew it wouldn't matter to him, but she continued. "Have you ever made the trip?"

He shook his head. "Been busy working since I was sixteen. I don't have time for such luxuries."

She gave him a curt nod of acknowledgment. "Well, it is a luxury to be certain. I very much enjoyed the time with family."

He said nothing for a moment, then gave a shrug. "If you don't mind, I'm looking for my brother."

"Your brother?" Chantel questioned. "I sometimes forget you have a brother."

"There's no need for you to either remember or forget it. As you will recall, our families are not exactly on speaking terms."

She gave a laugh. "Well, we're standing here speaking, so I suppose we've broken with that tradition. I always felt it was a silly one, anyway."

"You would. I've not yet known a Panetta to honor family in the same way we Calarcos do."

Chantel felt her ire rise. "Now, just a minute, Mr. Calarco. My family is a very honorable one. I simply feel that God's desire for us to live at peace with one another is far more honorable."

"You sound like my brother." He pushed past her to go into the store.

"Then he's a good deal smarter than you," she called after him, remembering Isabella's comment to irritate Dante if all else failed.

Dante turned and narrowed his eyes. "You sound as if you'd like to perpetuate the feud. Insulting me certainly isn't any way to make friends."

Chantel shrugged. "I wasn't attempting to insult you, but to speak the truth. I believe God's Word makes it clear we aren't to bear grudges, but rather are to bear one another's burdens."

"Will you preach an entire sermon here in the cold?" he asked, his voice dripping sarcasm.

Knowing she had to do whatever she could to keep him from searching out Orlando, Chantel smiled. "Mr. Calarco, I am hardly preaching.

No, I am simply stating that it seems uncalled for that we should be at odds. Our families might have had troubles in the past, but there is certainly no need to continue that now. America is the land of new beginnings. Perhaps it will take a new generation to put aside our differences. Especially now."

"What's so special about now?" Dante replied, looking at her oddly.

Chantel was momentarily taken off guard. There was no way she would betray her sister's trust. "Especially now . . . that you and I . . ." She tried hard to regain control of her thoughts. "Especially now that you and I have met like this . . . and discussed the matter." She squared her shoulders and looked at him with what she hoped was an air of confidence.

He shook his head. "I thought perhaps you were going to say now that your sister has seduced my younger brother into thinking he should marry her."

Her eyes widened, and any denials caught in her throat.

"I'm glad you're not attempting to tell me you know nothing about it," Dante continued. "Lying wouldn't fit with your desire to follow the Good Book."

Chantel drew a deep breath. "I have no reason to lie. Perhaps, however, you should consider that it might have been your brother who enticed my sister." She took a step closer. "After all, she is young and innocent."

"Ha!" he replied, leaning forward, his face very near to hers. "Innocence is hardly something your family would be familiar with."

"How dare you?" Chantel rose on tiptoe to better face him. "I offered you an olive branch—peace between us. And instead you choose to insult my family."

"Miss Panetta, I neither want your olive branches, nor your peace. I am not going to be the one to betray our ancestors."

"Our ancestors? Must you continue to hide behind them?"

Chantel realized she'd probably gone too far. Dante's face reddened, and he poked his index finger against her shoulder. "I'm not hiding behind anyone, and I'd thank you to remember it. You have a sharp tongue, Miss Panetta, and I'll not remain here to be berated by you regarding what you perceive as right and wrong."

"Chantel! There you are," Isabella said, coming from behind her sister. She took hold of Chantel's arm. "Goodness, it looks like you bought out the store."

"I needed a new coat," Chantel replied.

Isabella nodded knowingly and relieved her sister of the other purchases. "We need to get this sugar home to Mama." The sisters exchanged a brief glance, and Isabella smiled and gave a nod. "Mr. Calarco, good day."

Chantel didn't fight as Isabella pulled her along down the boardwalk. She couldn't resist one backward glance, however. It was a mistake to look. Dante stared back, and for just a moment Chantel feared he might actually come after them.

Dante was dumbfounded by the open way Chantel Panetta baited him. He was further surprised by the fact that he'd fallen for it. No doubt she'd been instructed by her sister to run interference for the young lovers. He kicked at the doorjamb and all but growled when Orlando appeared, looking for all the world as if nothing were amiss.

He held up a small sack. "They had the ointment Nonna wanted. We can go home now."

Dante grabbed his brother by the lapel of his coat and slammed him up against the wall. "You were meeting her again, weren't you? Don't even think to lie to me," he continued without giving his brother a chance to answer. "I just spent the last few minutes arguing with her sister."

Orlando looked at his brother for a moment,

then shrugged. Dante wanted to pummel him for his seeming indifference. "Like I told you, this has to stop. If I have to, I'll go to Mr. Panetta himself. I kind of doubt he knows anything about this romance."

"You wouldn't dare," Orlando countered, pulling away from his brother's hold.

"If you don't stop seeing her—and stop all this nonsense about wanting to marry her—I will." Dante turned for home. "Just see if I don't."

Chapter 4

Marco Panetta punched his brother's arm. "You ready to go?"

Alfredo looked up from the supper table with a nod. "Let me get my hat."

"You boys shouldn't go to town," Mama said, clearing dishes from the table. "You know it's no good for you. Save your pay, and don't let those foxes take it from you."

Marco ignored her pleadings. It was always the same. His mama didn't like that her sons frequented the local saloons and gaming houses. Marco went to her side and kissed her forehead.

"You worry too much, Mama. Alfredo and I just want a little time to play pool and maybe some cards. There's nothing in the Bible that says we can't enjoy the fruit of our labors."

"Bah! You don't read the Bible enough to know what it says," Mama retorted. "Better you should stay home and study Scriptures than go off to lose your money in drink and games. If you stay home, I could get Chantel to read to us."

"I'm not in the mood for a story, Mama."
He could see the worry on her face, but Marco
wasn't going to give in.

The two brothers encountered their father
on the way out the front door. He eyed them
suspiciously, then gave a shrug. "You boys
stay outta trouble," he commanded. "If the
marshal hauls you off to jail, I won't come
get you."

"Pa, we aren't going to cause trouble,
and we aren't looking to do anything that
would put us behind bars," Marco replied.
He brushed back his oiled brown hair and
grinned. "I just want to enjoy myself a little
bit. We had a hard week, and a little fun is
in order."

Their father understood this better than
their mother, but still he gave his boys a rather
reproving look. "Be careful. You know the
evils in this town. You know how dangerous
it can be."

Marco and Alfredo nodded. "We will be
careful," Marco replied. "We'll just go see
Leo and no one else."

Leo Fortino owned the Fortune Hole Saloon and Gaming House. It was a favorite
among the Italians who enjoyed Fortino's
homage to the old country. He employed
Italian girls to entertain and dance. There
were even painted murals on the walls of

the saloon depicting Italian landmarks and scenery.

Marco and Leo had become fairly good friends over the course of time. The two were around the same age, and Leo had a strong interest in Marco's sisters. More than once he'd encouraged Marco to introduce him properly to Chantel and Isabella. Of course, Fortino would never be considered an acceptable suitor for either one. Marco knew his mother wouldn't allow for her daughters to court a saloon owner. Especially one with a reputation like Fortino's. The man and his place were notorious for fights—even killings.

The Fortune Hole was packed to capacity, as was expected on payday. Marco and Alfredo made their way to the bar where Leo was busy marking figures in a book while the man standing in front of him counted out money onto the bar.

"You sure you wanna put it all in the safe?" Leo asked the man. "You don't wanna spend a little on the tables?" He grinned at the man and rubbed his well-trimmed mustache. "They're paying out tonight."

The man looked longingly over his shoulder and then back to Leo. "Jes putta the money inna the safe. My wife, she threatened to poison my food if I lost our money at the cards again."

Leo laughed heartily, and even Marco couldn't help but grin. The threat of an Italian wife was not to be taken lightly; however, such an extreme reckoning was unlikely. The man took a receipt from Leo, gave Marco and Alfredo a nod, and, with one last look at the gaming tables, exited the saloon.

"He'll be back later tonight," Leo declared. He put the man's money in the safe behind him and turned back to the Panetta brothers. "What can I do for you two?"

"We're here to deposit our earnings, too," Marco said, putting his money on the bar. "Of course, not all of it."

Leo smiled. "Of course not. If you're feeling lucky tonight, there's going to be a high-stakes game in the Snake Room. When I finish up here, I'll be dealing."

Marco glanced toward the door across the room. This exit led to a short hall and several other rooms, one of which was known for its more intense games. Most saloons had a snake room where men could lose their lives as easily as they lost their money. Even so, it was one of Marco's favorite places to spend his time.

"Sounds challenging," he said, looking back at Leo.

"It should be."

He counted through Marco's money and

wrote a receipt. While many of the immigrants didn't trust the banks to handle their money, they were less guarded with their favorite saloonkeeper. Many of the bar owners kept the miners' wages for them in the house safe. They spent most of their money in the saloon anyway, so it seemed only appropriate.

After seeing to their deposits, Marco and Alfredo made their way around the room. They each ordered beers and flirted with the women who served them. One of the girls named Bianca was a favorite of Marco's.

"You are here for some fun, no?" she asked in thickly accented English.

"I'm here for the best time money can buy," Marco declared. He nodded toward one of the gaming tables. "You wanna be my lady luck?"

Her dark eyes flashed as her sensuous mouth widened in a smile. "I wanna be whatever you want me to be."

Marco lost track of Alfredo for a time and concentrated on Bianca and the games at hand. He lost and won several hands of poker, then grew bored and headed to the Snake Room. Bianca clung to his arm possessively.

"We could go to my room," she whispered low.

"Leo's expecting me," Marco replied, giving her a wink. "I feel lucky tonight. Maybe I'll win a big fortune, and we can run away together."

She pouted and moved to stand in front of the closed door to the Snake Room. "You tease me, but you know I adore you. I will run away with you, Marco."

He nodded, knowing she would run away with anyone who would take her from this life. He couldn't blame her for trying. "Come on, now. We can't keep Leo waiting."

Giving up, Bianca opened the door and stepped aside. True to his word, Leo was now dealing cards to several men. Marco recognized some of the players. Most were well into their cups, enjoying the cheap liquor. With a shot of whiskey selling for ten cents and a twelve-ounce schooner of beer for a nickel, it was often said, "There's a whole lot of drunkenness to be had in a dollar."

Feeling rather sober in light of this new company, Marco tossed Bianca a nickel and told her to fetch him another beer. She gave a playful nip to his earlobe before slinking off across the room and out the door. Marco knew that she would try to entice him to spend the night with her, but he would refuse as he had done in the past. Drinking and gaming was one thing, but he would not grieve his mother by associating with the local soiled doves. After all, a man needed to have his standards.

Leo motioned him to take a seat at the table. Marco moved closer but didn't sit. One of the drunks took a look at his cards. "I'll take one," he commanded, discarding the same.

The bar owner smiled and dealt a seven of clubs. The drunk moaned and fell back against his chair. "I fold."

The man at his right shook his head. "Ain't natural you losin' another hand." His slurred Italian was barely understandable.

"Maybe you boys should call it a night," Leo said, gathering the cards.

"Not until I win back my money," the first man declared.

Marco knew the man only by reputation. The boys at the mine called him *Coscia d'agnello* or Leg of Lamb, because of the Italian revolver he carried. The pistol held that affectionate nickname, and so it seemed natural to carry it over to the only man in their area to own one. However, the man was also known for a temperament that was far more aggressive than any lamb.

"Let's go again," the man demanded.

"You in this time?" Leo asked Marco.

He considered refusing, then thought better

of it. The tension was already palpable, and Marco didn't want to offend Leo by refusing. He took the seat beside Leg of Lamb and pulled some money from his pocket. "I might as well." Bianca appeared just then with his beer. Marco took a long drink as the woman began to rub the knots in his neck.

"Let's see if lady luck is with you now," Leo said and began dealing the cards.

The next few hands went peacefully, much to Marco's relief. Lamb won enough back to remain intrigued and said nothing more. Marco didn't do so bad himself, although he couldn't claim quite the victory that Lamb was enjoying. The man bet aggressively as if he had nothing to lose, but when the cards failed him, he pounded the table with his fists. Losing didn't sit well, but with the next hand he recouped his losses and was content once again. It went on and on like this for the next hour.

Marco lost track of how many beers he'd had. His head was spinning and his vision blurred as he studied the cards in his hand. He had a pair of sevens, but little else. Lamb had already raised the stakes, and Marco didn't feel confident enough of his pair to continue. He folded instead and drained the schooner once again.

"You want another?" Bianca asked.

He looked at her, knowing she was still hoping he would pay for her services. Instead, Marco took several coins from his winnings and handed them to her. "I'm done for the night. You were good company, so this is for you." She smiled, but he could tell she wasn't pleased. Even so, she knew when it was time to leave.

Lamb roared in approval as another hand went his way. Marco started to gather his money, but Leo put out his hand.

"The night's still young. Stick around."

Marco couldn't suppress a yawn. "I'm done in."

"Nonsense," Leo said. "You're doing just fine."

Marco shrugged and leaned back in the chair. "I guess a few more rounds won't hurt."

With Lamb's confidence returning, he became more reckless as other players came and went. He also became more boastful and outrageous with his comments. Marco couldn't imagine that Leo would put up with the man for long, but the barkeep said nothing and just continued dealing the cards.

The hours blurred together and Marco found himself wishing he hadn't sent Bianca away. His mouth felt dry—full of cotton stuffing. He would have enjoyed a drink right about now. Especially in light of the game's intensity. Lamb now seemed bent on showing Leo up. He argued and snarled insults when the cards weren't to his liking and sat back in smug satisfaction when things went his way. However, when another losing streak seemed to hit, Lamb began to cheat. At least Marco thought he was. The beer clouded his mind, but it seemed from time to time the man played some sort of sleight of hand. Even so, Marco couldn't be sure enough to challenge him.

The other players eventually cleared out, leaving Leo, Lamb, and Marco to their game. Alfredo ambled in after a time, and Marco could see that he had grown bored with the place.

"I'm headin' home," he told Marco.

Without warning, Leo jumped to his feet and pointed at the table. "You shouldn't have laid that ace on the table, Lamb. I don't hold with cheating around here."

Before Marco realized what was happening, Lamb had drawn his revolver. With drunken hands he waved the pistol at Leo. The barkeep seemed undaunted.

"Alfredo, on your way out I'd appreciate it if you'd get the marshal in here. He needs to arrest this dirty rotten cheat."

"Nobody's . . . 'restin' me." Lamb's words

were hopelessly slurred. He pointed the gun at Marco for a moment, then seemed to realize Leo was the one he wanted to shoot.

Alfredo hurried from the room, leaving only Marco, Leo, and Lamb in the Snake Room. Marco edged away from the table while Leo shook his head in disgust. "You can't always get your way with a gun."

Marco wasn't so sure. He took another step back and realized he'd hit the wall. There was nowhere else to go.

"You're the cheat," Lamb began again. "You . . . you . . . robbed me. I'm a better player than that."

"You're a stupid drunk," Leo said, and to Marco's surprise he charged at the man. In one sleek, catlike move, Leo grabbed the weapon and pressed the barrel of the gun under Lamb's neck. When the pistol fired, Marco's hands flew to his chest as if he'd been shot.

"That's that," Leo said, stepping away from Lamb as his body crumpled to the floor.

Marco didn't know what to say. His head was spinning from the liquor, and his ears were ringing from the close proximity of the gunshot. Leo glanced at the table a moment, then gathered the remains of Lamb's winnings for himself.

When Alfredo and the marshal entered the

room moments later, Marco was still staring dumbly at Lamb's motionless body.

"What happened here?" the lawman asked.

"Caught him cheating. Guess he couldn't bear the shame," Leo said, gathering his chips and cards. "Killed himself."

The marshal looked to Marco, then knelt down to check the body. "That right, Panetta?"

Marco blinked several times, hoping it might clear his head. It didn't. "What?" he asked, stalling for time. He looked to Leo, who only gave a slight nod.

"I asked if that was right," the marshal replied, looking up.

Nodding, Marco affirmed his friend's statement. Maybe it wasn't like it seemed. Maybe the liquor had clouded his understanding. After all, Lamb had been cheating—even Marco was sure of that. Blood pooled on the floor, and the sight of it turned Marco's stomach.

He clutched his belly. "Alfredo, I need to get outta here."

They'd no sooner hit the street than Marco lost the contents of his stomach. In the dim glow of light from the street and buildings, Marco imagined it was blood. He shuddered and heaved again.

When the nausea passed he straightened. "Get me home."

Alfredo took hold of his arm. "So what happened in there? Lamb really kill himself?"

Marco grunted but gave no other reply. Alfredo continued. "Marshal says there's been a lot of dying going on at Leo's. Lot of suicides. Don't you think that's strange?"

He had no desire to discuss the matter further. "Shut up and get me home, Alfredo. I gotta lie down."

Chapter 5

Chantel shifted her weight to get comfortable in the hard-bottomed chair. Around her, dozens of women sat speaking in hushed whispers. Most of the women were dressed in their Sunday best, even though it was a weekday. There were very few events to dress up for in Ely, and having an out-of-town speaker was definitely one of them. Today they would hear from a traveling minister, the Reverend Black, who had once been a slave to the demon alcohol. Because the event was held on a weekday, it was attended primarily by women. However, Chantel spied a few men among the numbers.

The Finnish Temperance Society assured their audience that this man's stories would convince any doubters, no matter their ethnicity, of the problems liquor could cause. Chantel was surprised that her mother had wanted to come, but Isabella confided that ever since Marco and Alfredo had started frequenting the local saloons, their mother had taken a strong stand against alcohol. The only exception was the wine she sometimes used in cooking.

"They have quite the crowd," Chantel murmured in her sister's direction.

Isabella smoothed down the ruffle of her white muslin blouse and leaned closer. "They are planning to build a Temperance Hall, and this is how they raise money. The speakers get paid, of course, but the rest of the money they charge to attend the event goes into the collection for the new building."

Glancing around the room, Chantel couldn't help but wonder what these women thought they could accomplish. Miners and loggers made up the bulk of the area's population. These hardworking men loved their liquor. They weren't going to be easily persuaded to give it up—new building or not.

"Ladies and gentlemen, I am Mrs. Maki. Welcome to our monthly lecture," a severe-looking woman announced from the podium. "It is our desire to further the elimination of alcohol from our society. We see its evil effects daily here in Ely, and around our state thousands upon thousands suffer from the affliction of drunkenness, alcohol enslavement, and other abuses. It is up to God-fearing people to take a stand and reclaim the nation's people and save our children. We are hopeful that you will aid us in this endeavor."

Chantel joined the others in clapping. She didn't really know, however, if it was possible to eliminate the consumption of alcohol. It seemed to her that so long as there were men seeking to ease their miseries and forget their misfortune, there would be customers for liquor. As her brother had once told her, whiskey and beer were big business. As long as there was money to be made, men would find a way to keep the industry running. Not only that, but if the various temperance societies had their way and the substance was abolished, something else would rise up to take its place.

"The Reverend Black has traveled from Duluth to speak to us today," Mrs. Maki continued. "This man knows firsthand the sordid details of a life consumed by alcohol. Before he gave his life to the Almighty, he gave it to the bottle. Only the hand of God was able to pull him back from the very pit of hell, where liquor had taken him." She looked to the side of the stage where the small, unassuming man sat dressed in a black suit. "I ask that you would listen carefully to what he has to say and give him a warm welcome. Reverend Black, please come and impart your wisdom to us today."

The audience again applauded as the short, frail man made his way to the podium. Chantel wondered if this tiny man could even begin to speak loudly enough for them to hear at the back of the room. She didn't have long to worry about it, however. For all his smallness of stature, the Reverend Black had a most commanding voice.

"Alcohol is the devil's drink," he boomed out to the crowd. "There is nothing of the Lord Jesus in a shot of whiskey. Nothing of our heavenly Father in a bottle of wine or a glass of beer." He pointed his finger at the congregation. "But I can tell you don't yet believe me."

Chantel dared a glance to her left and then to her right. She didn't see anything to indicate that the reverend's words weren't believed. Chantel jumped, as did many in the audience, when Reverend Black slammed his Bible against the lectern.

"God in heaven demands you hear my words and believe. Alcohol will lead to the destruction of our nation, just as it has many others. There are entire countries now long destroyed and forgotten because of this tool of Satan.

"Oh, it starts out simple enough. After all, even the Good Book talks of taking a little wine for your stomach." He slammed the Bible again, and the noise echoed throughout the otherwise silent room.

"But the men and even women of this great

country know nothing about taking 'a little.' This is a country of extremes—of plenty. We take a great deal when a little would do. We demand the king's portion when we have need of no more than a pauper."

Despite the cold temperatures outside, Chantel was beginning to feel the heat of this man's passion. She had been raised in a culture where wine was commonplace. No one gave it a second thought if it was served with meals. In fact, it would have been questioned had it been absent. Even so, her mother and father had never been much for its consumption, and they certainly had no taste for whiskey. Chantel knew, however, that her mother feared for her sons. The town's many saloons enticed them, and she'd already witnessed her brothers becoming sick from drinking too much.

"Friends, I tell you that God is not pleased. He is not happy with our refusal to act. He calls for His children to put an end to this madness. He commands us in His word to be not drunken, yet we allow for drunkenness in our towns and even, dare I say it, in our homes. We not only allow it—we encourage it. We welcome it in like a long-lost friend, then grieve when it robs us blind or kills those we love."

The Reverend Black's rebuke went on for

over half an hour before he began to speak on how he had once been a slave to whiskey. "As a boy, I was introduced early to whiskey," he announced. "Godless men surrounded me and my days were dark. I sought comfort and refuge, but there was none to be found—except in a bottle. And what a sweet seductress that bottle was. She called to me as a Jezebel might, enticing me, promising me what she could not hope to give. I was taken in."

He stepped away from the podium, leaving the Bible behind. Balling his fists, he raised them toward the ceiling. "I was deceived!" he bellowed. Murmurs arose from the audience, but he held his ground and continued. "The great Deceiver himself—Satan—convinced me with his lies that there was nothing wrong in this indulgence, and so I drank.

"And I didn't just drink a little. Oh no." He shook his head vehemently. "That is part of the seduction. It starts with just one glass, but it ends, my friends, in death!"

A group of women on the far side of the room began to applaud, drawing the rest of the audience in rather awkwardly. Chantel could see from the looks on the faces of some of the women that they weren't quite sure what they were clapping for.

The reverend momentarily slowed down, as if to regroup his thoughts. He kept his audience waiting several minutes, in fact, while he went to a small table and poured himself a glass of water. Once he'd taken a long drink from the glass, he set it back down and returned again to the lectern.

"Liquor is only one part of the problem," Reverend Black began in a less imposing voice. "The companions of alcohol are many. Gambling, prostitution, thievery, and all manner of addictions and abuses walk hand in hand with liquor. My friends, they are the best of acquaintances and revel in each other's company. If you doubt me, you have only to look as far as the saloons and brothels in your town."

He began to pick up speed and volume. "For good Christian people to sit back and do nothing—to look the other way when sin rears its ugly head—is in and of itself . . . sin! You are sinning if you sit idly by and do nothing to put an end to this problem. Furthermore," he said, once again pointing his finger, "if you continue in this sin, you will burn in the pits of hell for all eternity!

"Yea, even if you allow this sin, you will be found guilty. I tell you, have nothing to do with these people! Have no fellowship with them. Turn away from their wickedness, avert your eyes, and let Satan have them!"

If it had been possible to leave unnoticed, Chantel might have gone. The man spoke the truth about the damages caused by drinking, but he seemed completely focused on judgment—not in the grace and mercy to be found in Jesus.

Furthermore, what if those who drank to excess were unable to break away from the stronghold of liquor on their own? Would God truly condemn the man or woman who was trapped in their life's woes while others turned away? And what of bearing one another's burdens? Should Christians not reach out in love to help one another? Did God not call them to love even their enemies?

The speaker continued to rant about sin for nearly forty minutes, and Chantel found herself praying he would grow tired and conclude his tirade. She hated the ugliness of the saloons, brothels, and gaming houses just as much as the reverend seemed to. However, she couldn't imagine that hatred would result in the change he was seeking. A dozen Bible verses ran through her mind that suggested God would have her show love and mercy.

Reverend Black appeared to be winding down as he moved into rhetoric regarding what each individual could do to aid the cause. He told them how money was needed to further the mission and encouraged the audience to give above and beyond their regular tithes to the church, to see that the Temperance

Movement was strengthened. By the time the noon whistle sounded, he had concluded his lecture. Mrs. Maki retook the stage to thank everyone for their time and attention.

Mama looked to Chantel and smiled. "He had quite a bit to say, didn't he?"

Chantel nodded and turned to speak to Isabella but found her gone. "Isabella didn't lose any time getting out of here."

They both looked around the room to see if they could spy the younger woman. "No doubt," Mama began, "she's hungry. I know I certainly am. I thought we would have been home well before now."

Chantel stood and did her best to stretch without seeming unladylike. Her blue-and-green-checked cheviot jacket fit her snugly, thanks to the well-drawn corset. It made a sharp contrast to a green woolen skirt that exactly matched the green of the coat. The outfit, however flattering, was not one to allow for much movement. Of course, a lady in public was not to be overly active.

"Oh, Maria, I'm so glad you came today," an older woman said in a heavy Italian cadence. "And, Chantel, how lovely you are. Italy must have agreed with you. That hat is quite darling."

Chantel smiled at the woman. The green-and-blue-pleated velvet toque was one of her favorites. "Thank you. It was a gift from my nonna."

"Mrs. Moretti," Mama exclaimed. "It's so good to see you up and around. I pray the ague didn't leave you too weak."

"No, no. I feel much better," she replied. "I think this reverend, he want to change the tiger stripes to spots, no?"

Mama chuckled. "I think he makes a good point, but I fear the men of this town won't abide by his concerns."

"I think no." Mrs. Moretti gave a *tsk*ing sound and muttered something in Italian that Chantel couldn't quite make out.

Leaving her mother to talk to the older woman, Chantel moved to the door to see if she could find Isabella. It wasn't like her not to at least tell them she was headed back to the house. She knew their mother would worry about Isabella walking off alone.

Mrs. Maki stood at the door and nodded to Chantel as she approached. "It's good you could come today, Miss Panetta. I know your people to be some of the worst drinkers in Ely."

Chantel's brow rose at this. "Excuse me?"

"Your people—the Italians. The Italians, Irish, and Germans probably consume more alcohol in this town than anyone. Seeing several Italian families represented here today makes me quite hopeful."

"Well, I'm glad we could accommodate you, Mrs. Maki," Chantel replied, not knowing what else to say. She glanced out the open door. "Have you by any chance seen my sister, Isabella?"

"Why, yes. She exited only moments ago. I saw her head off down the street to the north. I reprimanded her for leaving unescorted, but she said she wasn't feeling well."

Chantel frowned. "To the north, you say? Perhaps I'd better find her and see her home."

Mrs. Maki nodded, then turned to greet other guests. Chantel pulled on her wool coat and stepped outside to see if Isabella was perhaps still in sight. She wasn't. Going back into the building, Chantel found her mother speaking with several other women.

"Oh, good," Mama declared when Chantel arrived at her side. "I'm going home with Mrs. Moretti. She has a new lace pattern to show me. You and Issy go on home and get started on the ironing."

"Sí, Mama."

She waited until her mother and the other women headed back to their houses before deciding to go in search of her sister. It didn't make sense to Chantel that Isabella should head north. Then a thought crossed her mind. The mines were to the north of town, and it was lunchtime.

"Oh, Isabella, you didn't," Chantel murmured, making her way toward the north end of town.

She hadn't gone far, however, when someone called to her. Chantel turned abruptly to find Leo Fortino strolling toward her from one of the alleyways.

"Why, Miss Panetta, you are as pretty as a picture of springtime and roses."

"Mr. Fortino," she said with a slight bob of her head.

The man's grin only widened as he gave his mustache a brush with his index finger. "I was just telling your brother Marco that I'd like to come calling on you."

Chantel shook her head. "I don't think that would be wise, Mr. Fortino."

"Please call me Leo."

"I cannot. That wouldn't be appropriate." She glanced up the road, straining to see Isabella.

"But how else will we get to know each other better?" he asked, moving another foot closer.

Turning her gaze back to him, Chantel tried to sound nonchalant. "I have no desire to know you better, Mr. Fortino." He looked rather hurt, and she hurried to continue. "I'm sure you must be a very nice man—after all, Marco thinks highly of you. However, I'm not looking to court anyone, and when I do,

I am going to want a man who is strong in his faith—one who will accompany me to services on Sunday morning."

"I'm a businessman, Miss Panetta. I can hardly help the fact that my business stays open until the early hours of Sunday morning. It would be very difficult for me to attend services with you."

"Exactly," she said, nodding. "Which is why I refuse to do more than make your acquaintance and acknowledge you as a friend of my brother. Besides, I've only just returned from Italy."

"Ah, yes, and how was your travel abroad?"

"Very pleasant, thank you. Now if you'll excuse me, I need to catch up with my sister. She passed this way just a few minutes ago, and I'm told she wasn't feeling well." Chantel searched the city streets for some sign of Isabella.

"I could accompany you," he offered, not easily discouraged.

"No, that's quite kind, but I can manage." She started down the street before he could protest her actions.

"I'm not giving up," he said, calling after her.

Chantel rolled her eyes. "You might as well," she murmured, but kept moving.

Picking up her pace, Chantel glanced quickly

down each side street and alley, hoping she might catch sight of Isabella. It was only when she'd nearly given up all hope that she caught a glimpse of a young woman turning past the train depot.

"Isabella!" Chantel called out. Her sister either didn't hear her or didn't want to be found. Chantel hiked her skirts and began to run in a most unladylike fashion. "Isabella, wait!"

Rounding the corner of the depot, Chantel came to a dead stop as she again caught sight of the woman. It wasn't Isabella. She frowned and stared out across the short expanse to the Chandler Mine. The place was alive with activity and noise despite the noon hour. Miners moving around the grounds and train cars full of ore bore evidence to their hard work. Tree stumps dotted the ground between the rail lines and the mining shafts. Just enough land had been cleared to allow for heavily rutted roads. It was filthy, cold, and unappealing.

For a moment Chantel just gazed toward the mine. Many of the men were enjoying their lunch outside in the cold. It had to be better than being stuck down in the mine all day. But she knew she should get away from the area, and quickly. Where had Isabella gotten off to?

Remembering things her sister had said

about meeting Orlando near the mine, Chantel tried to imagine where the young lovers would hide their rendezvous. There were shaft towers and trestles, mining shacks and equipment scattered across the expanse, but Chantel couldn't imagine her sister walking out into the midst of it.

With a growing fear for her own safety, Chantel hurried back toward Camp Street. She made her way south and thought she'd managed to go unnoticed until a reproving voice called her name. Realizing she'd been found out, Chantel stopped and faced her accuser.

Dante Calarco eyed her quite suspiciously. "Miss Panetta, what in the world are you doing over here?"

She bit her lip, wondering what she should say. She could tell him she'd come to see her brothers or father. Maybe she should just say she wanted to see the mines, and against her better judgment she'd come on her own. Words failed her, however, and she could only return Dante's intense gaze.

He seemed to immediately understand. "She's gone to see him." He looked around the area, then returned his gaze to Chantel. "Your sister is out here somewhere with my brother, isn't she?"

Chantel knew she couldn't very well lie. "I

think so. I can't be sure. I didn't see her come here, but . . ." She fell silent. He wouldn't care about her reasons or thinking.

"Your sister is ten kinds of fool to expose herself to the dangers here." He narrowed his eyes and shook his head.

Chantel noted the filthy trousers tucked into well-worn black knee boots. She let her gaze travel up the length of him and felt her heart skip a beat when she again met his stare. Rational thought left her momentarily, but Dante either didn't notice or care.

"If I find her, I'll give her what she should have been given a long time ago," Dante said, his jaw clenched tight.

"And . . . ah . . . just what would that be?" Chantel asked, still barely able to think.

He glared at her. "A spanking."

This snapped Chantel out of her strange fog. "You wouldn't dare touch her! It would cause an even bigger rift between our families if you did such a horrible thing. I'll find her and I'll get her home, but you keep your hands off of her!"

She didn't wait to hear anything else he had to say. Instead, she marched on with new determination, hoping that her sister and Orlando would have the good sense to meet closer to town rather than the mine.

Only after she'd gone a block or so did

Chantel realize the hopelessness of it all. She slowed her pace and tried to figure out what she should do. There really was nothing to be done, she supposed.

"I might as well go home," she told herself. She knew Isabella was capable of taking care of herself. After all, she'd done so for the entire year Chantel had been in Italy. Shaking her head, Chantel whispered a prayer.

"Oh, Father, watch over my sister. She's not using her head, but rather letting her heart make all her decisions. Please keep her safe and bring her home without any trouble."

Of course there would still be trouble of some sort because Dante Calarco knew his brother was once again meeting with a Panetta. Chantel swallowed hard and squared her shoulders.

"Let him make trouble," she muttered.

Chapter 6

The weeks passed and with it came the snows. St. Anthony's construction was finished and the church was dedicated just before the first of December. Everyone was excited to celebrate the Christmas season in their new building. Chantel was more relaxed now that the cold weather kept Isabella closer to home. She knew her sister still planned to marry Orlando Calarco, and she'd done her best to encourage Isabella to confide in their mother. Even so, Isabella was hesitant. She knew there were few secrets between her parents, and she feared how her father would respond.

"He won't understand at first," Isabella had told Chantel. "But maybe if I marry and then let him know, he'll realize that he has to accept it."

Chantel disagreed, but Isabella begged her to remain silent on the matter. In time, she promised, she would tell their mother.

Working at her tatting in the warmth of their front parlor, Chantel couldn't help but notice her mother's busy hands. Mother delighted in making Chantilly lace and could fetch quite a price for it if she'd been inclined to sell it. Usually, however, the lace was given as gifts or sewn into new clothes for her daughters.

Isabella worked across the room in silence. She sewed pleats on a buttercream-colored bodice. The piece was to be part of a new gown, and Chantel wondered if it might become her sister's wedding dress.

A knock on the front door sent all of their gazes in search of the source. Chantel was the one nearest and got to her feet. "I'll answer it." She made her way to the door and opened it to find a delivery boy.

"This here is for Miss Chantel Panetta," the boy declared, holding up a small wooden crate.

"You may place it on the hall table," Chantel said, pointing. She reached into her chatelaine and procured two pennies. She smiled and handed them to the boy. "Thank you."

He grinned from ear to ear and pocketed the coins. "Thank you, miss." He doffed his cap and hurried from the house.

"What is it?" Mama called from the parlor.

Chantel lifted the wooden box and brought it to show her mother and sister. "Apparently I am the recipient of a gift."

"Oh, do open it!" Isabella said, looking quite excited. "I love surprises."

"Who is it from?" Mama asked.

Shaking her head, Chantel pried at the

wooden top with her fingertips. "I have no idea."

"You need a hammer for that," Mama advised.

Nodding in agreement, Chantel went to the kitchen and retrieved her mother's household hammer. "I can't imagine who would send me a gift," she said as she returned.

"Yet there it sits," Isabella said with a grin. She had cast aside her bodice to hover near the box. "And it is the holiday season. Why, before we know it, Christmas will be here."

Mama laughed and continued twisting her threads to make lace. "Sí, we'll have a grand celebration with everyone home. We missed you very much last year, Chantel. It didn't seem like Christmas with you gone."

The box yielded with a creaking groan. Chantel pushed aside the lid and maneuvered through the packing to find a card. She opened it and read it aloud. "'It's good to have you home again. From an admirer.'"

"And that's all?" Isabella said, looking over her sister's shoulder.

"That's all," Chantel admitted. She put the card atop the lid and dug back into the packing. One by one she pulled a dozen oranges from the crate. It was a rare and expensive gift to have in the dead of winter—especially this far north.

"Oh my!" Mama stopped her work. "Oranges?" She gave an exclamation in Italian. "What a fortune those must have cost."

"And we don't even know who sent them," Isabella declared. "But someone certainly has strong feelings for you, Chantel." She gave her sister a nudge. "Maybe there will be more than one wedding to come."

"What do you mean more than one?" Mama asked.

Isabella bit her lip and hurried back to her chair. She picked up the bodice. "Well, I'm sure there are weddings being planned in the community. I heard something just the other day about Margaret McGuire and her beau getting hitched."

Chantel could see her mother was less than convinced. She replaced the oranges in the crate, certain that the only man who could afford to send them was Leo. "Perhaps the time has come that you should let Mama know what's on your heart."

She took her seat and picked up her tatting shuttle. "After all," Chantel continued, "I believe you would have an advocate."

Mama eyed her daughters with great curiosity. "What is this? You are keeping secrets from your mama?"

Isabella looked wide-eyed at Chantel as if to question her sanity. Chantel gave her the slightest nod of encouragement. "She's right, you know. Let's just have this out."

Isabella fidgeted with the bodice for a few seconds, then tossed it aside. "I'm in love."

"But why should that be a secret from your mama?" The older woman looked deeply wounded. "I thought we were closer than that."

Isabella came to kneel beside her mother. "We are, but you may not like what I tell you, and I wanted to spare your feelings."

Mama looked to Chantel. "But your sister, she knows?"

"Sí, Mama."

"Then you had best tell me." Mama let the bobbins rest against the small pillow where she'd pinned her lace pattern.

"I am in love with Orlando . . . Calarco."

Mama's mouth fell open in a silent *O*. Isabella took hold of her mother's hands. "I cannot bear to hurt my family, but this feud between us and the Calarcos is ridiculous. Who cares that a silly mule was accidentally killed fifty years ago? Orlando and I believe that if we marry, we can put this matter to rest once and for all."

"*I santi ci preservi!*" Mama whispered. Saints preserve us.

"I don't think even the saints can help this, Mama," Chantel replied. She wrapped the thread around her left fingers and worked the shuttle to make a ring.

"I love him, Mama. And he loves me. We want to marry but figure we'll have to elope."

For several minutes their mother said nothing, but Chantel could see that she was deep in thought.

"Your papa and brothers will be . . . ah . . . surprised," Mama finally said.

"I'd rather not tell them just yet, Mama." Isabella got back to her feet and smoothed out her gown. "Orlando and I figure to elope after the New Year. We didn't want to cause problems for anyone over Christmas. I love you all so much." Isabella turned to Chantel. "I never wanted to hurt anyone."

She took her seat again and picked up her sewing. "I'm making my wedding dress."

Mama looked at the piece and then back to her lace making. For several long minutes she said nothing. Chantel could see the troubled expression on her mother's face, however. She knew this would not be an easy matter to deal with.

Finally Mama looked at Isabella. "This black lace I'm working on would hardly be suitable for a wedding gown. Chantel, you brought back a good deal of tatted lace, did you not?"

"Sí, mama."

Her mother nodded. "You'll need some lace

for your gown," she said, continuing to nod. "A wedding dress should have lots of lace."

Isabella grinned. "Thank you, Mama."

Chantel understood this was their mother's way of accepting the news—perhaps even approving it.

"And you'll say nothing to Papa and the boys?" Isabella asked hopefully.

Mama nodded. "I say nothing for now. But, Issy, you know in time you will have to tell your papa."

Isabella nodded. "I know, but I'm praying for just the right time."

A long and mournful blast from the mine's whistle sounded and continued to do so for far longer than any noonday lunch signal. Chantel saw her mother's face pale, and Isabella jumped to her feet.

"Something's wrong at the mine!" her sister exclaimed. "We must go."

She threw the bodice aside once again and ran for the hall. Chantel put aside her tatting, tucking it into her chatelaine before helping their mother to her feet.

"I'm sure Papa and the boys are fine."

Mama's eyes met Chantel's. "We must pray for the men."

"I'm already praying, Mama." She helped her mother into her woolen coat and then retrieved her own while Mama secured her bonnet. Isabella waited anxiously, wringing her gloved hands nervously. Chantel knew she was worried about her father and brothers, but she was also concerned about Orlando. What if the young man had been killed? What if Papa or Marco or Alfredo had suffered injury or death? What would any of them do?

They hurried with hundreds of other people to make their way to the mine. The mass confusion did nothing to reassure Chantel that everything would be all right. The dust in the air seemed far thicker than usual, she thought, and when someone mentioned a premature explosion, she couldn't help but fear the worst.

"Does anyone know if there are miners trapped below?" she asked as they joined a crowd of women who had gathered close to the problem shaft.

"They say a half dozen or so," one of the women responded. She held a rosy-cheeked baby on one hip, while a small girl held tightly to her skirt. "Nobody knows yet what happened."

As the minutes ticked by in agonizing slowness, Chantel began to search the crowd for her brother and father. When she spied Dante Calarco, she breathed a silent prayer of thanks that he was all right before she even realized what she was doing. Uncertain of why the sight of him caused her to react in such a way, she shook her head, then scanned the faces about her once again. When she finally caught sight of her brothers, she shouted to them.

"Marco! Alfredo! We're over here!" She waved and pointed to them. "See, Mama, the boys are fine."

"Where's your papa?" Mama questioned as her sons closed the distance between them.

"He's . . . he's trapped, Mama." Marco's expression was grave. "I don't know how bad it is. Alfredo and I had just headed up the shaft to see a load of ore to the top. Then the explosion came. We don't know what happened."

Mama's eyes remained dry, but Chantel could hear the sorrow in her mother's voice as she pounded her fist against her breast. *"Cuore del mio cuore."* Heart of my heart.

It was something Chantel had often heard her mother call their father. She put her arm around Mama's shoulders and looked to Marco. "What are they doing to get them out?"

"There's a whole team down there digging."

As if to offer proof, someone called out, "They're bringing one up!"

The crowd fell silent. It was a heavy, eerie silence that wrapped itself around the gathering like a shroud. Chantel gave a shiver, but not from the cold. Father Buh moved toward the shaft opening. When the man's lifeless body was brought out of the mine, the priest knelt beside him.

"I cannot see who it is," Mama said, gripping Chantel's arm hard.

"It's not Papa," Alfredo said. He moved away from them to draw closer to the dead man. In a moment he returned. Across the way a woman began to wail in anguish. "It's Paulo Conti," he said, meeting Chantel's eyes.

The painful waiting continued, punctuated by the sobbing of several women. As the women figured out which of their family members were safe and which were unaccounted for, the crying grew louder. Many of the Panettas' dear friends gathered around the family to offer Mama and the family comfort. Each knew it could well be their loved one buried beneath the rubble next time.

"They're sending another one up."

Marco and Alfredo hurried toward the shaft opening. Machinery hummed and the ground even shook a bit. Chantel knew her brothers would let the family know if it turned out to be their father. She saw her sister, who was busy scanning the crowd for Orlando.

"Secure the hoist!" someone called.

Hearing this, Chantel moved away from her mother. She knew the other women would see to her and for reasons beyond her understanding, she needed to see what was happening. She drew closer to the shaft tower where earlier she'd seen Dante. He wasn't there now, but several other men were.

Boldly, knowing it wasn't her place, Chantel moved toward the men. "Do they know what happened?" The men looked at her oddly. "My father is down there—he's one of them."

Understanding instantly filled their eyes. "Premature explosion," one of the men explained. "A charge went off in the area where the men were working. No one knows why. It collapsed the stope."

The blood- and dust-caked body of the next man surfaced, and Chantel could see that it wasn't her father. She didn't know who the man was, but he was hardly more than a boy. Father Buh moved from Mr. Conti's body to the still youth. The priest moved the boy's arm to place it atop his body, revealing a broken bone through a huge gash in the forearm.

She shuddered and turned—right into the arms of Dante Calarco. He said nothing as she pushed away, but when their eyes met she could see his sadness. "Orlando?" she barely managed to whisper.

"He's fine. My father, too."

She nodded. "My father . . ." She couldn't say anything else.

"I know," he replied in a whisper.

She looked back to where the Conti family was lifting up the body of their fallen loved one. Sadly no one came forward for the younger man. Chantel felt a deep sorrow for the unknown boy. Surely someone—somewhere—loved this boy-man.

"Do you know him?" she asked Dante.

"He was new. His name is . . . was Samuel."

She nodded. "Does he have no family?"

"I don't know," Dante admitted.

"You know that explosion could have been set early on purpose," Chantel heard someone say behind her.

Someone else picked up the conversation, apparently not seeing Chantel and Dante. "You know them Panettas and Calarcos have been fighting for a long time, and them Calarcos handle explosives."

"Seems a foolish gamble just to get rid of your enemy," another man joined in. "Makes no sense to risk everyone's livelihood that way."

Chantel swallowed hard, then noticed Dante was watching her closely. She bit her lip to keep from asking him about the comments. It was clear he had heard the men talking, just as she had.

She gestured toward where her family had gathered. "I should get back to my mother," she said, feeling awkward.

Making her way through the crowd, Chantel

resumed a place beside her mother. "It's a young boy named Samuel." She then looked to Isabella. "Orlando is all right. Dante told me." Isabella closed her eyes, relief washing over her face.

Mama took hold of her daughters' hands. "We must keep praying for your papa."

"I am." Chantel turned back to where Dante stood. His dark eyes seemed to look right through her. "I am, Mama." Her voice barely sounded, while Isabella, eyes closed, appeared to already be in prayer.

Nearly an hour later they announced they were bringing up another man. Chantel's feet and face felt frozen, but there was nothing to be done. None of her family would leave the area until they knew the truth about her father.

Again the body was brought up from the shaft and laid out on the cold ground. "He's alive!" someone called. "Get Dr. Shipman!"

"It's Panetta," someone else declared.

Chantel felt her mother tremble. "I must see him," she said. Marco and Alfredo were nowhere to be found, so Chantel took hold of her mother's arm. "Come, Mama. I'll get you up there."

She pushed through the onlookers, pulling her mother behind her. They were very nearly to where her father lay, when Marco appeared. "He's alive, Mama. He's unconscious, but he's alive."

He took over and led their mother to her injured husband. Chantel felt strangely alone. She crossed her arms and tucked her frozen fingers under her arms. She again found Dante watching her from across the way. She couldn't explain the look in his eyes, but for just a moment, it resembled guilt. Surely he didn't have anything to do with this accident.

Dr. Shipman ordered several men to take Chantel's father to his office and makeshift hospital. Chantel and Isabella followed after their brothers and mother. Neither spoke, but they held each other's hand like they might have when they were young.

"He will be all right, won't he?" Chantel heard her mother ask Marco.

"The doctor doesn't know, Mama. We have to be strong and wait," he replied.

Chantel noticed how much he sounded like their father. Taking charge the way he had, she could almost imagine her father as a younger man. She thought again of young Samuel. Poor boy. It could just as easily have been Marco or Alfredo. The three of them generally worked close together. If someone had wanted to end their lives, it would be relatively simple—just wait until the trio was isolated and working alone. She felt disgusted by her thoughts and pushed aside the growing suspicion she felt.

At the doctor's they sat in an outer waiting area while the doctor and his staff worked to save Giovanni Panetta. The family members alternated between pacing and sitting, but all the while they prayed. Chantel had never known her brothers to be overly religious, but even they were attentive to Father Buh as he spoke words of encouragement and hope.

Chantel took out her tatting and began to work at the rings and chains. She found the work helped to soothe her weary nerves. She wove the shuttle back and forth between her fingers, begging God to save her father.

When Dr. Shipman finally appeared, she had created quite a length of trim. The doctor offered a stern expression. Only then did Mama begin to sob. Marco put his arm around her shaking shoulders. "How bad is it?" he asked.

Chapter 7

Dante saw his father speaking with the mine captain and knew he was giving an accounting for every stick of dynamite and every bit of nitroglycerin. He couldn't help but notice the looks of the people around him. They watched him and his father with an expression that suggested blame. Even so, no one said anything about it—at least not to his face.

By the time his father joined him, Dante had seen them move two more men from the mine. Both were badly hurt, but alive.

"Where's your brother?" Father asked.

"I sent him to let Nonna know we were all right. What did the captain have to say?" Dante asked.

"He said there will be a thorough investigation to figure out what caused the collapse. Neither of us is convinced that there was actually an explosion. The noise heard might simply have been a large piece breaking loose. That in turn could have weakened the entire structure."

Dante nodded. "I think plenty of folks see

it otherwise. I heard some of the talk. They want to pin it on the old feud."

His father shrugged. "I'm never heartbroken to see a Panetta die."

Rage heated Dante's face. "How can you say that?" He lowered his voice considerably. "We aren't murderers. But talk like that will convince folks we are."

His father seemed surprised by Dante's reaction. Again he shrugged. "You are right. We are not murderers, but if God chooses to remove Panettas from the earth, I for one will not mourn."

Dante shook his head at his father's comment. "Men lie dead and others are injured—and this is your thought on the matter? With this response, it's no wonder people suspect we set an explosion to kill."

His father swore and spit. Moving closer to his son, he raised his fist. "You forget yourself, Dante. I am your father and you will show me respect. *Capisce?*"

"Yes, I understand."

Dante watched his father move off toward one of the other mine shafts. To him this was just an unexpected interruption in the day's work—at least it seemed that way. It was already growing dark, and soon their shift would be over and the next shift would come on. A great many men would be needed to clear debris and ore from the collapsed stope. If luck was with them, tomorrow it would be back to the same routine and they would learn if the injured men had survived the night.

Frowning, Dante couldn't help but wonder about Panetta. He hadn't looked good when they'd pulled him from the shaft. If he died, what would happen to Chantel and her family? Marco and Alfredo were perfectly capable of seeing to their family's needs—if they were inclined to stop spending so much of their money in the saloons. Marco had gained a reputation for his drinking at the Fortune Hole, and both boys seemed to have a passion for gambling.

Dante clenched his jaw. It was impossible to forget the grief in Chantel's eyes. If her father died, Dante knew she would be heartbroken, and for reasons he couldn't begin to share with his father, he didn't want to see that happen.

"They're bringing up the last of them," a man called from the shaft.

Dante made his way to the area and waited while the final victim was brought to the surface. When he heard that the man was still alive, he offered his help to get him over to the hospital. The mine captain met Dante's determined look and nodded.

"Find out how the others are doing, Calarco, and get word back to me."

"Will do, Captain."

They made a makeshift litter from a long wooden plank and carefully balanced the older man's body on it. Dante knew the man, but not well. The men called him Spud because he always brought a baked potato in his lunch. He'd only recently joined them from another nearby mine.

Taking one end of the plank, Dante lifted in unison with the man who held the other end. A third man walked with them to keep the unconscious patient from rolling off. None of the men spoke as they made their way to Dr. Shipman's. Dante was grateful for the frozen ground. Even with the drifts of snow, it was easier to traverse than dealing with the mud.

Shipman's place was packed with people just as Dante had known it would be. But as they approached, the crowd parted much like the waters of the Red Sea had for Moses and the Israelites. Dante kept his gaze on Spud's pale face, afraid that if he glanced around at the people there, he would see accusation in their expressions.

They made their way up the steps and into the building where one of the doctor's staff directed them to take the litter. Once they'd deposited the patient on a table, the other men quickly exited the room. Dante, however, approached the orderly who prepared to tend Spud.

"Captain told me to ask about the men."

The man looked up and nodded. "Doc's busy working on one now. He thinks most of them will pull through, with exception to one man. He was pretty badly wounded."

Dante didn't want to ask which man. He was afraid of hearing the truth. If the man told him that the dying soul was Giovanni Panetta, he wasn't at all sure what his reaction might be. Spying Father Buh arriving to offer prayers for the new man, Dante left the orderly and went to the priest.

"Father," Dante said, giving a slight nod. "How are the men?"

"They are doing as well as can be expected. It's in the hands of God. Frankly, it's a wonder that any of them have survived."

Dante licked his dust-dried lips. "And . . . what of . . ." He was unable to ask about Panetta, the words sticking in the back of his parched throat. Dante noticed Chantel slipping out the front door. He decided to follow her and ask after her father. His report to the captain could wait that long, and besides, Dante would be inquiring after one of the mine's best workers.

By the time he exited Dr. Shipman's and made his way through the now less than cooperative crowd, Dante could see no sign of Chantel. He frowned, wondering where she might have gone. Heading east on Chapman Street, Dante kept a watchful eye for any sign of the young woman. He finally spied her on the boardwalk and hurried to catch up to her.

"Miss Panetta!"

She stopped and turned to meet him. Her face was tearstained and her eyes were red from crying. His heart sank. "Your father . . . is he . . ."

Chantel's brows knit together as if confused, then realization seemed to dawn. "He's going to be fine. His injuries are not life threatening."

Dante let out a heavy breath that he hadn't even realized he was holding. "I'm glad."

"Are you?" Her tone suggested disbelief.

"I am," he confirmed. "I wouldn't wish an accident like that on anyone."

"Not even your Panetta enemies?" she asked.

Dante shook his head. "That isn't my way. Neither is the setting of premature explosions in order to continue a vendetta."

Chantel brushed back errant strands of brown hair and fixed him with a hard gaze. "This has to end. It's ridiculous, and you know it."

Dante knew she was right and gave a hesitant nod. "It does need to end."

She looked surprised. "I'm . . . glad . . . you agree. Now perhaps our families can be friends."

"I wouldn't go that far," Dante replied. "I just agreed that the seeking of retribution should end. Not that this was an act of such," he quickly added. "Our two families would do better to simply ignore each other. Separate and go our own ways. I'm going to suggest to my father that we consider moving to the Mesabi Range and offer our services there." It was the first time he'd really considered such a thing, but it made perfect sense. There were other iron ranges, and it was pure stubbornness that had kept both families at the same mine.

"You would do that rather than choose to be at peace?"

"It will bring peace, believe me."

She shook her head. "We've not been in the company of your family until the last five years, and the animosity lives on. Especially in the old country. When I was in Italy, there were several incidents. This feud—this need to perpetuate the anger and hatred of generations—will never end . . . until someone chooses to forgive and let the matter go."

"It will take a great many someones, if you ask me."

Chantel raised her chin in a determined

manner. "Well, it has to start with someone. Someone who will take a stand and tell the others that enough is enough."

Dante didn't know what to say. He knew that what she said made sense from the perspective of lessons taught in Sunday services, but from family oaths sworn and honored . . . there would be no letting the matter go. Their very culture was steeped in such traditions.

"Are you heading home now? It's getting dark, and I could see you there safely," he offered.

Chantel's expression became guarded. "Ah . . . no. That's all right. I might need to stop at . . . ah . . . the Morettis' to let them know about my father." She looked as if she'd just decided this fact, making Dante more than a little suspicious.

"If you'll excuse me," she said and gathered her skirts. "Good evening." She hurried to the end of the boardwalk and stepped out into the street. She glanced quickly up one side and down the other before crossing.

Dante saw her glance back over her shoulder as if to see what he was doing. His suspicion grew. What was she really up to?

A thought crossed his mind. He'd not seen Orlando since he'd sent him to tell their grandmother news of the accident. Had Orlando come to the doctor's place—come and then escorted Isabella Panetta elsewhere? Dante certainly hadn't seen the younger woman at the hospital.

He frowned and watched again as Chantel paused momentarily to look over her shoulder. She was up to something, and she clearly didn't want Dante to be a part of it.

Chantel did her best to give Dante the slip. Isabella and Orlando were together at the Panetta home, planning a way to begin their life together.

"This accident has made it clear to us that we want nothing more to do with mining," Isabella had told Chantel when Orlando had shown up at the hospital. "Since the doctor said Papa would live, I want to talk to Orlando. If we are to elope, we must make plans now, while we have the chance."

Chantel had tried to talk her into waiting a few days, but her sister had insisted that now was the moment. They would never have another opportunity to meet like this, unseen by those who wouldn't approve.

Chantel had reluctantly agreed and promised to meet them at the house. "And then Dante had to be at the hospital," Chantel murmured. She glanced again over her shoulder before cutting across an empty lot. Dante was nowhere in sight.

She picked up her pace, noting the darkening winter skies. A chill went through her as the breeze picked up. *But it's more than that. Someone is watching me.* Again she glanced around but saw no one in particular paying her any attention.

Less than two blocks from home, Chantel began to relax a bit. She supposed it was silly to worry about being alone. After all, there was nothing she could do about it now. *I suppose I should have let Dante escort me home. After all, he was good enough to offer. But if I had and he had found Orlando there . . .* Her thoughts trailed off. She couldn't risk him finding his brother there with Isabella. No, God would have to be her lone protector tonight.

Turning onto their street, Chantel had all but forgotten her fears when someone took hold of her from behind. She let out a squeal as the iron hold tightened and whirled her around.

"Miss Panetta, forgive me for startling you. I just thought it strange to see you out here alone. Are you in distress?" It was Leo Fortino. She could make out his features from the streetlight, and his leering smile chilled her even more.

"Mr. Fortino," she said, nodding. She stared down at where his hand gripped her arm.

"I could hardly believe my good fortune when I saw you. However, you know this town isn't safe for a young lady to be walking alone at night."

The skin at the back of her neck tingled. "My . . . my father . . . my father was in the mining accident today. I was at the hospital with my family."

Leo frowned. "Will he live?"

Chantel nodded and tried to pull away from Leo's hold. He did not loosen his grip. "He's hurt, but Dr. Shipman says he'll recover."

"He's lucky. I heard others died," Leo replied.

"Some did," she admitted. "There were a couple of other injured men. I don't know how bad their wounds were, but Dr. Shipman was seeing to them with the help of another doctor."

"And your brothers?"

She nodded and tried her best to calm her shattered nerves. "They are uninjured."

Leo smiled. "So what's your hurry in getting home? Why don't you let me take you to supper?"

"I can't do that, Mr. Fortino. My sister is awaiting news of our father." Chantel again tried to pull away, but this time Leo took hold of both arms.

"You don't need to go just yet. I won't bite, you know."

Chantel swallowed hard. "Mr. Fortino—"

"Leo," he insisted.

She didn't want to argue with him about the inappropriateness of her calling him by his first name. "Leo, I need to go. Walk with me if you must, but my sister is waiting."

"She'll be fine. You look like you need a hot meal, and I know just where we can get one."

"I believe the young lady said she needed to go."

Chantel looked up to find Dante Calarco emerging from the shadows of the alleyway. Never had she been so glad to see anyone in her life.

"I don't believe this is any of your business, friend," Leo said, but he let go his hold on Chantel in order to face Dante.

"I'm making this my business," Dante insisted, taking another step closer to Fortino.

Chantel watched the two men square off, and when the sound of other people coming down the street could be heard, she saw Leo give a shrug.

"I can take you to supper another time, Miss Panetta. Please tell your brother Marco that I'll have drinks waiting for him and Alfredo. I'm sure after a day like today they could use one."

He turned and made his way through the group of women and children who were approaching. He tipped his hat, and Chantel heard him offer them greetings in Italian before she shored up her nerve and met Dante's searching face.

"Thank you," she murmured.

One of the women recognized her. "Chantel, how is your father?"

Another of the women recognized Dante. "Is Mr. Calarco bothering you?" She waggled her finger at Dante. "I heard tell it wasn't an accident that happened today."

Chantel shook her head. "It was exactly that. Just an accident. Furthermore, Mr. Calarco isn't bothering me at all."

The women looked skeptical and the first one spoke again. "And your father?"

"The doctor says he'll recover, Mrs. Nardozzi. Mama and the boys are still at the hospital with him."

Another of the women spoke up. "You tell your mama we'll be bringing by food to help."

"I'll tell her, and thank you. I know she'll appreciate seeing you."

"We'll be preparing food for the other families, as well," Mrs. Nardozzi said. "If you and your sister have time, come join us at my house. Many hands make light work."

"I'll try to get away," she promised.

"And you're sure that you're all right?" Mrs.

Nardozzi glanced again to Dante, and the other women did likewise.

"I'm fine," she assured them. "Mr. Calarco was just inquiring after my father. I should go. Isabella needs to know about Papa." Chantel breathed a sigh of relief when the women didn't question her further. Instead, they bid her good evening and urged their children in the direction of home. Once they were well down the street, Chantel turned to Dante.

"I should get home."

"I'll come with you," Dante said.

"No, that won't be necessary. Truly. I'll be just fine. It's just another block."

"I know where it is," Dante said, taking firm hold of her elbow. "I also know that I'll most likely find my brother there with your sister."

Chantel was grateful for the dim lighting because she was almost sure the color had drained from her face. How had he figured out the truth? She'd said nothing to give the couple away.

"You are certainly quiet now," Dante said with a hint of amusement in his voice.

"What's to be said? You've made up your mind to stick your nose where it doesn't belong." Chantel was rather surprised at her own rudeness, but the man's tone irritated her.

To her surprise Dante laughed, only making

matters worse. "Like I told Fortino, I'm making this my business."

Chantel jerked away from his hold. "And I'm not having it!" She stamped her foot as if to emphasize her words. "You have no right to barge into my home. I won't admit you." She pushed her index finger into the middle of his chest. "You Calarcos may think you can force your will upon the Panettas, but I have news for you."

"Do tell," Dante replied, his voice now sober.

"I won't be bullied by you or anyone else. If my sister wants to marry your brother, then that is their business, and you have no right to interfere. Now leave me alone and don't follow me or I'll . . . I'll . . . well, you won't like it."

She stormed down the street, infuriated that he was actually chuckling at her. When Chantel reached the front door of her house, she turned and could see the shadowy outline of his form where she'd left him.

At least he didn't try to follow her.

Chapter 8

It was Chantel's turn to relieve her mother and sit with her father at the hospital. Smiling down at her father's sleeping form, Chantel shifted in her chair and began tatting again.

"Ah, keeping busy, I see," Father Buh said as he came for his daily visit.

Chantel smiled. "Father, it's good to see you."

"And you, Miss Panetta. I know your mama is quite delighted to have you back."

"Her papa is as well," Chantel's father said, opening his eyes.

Father Buh stepped to the side of the bed. "Sorry if we woke you."

"That's all right. I was hoping to speak with you today," Papa replied.

Chantel was surprised by this. She'd never known her father to seek out counsel from their priest.

Father Buh drew up a chair. "Well, I've always time for a parishioner."

"Should I leave you, Papa?"

Chantel's father shook his head very slowly. She could see the pain in his eyes even at this small effort. "Stay. What I have to say is nothing to be hidden." She smiled and turned her attention back to her tatting.

Papa sighed, then began to speak. "Some say, Father Buh, that this was no accident."

"I have heard as much myself. However, I'm also told that in the days that have followed, no one could find anything that suggested otherwise."

Papa seemed to breathe a sigh of relief. "I'm glad." For a moment he closed his eyes and then reopened them. "Do you suppose God allowed such a thing to happen for the purpose of . . . well . . . teaching?"

The old priest smiled and stroked his beard. "A good question. I for one am of the belief that nothing happens by chance. The Lord foretold of troubles and tragedies that would afflict our days."

"So an accident like this could be one of those troubles and nothing more?"

"Of course," the priest replied.

"And that trouble could be allowed by God to teach a man a lesson, could it not?"

"Oftentimes that is the case, my son. Why do you ask?"

Chantel was intrigued by the conversation, but didn't want to appear overly interested, lest she be asked to leave. She'd never heard her father give anything such a deep spiritual consideration.

"I just feel that there's something here that I'm supposed to see," her father finally admitted. "It's like a restlessness that won't let my soul be at peace."

Father Buh nodded. "I have seen such unrest on many occasions. At times our Father in heaven niggles at the soul to get our attention. Other times, when we are less than willing to receive Him, He does allow for other ways to awaken us to His calling."

"Like facing death?"

"Very often that can be the case. Many a man has changed his ways when death looms. I've sat with men who were about to be hanged and heard their great sorrow and repentant words. I've no doubt in my mind that most of those men, if given another chance at life, would have changed their ways and done things differently. Are you one of those men, Giovanni?"

Chantel couldn't pretend not to want the answer to that question. She continued to tat, waiting anxiously for her father to speak. It seemed to take forever.

"As you know . . . our family," Papa finally began, "are enemies of the Calarcos. The disagreement goes way back, and both sides are guilty of . . . guilty of . . ." His words faded as if he couldn't quite figure out how to explain the matter.

Father Buh had no such trouble. "Guilty of perpetuating the disagreement?"

Papa nodded and closed his eyes. "Perpetuating . . . yes."

"And what is God saying to you about this?"

Chantel glanced over and found her father's face tighten, as if the pain were suddenly too great. She thought to ask him if he needed more medication, but something held her silent.

"I think . . . I believe God is telling me that it must end. That we are wrong for our actions." He opened his eyes and his face relaxed. "I believe He spoke to me."

The priest smiled and reached out to pat the man's bruised and scratched hand. "Sometimes God speaks in a whisper and sometimes in the collapse of rocks and iron ore. And always His words offer us a choice."

"A choice?" Chantel's father asked. "What do you mean?"

She could see that her father was growing quite tired, but he continued to press the priest for understanding.

"You believe God spoke to you," Father Buh replied. "I believe God speaks to all of His children. Do you remember your training as a child?"

Papa gave a single nod.

"A man who is without a Savior is without

hope. We cannot be cleansed of our sins without God's grace and the sacrifice of our blessed Savior. We are utterly and completely left to condemnation and darkness, by our own choice. And," he continued, "we are ushered into forgiveness and light by a choice, as well. If we acknowledge our sinfulness—our evil nature—and repent, we choose that light. To reject it is to cast aside the slain body of our Lord Jesus and all that He did for us at the cross. It is to mock the empty tomb and despise the resurrected Savior."

"I have never sought to . . . reject God," Chantel's father said, his voice weak.

"My son, it is in our very nature to reject authority. However, God has made a way for us to come unto Him, and that is through Jesus."

Papa looked at the older man. "And past mistakes can be forgiven?"

"Are you willing to be forgiven? Are you willing to confess your sins?"

Chantel's hands stilled as she looked at her father. He seemed to feel her gaze upon him and gave her a smile. "I am," he whispered. "I want to be at peace with God."

"Then," the priest said, "we must pray."

Dante sharpened one of his grandmother's paring knives on a whetstone as she bustled around the kitchen. The aroma of her delectable lasagna filled the air, and his stomach growled in anticipation of the meal.

Turning his attention to testing the knife's edge, Dante couldn't help but think of Chantel Panetta. Her tongue was sharp when she was riled. He thought of her threat to him and the way she had stood her ground in defense of her sister and his brother. It brought a smile to his face remembering how unafraid she'd been—at least in dealing with him.

"Ah, you must be thinking of a young lady, no?" Nonna said, eyeing him with careful scrutiny.

Dante startled at this. His grandmother always seemed to have an uncanny way of getting the truth out of him. "I was, in fact. I was thinking of you and how blessed we are to have your amazing meals."

"You are a poor liar, Dante Calarco. Better to ask God's forgiveness than continue," she said, shaking her finger.

He laughed and shrugged. "Well, it was partly true. Your lasagna is my favorite, and you know that full well."

"Sí, but there is something more on your mind, I think."

Dante opened his mouth to reply, but just

then his father and Orlando came into the kitchen from outside. Both looked half frozen.

"It's cold out there," his father declared. "Cold that goes right to the bone."

Orlando slipped from the room, but their father went to the hot stove and warmed his hands. "Some say it's a gonna be a bad winter."

"They always say that," Dante replied. "And this far north they have good reason." He thought it just as good a time to bring up his idea of moving. "Maybe we should think about relocating. This isn't the only iron mine in Minnesota. Maybe we should go south to the Mesabi Range."

His father looked at him oddly. "Why would we leave perfectly good jobs and do that?"

Dante switched to English so his grand-mother would have more trouble keeping up. "Well, I was just thinking that if we were to move a little farther south, it might be good for Nonna. If we suffer from this cold, just imagine what it's like for her."

His father cast a glance toward his mother-in-law and then back to Dante. "Has she complained?"

"No, of course not. You know that isn't her way. It was just something that came to mind." In fact, it would be the perfect solu-tion for getting Orlando away from Isabella Panetta.

And for getting me away from her sister.

Dante pushed that thought aside and got up to put away the whetstone. He handed the knife to his grandmother and again spoke in her native tongue. "I believe this will do."

She put her thumb to the edge and nodded. "Sí. *E'perfetto.*" She looked to Dante's father. "Vittorio, are you ready to eat?"

The man nodded and moved from the stove. "I'll go wash up."

They were soon seated at the well-worn kitchen table with steaming plates of lasagna, crusty bread, olive oil, and freshly grated cheese. It was a veritable feast as far as Dante was concerned. He dug into his food, hoping there might also be some cannoli for dessert.

"The mine owners are pushing to have the saloons closed all day Sunday," his father informed them.

"That won't go over well," Dante replied.

"No, it won't," his father said, tearing a chunk of bread to dip in the oil. "The miners claim that the men are too often unable to work because of their Sunday drinking. They believe if the saloons are closed, the men will be more likely to show up to work on Monday."

"I doubt the saloon owners will allow for it," Dante replied. Orlando kept his eyes fixed on the food. No doubt his mind was on Isabella.

"They may not have a choice. Ely will soon incorporate, and when it does there will be all sorts of new laws. In order to acquire the mines into the city limits, those in charge will have to be willing to yield something in return. This will be a good first step. The taxes brought in by the mines will far outweigh any benefit of having an open saloon on the Sabbath."

"The men should be in church on Sunday," Nonna added. "If the saloons are closed, maybe they will go with their families to church and spend time with their little ones."

"I doubt it, Mama Barbato," Dante's father replied.

"Well, once the mines are incorporated and the town has a taste of increased monies, it will only whet their appetites for more," Dante replied. He wasn't much for drinking and seldom wasted his money at the saloons or gambling halls. He had saved a great portion of his wages over the years and even now knew that he could most likely buy a home of his own if he had the desire. Of course, leaving the comfort of his grandmother's tender care for life on his own held no appeal.

"You're quiet tonight, Orlando," Nonna interjected. "Are you ill?"

"No, Nonna. I'm fine. Just a lot on my mind," he replied. "The food is really good. Thank you."

Dante could see that his grandmother was less than convinced, but she said nothing more. Dante couldn't help but wonder if his brother's moodiness had to do with his meeting with Isabella Panetta. Or perhaps the accident at the mine had left him more rattled than Dante realized. Either way, his brother was clearly not himself.

"Marilla's letter says that she could use as much tatting and Chantilly lace as we have to sell," Mama said, looking up from the missive as the family enjoyed a quiet evening in the warm sitting room. Outside the wind howled, but the house was a perfect refuge.

Marco poked at the fire and added another log to keep the room toasty. Isabella worked feverishly on her sewing, and Chantel couldn't help but wonder just how soon the young couple would elope. She hadn't had a chance to really speak to her sister on the matter since the accident last week.

Papa rocked quietly, a warm wrap tucked around his legs. He'd only been home a day, but Chantel could tell that he was feeling much better. He said there was something about being among his loved ones that made him heal all the faster.

Mama continued. "She also says that she will be sending a Christmas package soon, although she wishes we could join her for the holidays in Duluth."

"Aunt Marilla always sends such wonderful gifts," Chantel replied. Her wealthy widowed aunt was most generous with her dead husband's money. Uncle Gaetan Faverau had made a small fortune and never failed to spoil his childless wife, and she in turn had learned to do likewise with her family.

"It would be wonderful to see her again," Isabella surprised Chantel by adding. "Maybe Christmas in Duluth would be possible, Papa?"

"We can't leave our jobs to go gallivanting off like that," Marco said before their father could speak. "The mine captain has already been complaining that production is behind. Quotas have to be met."

"I heard them say we'll be going to twelve-hour shifts before Christmas," Alfredo added.

"That's hardly fair," Isabella pouted.

"Fairness never figured into iron mining," Marco countered.

"I've been thinking," Papa began, "that God has given me a second chance to live a better life."

His sudden declaration immediately caught the attention of his family. Mama smiled and nodded as if she knew what he would say next. "I think," Papa continued, "that it is time for us to put our affairs in order. To set our lives right before God."

Chantel saw Marco frown. "And what do you mean by that, Papa?" he asked. "I suppose you'll want us all confessing our sins and attending church regularly." Marco sounded sarcastic and unimpressed.

"What I want . . . is an end to the fighting," Papa replied. "I want to make peace with the Calarcos."

Chapter 9

As Christmas neared, the mine owners mandated twelve-hour shifts for their workers to meet their promised quotas. It seemed the entire nation, possibly the world, was hungry for Minnesota's very pure Bessemer iron ore.

Dante knew the hours were hard on his father, whose age often seemed more apparent in the cold months of winter. The damp cold of the north was only exacerbated by time spent deep in the mine. There the dampness was aggravated by seepage from the ground water and occasional unearthed springs. The pumps ran regularly to keep the mine shafts dry, but it did nothing to help the heaviness of the air. Most of the men who worked underground had a perpetual cough, and Dante's father was no exception.

These circumstances made Dante consider moving a natural solution. Of course, if they continued mining work, it would be damp and cold no matter where they went. But surely a warmer location would give his father's lungs time to dry out. And there were a great many states where mining jobs could be had, especially for men who were skilled in handling explosives.

Of course, his father really hadn't given any serious consideration to the idea. Dante had talked to him on several occasions, reminding his father that there were better places to live—places that would be easier on Nonna. Since first mentioning the idea of moving south, Dante couldn't help but think it would solve all of their problems. If he could just get Orlando away from Ely and Isabella Panetta, he would surely forget about his idea of marriage. Didn't the saying go, "Out of sight, out of mind?"

Making a careful check of his explosive supplies, Dante was surprised when he looked up to find the Panetta men coming his way. He closed the wooden lid on a crate of dynamite and turned to face them. Marco and Alfredo walked on either side of their father. Their soft mining caps were aglow from the small candle affixed to the canvas rim. Mining was dirty, dark work, and the candles were standard operating equipment. Even so, it wasn't something he wanted close to the explosives. Holding up his hand, Dante hoped they wouldn't take offense.

"I've got dynamite here."

The younger men stopped, but Mr. Panetta reached up to extinguish his candle, then slowly stepped forward. "I wonder if your father is nearby."

Dante looked around. "He was here a moment ago." He felt apprehensive and narrowed his gaze. "Is there a problem?"

"Hasn't there always been a problem between our families?" Panetta replied. "I've come to make peace."

"Peace?" Dante wasn't at all sure he'd heard right. "You want to make peace between our families? Here? Now?"

"I do." Panetta's dark-eyed gaze pierced deep into Dante's soul. They were eyes that reminded him much of Chantel's. Dante forced the thought away. He couldn't allow himself to think about her.

"I think it's well past time," the older man added. In Panetta's expression was a look that suggested true regret.

Dante was about to speak when his father came up from behind him. "What are you doing here?" he asked Panetta. Stepping between his son and the older man, Calarco pointed his finger. "We do our jobs; now go do yours."

Mr. Panetta squared his shoulders. "I've come in peace, Vittorio."

Dante's father spit on the ground in disgust.

"There can be no peace between us. Our ancestors cry out from the grave that you would even suggest such a thing."

"That's just my point," Panetta said, his expression softening. "I was nearly one of those ancestors. That accident," he said, stressing the word, "opened my eyes to the futility and stupidity of our feud."

Dante's father raised his fist. His face reddened. "You would dare to say my people were stupid. I should cut out your tongue. I should kill you for saying such a thing."

Dante feared his father's words would only serve to rile the Panetta brothers, but they stood back and said nothing.

"I'm suggesting that both of our families were mistaken," Panetta replied. "God calls us to peace, and I'm here to extend that peace to you and your sons."

Again Dante's father spit, and this time he swore, as well. Dante kept his gaze fixed on the three Panetta men, fearful that his father's anger would cause one of them to start trouble. They did nothing, however. *Maybe they are just as tired of this nonsense as their father*, he thought.

"Vittorio, we can make peace and put an end to this," Panetta said, limping forward.

Dante wondered if the cold damp of the mine caused the man's pain to increase. It seemed he hadn't limped quite so much when they'd first approached. Calarco pulled back and held out his fist.

"I make no peace with you. Calarcos have nothing to do with Panettas! Nothing except death!"

Giovanni Panetta halted and crossed his arms. "Then perhaps you should tell that to your son."

Calarco looked to Dante with an unspoken question in his expression. Dante didn't have a chance to say a word, however.

"Not that one. I'm speaking of your youngest—Orlando. It would seem he's quite content to have something to do with Panettas. Particularly my daughter Isabella."

"It's a lie!" Calarco raged. "A Panetta lie! My boys—they do not touch your daughters. They would not dishonor their ancestors and family that way. They know better."

"And I say otherwise. You should maybe ask Dante. My daughter tells me he knows all about it."

Dante felt as if the man had sent him a hard blow to the midsection. He stiffened as his father turned accusing eyes on him. How could he admit to knowing about this ordeal without causing his father even greater shame?

"*E'colpa mia,* Papa. All my fault. I've tried

my best to put a stop to it," Dante found himself explaining. "It's the biggest reason I suggested we leave Ely." By now several additional miners had gathered to see what the raised voices were all about.

"You knew, but you say nothing to me about it?" His father's eyes narrowed in anger. "I will deal with you later. I will deal with you both, but for now, I say no more." He turned back to Panetta. "I will put an end to this thing myself."

"Wouldn't it just be better to make peace between us?" Panetta again tried. "Nearly dying gave me a great deal to think about. I spoke to Father Buh, and he helped me to see that sometimes God gives us a second chance to make things right. He believes that God is calling us to make the peace."

Dante's father opened his mouth to speak, then closed it just as quickly. No one would speak out against the local priest. The man was loved by everyone, whether they attended St. Anthony's or elsewhere. Calarco looked at the gathering of fellow miners and muttered several expletives under his breath.

"I do not believe God tells us to make this peace. I believe God would tell me, if this were true. I will honor my people . . . the pledges of my father and his father before him. I am a Calarco, and there can be no peace with you." He turned and proudly stalked away.

Dante was left to face the Panettas. He understood his father's frustration. He was embarrassed by not knowing what was happening under his own nose. For his son to disrespect him in such a way was a humiliating thing. For his enemy to point it out made matters even worse.

Mr. Panetta looked to Dante. "I am sorry. I do want an end to this fighting. I tell you here and now, this feud will not continue because of us. It is finished."

The Panettas turned to go back to their tasks. Dante said nothing to stop them and nothing to agree with them. He couldn't very well do either one without causing his father further shame.

Chantel giggled like a schoolgirl. It was nearly Christmas, and the festive spirit was upon her. With the holiday just days away, Chantel found herself caught up in the joy of the occasion. She thought of the hidden presents she'd brought back from Italy. She had something for each member of the family and knew they would be quite happy with the gifts. Especially Mama.

Then there were the parties; informal, but well-attended gatherings of family and friends. Every night it seemed someone held open their home for visitation and refreshments. It might have been exhausting had it not been for the happiness the season brought.

Of late, Chantel had been kept quite busy at home with baking and creating little bags of goodies for the neighborhood children. She had brought home many of her father's family recipes and was anxious to try them all. Already she had compared some of the dishes with recipes from her mother's family. Mama was French-Italian, while Papa's ancestors had originally come from farther south of Rome, eventually resettling in the northern wine country. The recipes they cherished were often similar, but sometimes very different.

With her list of needed ingredients in hand, Chantel found herself perusing the shelves of one store and then another in order to find everything they would need. It was helpful that additional stores had come to Ely in her absence. Helpful, too, that with the growing population sporting so many Italians, the storekeepers had started paying more attention to that culture's culinary needs.

The clerk stepped forward to help her and smiled. "What can I do for you today, miss?"

She checked her list again and drew out two small glass jars. "I need a quarter cup of cinnamon and a quarter cup of anise."

The clerk took her jars and turned to the labeled spices behind him. Rows of bottled spices were filed alphabetically and set at a level that was easy to access. Some of the other stores used drawers or tins, but Mama preferred the spices to be kept in glass.

As the man began to measure out the anise, Chantel was surprised by a friendly greeting.

"Buon giorno!" Mrs. Barbato said with a smile. The old woman seemed quite jolly. She wore a bright red bonnet and scarf that very nearly matched the hue of her cheeks.

"Good . . . morning," Chantel replied rather hesitantly.

"You are well, yes?"

"Sí." Chantel felt rather awkward. *"E tu?"*

"Sí, I am well. I came to town with friends." She nodded toward Chantel's basket. "I see you are shopping to make your Christmas goodies." She motioned to her own basket. "As am I."

Chantel relaxed. There was nothing wrong in having a conversation with Mrs. Barbato, even if she was Dante's grandmother. "We've been getting ready for the holidays. My brothers are quite fond of sweets, but my sister Isabella is even worse. For such a tiny girl, you wouldn't think she could eat so much candy without getting fat."

Then the old woman laughed and patted her waist. "I am fond of it, too. Especially *Torrone*. You will make some, sí?"

The traditional Italian Christmas candy was a favorite of Chantel's brothers. "Sí. Mama has been shelling almonds and hazelnuts for days. My brother Marco could eat his weight in Torrone."

Mrs. Barbato chuckled. "Ah, so could my Dante and Orlando. They are spoiled, but I love them so."

"My Nonna Panetta taught me to make *struffoli* a little different from my mama's recipe, so I'm anxious to try that, as well." Chantel tried not to show her discomfort at the mention of the woman's grandsons.

"There are many ways to make it. I like the dough to have lemon and orange zest," the old woman declared. "Then I make the honey mixture with just a hint of clove."

"So does Nonna Panetta."

The woman laughed. "Sí, we sometimes shared our recipes when we could. Now for the candied fruit—does your nonna still include candied melon rind?"

Chantel had known the two women had grown up in the same town, but hadn't realized that Nonna Panetta and Mrs. Barbato

had ever spoken, much less exchanged recipes. "You know my nonna?"

Mrs. Barbato's smile dimmed only a bit.
"Sí, but our families . . . they did not like us
to be friends, so we didn't speak of it."

"I can well imagine," Chantel replied. She
glanced around all of a sudden, almost fearful
that someone might have overheard. "I suppose I'm surprised that you're even speaking
to me." She gave a nervous laugh to ease her
own embarrassment at the situation.

Mrs. Barbato sobered considerably. "I ask
myself, would our Blessed Lord speak to you?
And of course He would." She smiled again.
"So I speak to you, as well."

Chantel nodded. "I'm glad. You know my
papa was hurt in the mine collapse a while
back."

"I knew that. Is he well now?"

"He's much better. He took a hard hit in the
hip and it makes him walk with a limp, but the
doctor said perhaps in time that will diminish.
The accident changed him, Mrs. Barbato. I
know he tried to speak to Mr. Calarco about
it, but he wouldn't hear him out."

"He talked to Vittorio?"

"Sí, at the mine. But Papa said Mr. Calarco
wouldn't listen." Chantel shrugged. "I know
Mama was hopeful the bitterness between
our families could end."

"And what of your papa? What did he say to Vittorio?" Mrs. Barbato seemed quite interested to know.

"He feels that God would have our families put aside the feud. He thinks we should let the past be in the past and that the fighting should cease."

For a moment, Chantel wasn't sure that Mrs. Barbato had heard her. The old woman had bowed her head, and when she raised it again she had tears in her eyes. *Sia lode a Dio.*" Praise be to God.

Yes, Chantel thought, it would be glorious . . . had Mr. Calarco not rejected the idea. She shifted the basket to her left arm and nodded. "I was happy to hear that Papa wanted to see an end to it, as well. But Mr. Calarco refused to even listen. He said that Papa was disrespecting our ancestors."

"Foolish man. He cannot see how bad this is for the future." She fell silent a moment, then met Chantel's gaze and added, "For your sister and my Orlando."

Chantel nodded and drew a deep breath. She hadn't been sure what the old woman might have known about the young couple. It was a relief to find out she knew the truth. "My sister loves Orlando very much."

"And my grandson, he loves her. They wish to marry."

Chantel felt the weight of the secret ease a bit. "Sí." She reached out and touched Mrs. Barbato's coat. "I fear for them."

The older woman shrugged. "The Bible says there is no fear in perfect love. Perfect love casts out fear. We have that love in our Lord. They do, too. We needn't fear for them. Father in heaven, He will guide them."

"Here are your spices, miss," the clerk interjected. "Should I put it on the Panetta bill?"

Chantel took the bottles. "Yes. My father will be in to pay on Saturday."

The man nodded and turned to Mrs. Barbato. "And what can I get for you?"

She handed him a list. "I hope you have all of this in stock."

The man looked over the list and nodded. "I believe we do. Let me get right to work on this." The front door opened, sounding the bells that hung overhead. The clerk called out a greeting to two new customers before turning back to his work.

Chantel tucked the spice bottles in her basket. "I suppose I should be going."

"The baking will not do itself," Mrs. Barbato said, smiling. "But you have your mother and sister to help, and that is always more fun. I used to love baking for the holidays when we would all get together and share the work and tell stories of long ago. We laughed and ate—it was the best of times."

"We did that at my Nonna Panetta's last Christmas. It was wonderful. You remind me very much of my nonna. While I was in Italy, I missed my family here, but now that I'm here, I long to sit and listen to Nonna tell me stories of the old days and of our family."

Mrs. Barbato patted Chantel's hand. "When you want to talk to your nonna, come and see me instead. You can talk to me, and I will tell you stories about the days gone by and of the family. I know it won't be the same, but I will be happy to tell you what I know."

The offer was more precious to Chantel than she could explain. *"Grazie,"* she whispered. "That means so much to me."

"And you don't worry. I will speak to Vittorio. I will tell him he displeases God when he refuses to forgive. I will pray, too, that God will speak to his heart."

Chantel didn't think before saying, "And to Dante's heart, as well."

Mrs. Barbato smiled. "I think his heart is already changing, but I will pray for him, too. He is a good man—Orlando, too. I have raised them as I would have my own sons, and I know their hearts. They love their papa and do not wish to disrespect him. Still, I think if their father will listen to our Lord, then the son will do the same."

"I hope so," Chantel replied, feeling the strangest flutter in her heart at the thought of Dante coming to her in peace rather than anger. "I pray so."

Chapter 10

Christmas Eve arrived, yet the men trudged off to the mine as they usually did, leaving the Panetta women to prepare for that night's feast. An Italian Christmas called for several days of feasting, and Christmas Eve was just one of many. For Chantel, it was one of her favorite times of the year. She loved working with her mother and sister to create the special meals. She loved having her family all around her. When they'd been younger, she and her sister would go ice skating and sledding with the boys. Sometimes Chantel wished they could go back to those days when life seemed much less complicated. She sighed. At least they'd all share Christmas together.

The mine didn't often close, but the owners would cease work Christmas Day. There were precious few days of rest in the mining industry. Chantel thought it a terrible way to treat people. She had read not long ago that the United States Congress was working on new laws to address work hours and improvements to industrial jobs. Dangers were always great in any job that involved heavy machinery and explosives, and she would be glad to see new regulations enforced that might keep her father and brothers safe. For now, however, they would simply rely on the Lord and hope that each man would be mindful of their duties and the dangers.

Mama entered the kitchen humming a Christmas tune and carrying a large bowl of candied orange rind. They had worked for weeks to candy cherries, as well as orange, lemon, and melon rinds for the Christmas struffoli. Chantel couldn't help but lean over and take a piece of the sweet treat. "Mmm, I just love candied orange rind."

"It's always been impossible to keep you out of it," Mama said, putting the bowl on the counter. "Even when you were a little girl, it was your favorite." She checked the cloth-covered struffoli dough. "It's risen nicely. We can roll it out now. Is the oil ready?"

Chantel nodded. "It just needs to heat up. I was waiting until closer to time for the frying. I didn't want it to burn."

Her mother nodded and pressed her hands into the dough with one hand while sprinkling flour out on the cleaned countertop with the other. She pinched off a piece of the dough and began to roll it and sing a Christmas carol in Italian.

Chantel smiled. Christmas was her mother's

favorite time of year, and this year was special because Mama had all of her children around her. Chantel thought of her grandparents in Italy and wished they could have somehow come to America with her. In a sense they had, Chantel thought, smiling. While in Italy last year, she had spent her extra money to have a special photograph taken of her nonna and nonno, as well as another of the entire extended family. At least as many of them as could come for the picture. What a grand party that had turned out to be. Even now, Chantel remembered the joyous celebration and love that had been shared that day. The photograph would always be a special reminder.

Checking the fire, Chantel placed the large pan of olive oil on the stove and went to find the round-bottomed pan they used to heat the honey, sugar, and water mixture they would pour over the dough after it was fried. Isabella took that moment to return from her search for fresh cream and eggs. "Mrs. Merritt had plenty of both," she announced, coming into the kitchen. "Goodness, but it feels so much better in here than out there. I think we may be in for another snow. The sky looks so dark and threatening." She placed a basket on the large kitchen table and began to peel off her scarf and gloves.

"We're just getting ready to fry the struf-foli," Mama replied. "Put on your apron and help me roll out the dough."

Isabella shrugged out of her coat and went to hang it up before taking up her apron. "Mrs. Merritt says the Finnish are opening a school soon. It's to be a Finnish-American school."

"What's wrong with the school we already have?" Mama asked. "Miss Wilson is a good teacher, I hear."

Isabella shrugged. "But apparently she's not teaching the Finnish language and history."

"That is for the mamas and pappas to do, no?" their mother replied. "We are Americans now, so we should speak as Americans and let each family keep the language of their ancestors."

"I agree," Isabella concurred. "But apparently the Finnish people do not."

Chantel put the honey mixture on the stove to cook. She would boil it until the foam died down and the liquid turned yellow. At that point they would take it from the heat and add the struffoli and candied fruits. Then it would just be a matter of forming it. Mama always liked to make it into a holiday wreath. Chantel knew it didn't matter; her brothers and father would devour it no matter its shape.

There was a knock on the back door, and since Chantel hadn't yet started to help with the dough, she went to answer it. The cold air hit her face, but because of the heated kitchen it actually felt good. Mrs. Nardozzi's two youngest boys stood at the bottom of the steps, jostling each other.

"Mama sent us to recite our Christmas verses to you," the oldest boy said. He nudged his little brother. "You go first."

"Wouldn't you like to step inside where it's warm?" Chantel asked.

The older boy shook his head. "Mama said we couldn't. She said we had to stand here 'cause our boots are dirty."

Chantel nodded. "Very well. Please continue." Again the oldest boy elbowed his brother.

The youngest boy, who couldn't have been more than four years old, looked up at Chantel with wide dark eyes. "And, lo . . . a . . . lo," he stammered and let his gaze fall to the ground. "Lo . . . the angel of the Lord fell on them. . . ."

His brother ribbed him hard and interrupted. "He didn't fall on them, he came upon them."

The little boy pushed his brother away. "I can tell it." He looked back to Chantel, who did her best not to giggle. "And lo . . . the angel of the Lord . . ." He paused for a moment, gathered his composure, and continued. "The angel of the Lord came upon them . . . and the glory . . . of the Lord . . . shined around them . . . and they were sore and afraid."

Chantel put her hand over her mouth to hide her grin. She could only imagine that if the angel of the Lord had fallen on the shepherds, they would be sore and afraid.

"And the angel said unto them . . . Fear not: for . . ." His voice trailed off as his face screwed into a stern look of concentration. " . . . behold, I bring you good tidings of great joy, which shall be to all people." He grinned up at her and gave a bow.

"Very good," Chantel said, reaching out to tousle his brown hair.

"Now it's my turn," his brother declared. He filled his lungs with air and in one breath fired off the next few verses. "'For unto you is born this day in the city of David a Saviour, which is Christ the Lord. And this shall be a sign unto you; Ye shall find the babe wrapped in swaddling clothes, lying in a manger. And suddenly there was with the angel a multitude of the heavenly host praising God, and saying, Glory to God in the highest, and on earth peace, goodwill toward men.'" He barely got the words out before gasping in another deep breath. He grinned up at her, revealing two missing front teeth. "See, I know it really good."

"Indeed you do," Chantel replied. "And both of you did such a good job, I must reward you. If you will wait here, I'll get you some candy."

She went back inside and opened the cupboard, where little bags of goodies awaited. The neighborhood children had come steadily throughout the week to sing songs and quote Bible verses. As was the tradition back in Italy, the recipients of such visits would bestow treats upon their visitors.

"It's the two youngest Nardozzi boys," Chantel explained, taking two bags from the cupboard. "They quoted from Luke and did so quite nicely."

Mama smiled up from the long doughy snake. "Tell them I said well done."

"I will," Chantel replied. She hurried back to the boys and found them already distracted and pushing each other around. "Boys, my mama said to tell you 'Well done!' And now I have your gift." She held out the two bags. She had helped make little cloth bags for the candies and pointed to the drawstring tops. "Once you eat all the candy, you'll have the little bag for your marbles. Won't that be nice?"

The boys took the offering and beamed her a smile. "Grazie!" they declared in unison and ran for home.

Chantel watched after them for a moment, feeling a sense of longing. She envied her sister having found true love. Even as the thought came to mind, she prayed for forgiveness. Envy would get a person into trouble every time, her mother often said. Chantel pushed the thoughts aside and closed the door to the cold. There was plenty of work to keep her mind occupied. No sense letting sin ruin the day.

Marco ignored his conscience as he came upon the Fortune Hole. It was Christmas Eve and the family would be awaiting him at home, but he wanted a drink in the worst way. He entered the bar and immediately spied Leo standing with his back to the door. He was intent on a ledger book and didn't seem to even notice Marco until he'd come up alongside him.

"You ought to be more aware," Marco chided him. "Someone's likely to come in here and rob you."

Leo stepped back from the bar to reveal a derringer in his hand. He grinned. "I'm always very aware of what's going on—especially here in my bar."

Marco couldn't help but remember the night

Lamb had been killed. "I need a drink," he said, trying to force the images from his mind.

"On Christmas Eve?" Leo asked, laughing. "What will the priest say?" He closed the ledger and took it with him behind the bar. "Whiskey or beer?"

A large beer was more to his liking, but Marco didn't have the time to spare. "Whiskey." He put his money on the bar.

Leo furnished the drink and waited until Marco had downed it to hold up the bottle. "Another?"

Marco shook his head. "I need to go."

"Say, you haven't been here much since that little altercation with Lamb. I hope you aren't thinking of quitting on me."

He looked at Leo and could see the man seemed almost amused. "I don't much like getting drunk anymore. Clouds my thinking," Marco replied. He could still envision the blood pooling around Lamb's lifeless body— could still smell the gunpowder. Worse than that, Marco could well remember Leo's casual attitude about the entire matter.

Leo poured more whiskey into the empty glass. "This one's on me. Merry Christmas."

Marco hesitated and Leo chuckled. "Go on. You won't find me giving any other gifts." He recorked the bottle and put it under the bar. "One more drink isn't going to get you drunk. With any luck at all, you'll just enjoy your church services all the more."

Marco looked for several long seconds at the glass before picking it up and downing the contents. Leo smiled and nodded. "See, it's all just in the spirit of the holiday. Now, if you really want some fun, come around on New Year's Eve. We're going to have a high-stakes poker game that will beat 'em all."

"Thanks, but no. I don't think I will," Marco said, heading for the door.

"Suit yourself," Leo replied.

Marco left the saloon and made his way home without stopping. He knew his father and brother would already be there and that the family would be waiting for him to clean up and join them for the Christmas Eve feast. At midnight he would be expected to attend church with his family to remember the coming of the baby Jesus. His heart wasn't up for celebrating, however. As much as it irritated him that he craved another drink, the desire for alcohol held him fast in its grip, and all Marco could think about was returning to Leo's rather than heading to church with his family. Maybe he could slip away after supper.

"There you are," his mama declared when he tried to sneak in the back door. "I was just about to send your papa to find you."

"Sorry, Mama. I . . . ah . . . I had to take care of something." He kissed her on the cheek in a hurried fashion lest she smell the whiskey on his breath.

"Well, you're here now. Go get cleaned up and then we can eat."

He moved past her and through the warm kitchen. The succulent aroma of his mother's and sisters' cooking followed him through the house. Maybe a good meal would put the alcohol out of his mind. Maybe time with his family would help to ease his guilty conscience and bring him peace. But once again he pictured Lamb lying dead on the floor, his blood soaking into the rough wood planks. Peace seemed impossible.

Near noon on Christmas Day, Chantel gathered her family in the front room and announced that she had gifts from Italy to give to each of her family. "I could hardly restrain myself," she explained, handing out the presents. "I was so tempted to give them to you when I returned."

Mama looked at the square gift a moment. "This is such a surprise." She unwrapped the paper to reveal a photograph— nearly forty family members gathered for the occasion.

Tears welled and Mama clutched the photo to her breast. "It's wonderful."

"I'm glad you like it," Chantel said. She turned to her father. "Open yours, Papa."

He did so and held up the framed picture of his parents. "Oh, Chantelly Rosa, this is a precious gift." He looked at the woman and man a moment and then handed the portrait to his wife. "They look so old."

Mama nodded. "Oh, how I miss them." With her own parents now passed on, Mama considered the Panettas to be her mother and father.

Isabella had already unwrapped her gift and was quite excited at the sight of the brush and mirror set. "Oh, they're lovely and so beautiful." She turned them first one way and then another to catch the light.

"The mosaic pattern on the back is made with pieces of broken stained glass. I thought of you the moment I saw it."

"I'll cherish it always." She leaned over to kiss Chantel's cheek. "Thank you so much." There was a knock on the front door and, as if expecting someone, Isabella jumped to her feet. "I'll get it."

Marco and Alfredo had unwrapped their gifts by this time to reveal two beautiful marble shaving mugs, complete with marble-handled brushes. "A bit fancy for an iron miner, isn't it?" Marco asked with a grin.

"Nonno said it was the perfect gift for you boys, and who was I to say otherwise?" She smiled and motioned to their scraggly looking faces. "Maybe you could use them right away."

Isabella cleared her throat. "Ah . . . everyone, I hope you don't mind, but I invited Orlando to join us for the noon meal," Isabella announced from the hallway. Orlando Calarco stepped around from the entryway and took his place at Isabella's side.

The room fell awkwardly silent and for several moments all anyone did was stare at the young couple. They were all surprised to see a Calarco in their home, but it was Papa who welcomed the young man first. "Glad to have you. Merry Christmas."

Orlando stepped forward and shook hands with the older man. "Thank you, and Merry Christmas."

Chantel could see that her brothers were rather apprehensive, but they said nothing. They were well aware of their sister's interest in Orlando, even if they didn't yet approve of it.

"We were just enjoying Chantel's gifts," Mama said, holding up the pictures. "It's almost like having family from the old country here with us."

"And now we can feast and enjoy the day,"

Isabella said, taking hold of Orlando's arm. "I've already told Orlando what a wonderful cook you are, Mama."

Their mother blushed and put the photographs aside. Getting to her feet, she motioned to her daughters. "Come and help me, and then he will see what wonderful cooks you are, as well."

Isabella laughed and dropped her hold. "I'm not the best," she admitted, "but I'm learning."

Chantel could tell by the way Orlando looked at her sister that he didn't care whether or not she could cook. It was true love between them. No matter that their families had been at odds for generations. Their feelings for each other easily surpassed that obstacle. *I wonder if it will be enough when Mr. Calarco disowns his son.*

She said very little as they worked to set dinner on the table. She said even less as they joined together for the meal. As the minutes slipped by, she found herself more and more withdrawn. How was it that love had come so easily to Isabella and not to her?

After a while it seemed as if Orlando had always been a part of their family. Even Marco and Alfredo had forgotten their earlier hesitation. They now laughed and shared stories with Orlando as if he were part of the family.

Mama and Papa seemed to enjoy his company, as well. It might have been one of the most pleasant dinners Chantel had ever enjoyed had it not been for her own frustrations and longings.

It's silly, she told herself. *Silly to fret over something that cannot be helped. In time, I will find love.*

She couldn't help but think of Dante. His dark eyes and piercing gaze flooded her memories. She could see something of him in Orlando, but where Dante was more serious and intense, his brother was easygoing and lighthearted.

"The food this holiday has been the best we've ever had," Papa declared. "You ladies have outdone yourselves. You have my undying gratitude."

Without warning there was a heavy pounding on the front door. Marco was closest and got up to answer it without hesitation. Chantel heard him say hello, but then Dante Calarco stormed into the room and grabbed Orlando by the shirt and yanked him to his feet.

"What are you doing here? You know that our father has forbid you to see her." He glanced around the table. "And yet you come here to celebrate Christmas? What of your own family? What of Nonna? She's wondered all this time where you were."

"I'm sorry," Orlando said, pulling away from his brother's hold. "I can't abide by what Papa wants. I love Isabella, and we intend to marry. No one is going to come between us. The Panettas want peace, and so do I. If Papa can't accept that, then he'll have to disown me."

"You think he won't? And if he disowns you, that means we all must, or don't you realize that?" Dante questioned. He threw a glance at Chantel and shook his head. "Did any of you stop to think that this might only serve to make matters worse?"

"How can love ever make matters worse?" Chantel asked without thinking.

Dante scowled. "You and your foolish notions. Love has been the cause of nations going to war."

"Son," Papa said, getting to his feet, "why don't you calm down and join us. There's still plenty of good food to share."

For a moment Chantel thought Dante might consider it. He looked around the room and at the table as if contemplating the various dishes there. Finally he shook his head. "You've all gone mad. Especially you," he said, turning back to his brother. "You think you can dance to this tune, but you've not yet paid the piper. Now I'm taking you home and that's the final word on it." He reached out again to take hold of his brother, but without so much as a word, Orlando put his fist into Dante's nose.

Chantel couldn't help but cry out. Dante turned his stunned face to her only momentarily before his eyes rolled back and he sank to the floor. Orlando had knocked him out with a single blow.

Chapter 11

To Dante it seemed as if he were rising up out of mist. Darkness clouded his vision and yet he could hear voices. The words made little sense, however. He opened his eyes and fought against the gray veil until he could make out the faces of two women. Chantel and Mrs. Panetta hovered over him. But why?

"Rest a moment," Mrs. Panetta commanded. "You took quite a blow. Your brother, he packs a wallop, no?"

His brother. Orlando. Dante closed his eyes tightly and pain shot across his face. Orlando had hit him. Hit him hard. Opening his eyes again, Dante could see he was lying atop a bed.

"What happened?" he couldn't help but ask.

Chantel reached up with a cloth and gave a shrug. "You thought he needed to leave. He didn't want to leave." She put the cool cloth over the bridge of his nose. It felt good, but Dante wasn't inclined to tell her that. "So he hit you."

"You need to learn to let bygones be bygones," Mrs. Panetta told him. "The past needs to be put aside. It's Christmas, after all. If we cannot get along on the day of our Lord's birth, then when can we?"

"That's just my point," Dante said, trying to sit up. "We can't get along. Our families will never get along."

Mrs. Panetta pushed him back down. "They can't so long as people say they can't. Now you rest. You may have a broken nose. You bled a good bit. Rest and let your body regain its strength."

Dante nodded, fighting against the dizziness that caused his vision to waver. "Our father will come looking for us if we don't get home soon. He sent me to find Orlando."

"Why would he come looking at our house? Did you suggest Orlando had come here?" Chantel asked.

"Ever since your father told him that Orlando was involved with your family, I know he's been suspicious. It seems likely he would consider the possibility."

Mrs. Panetta nodded. "Your papa, he seems suspicious of everything. My Giovanni went to make the peace with him and still he would not shake hands. He believes the worst about everyone, and for that I am sorry. Sorry for him."

Dante closed his eyes for a moment. It had been a long time since anyone had hit him that hard in the face. Maybe Mrs. Panetta was right. Maybe he just needed to rest for a moment. He tried to wriggle his nose just to test it out, but pain shot through his face like a white-hot fire.

"I'll get some ice," Mrs. Panetta declared. "He's starting to swell."

She was gone by the time Dante reopened his eyes. Chantel sat watching him carefully as if he might fall off the bed. He shook his head in a short, brief manner. "This isn't going to work."

"What?" Chantel asked.

"Orlando and your sister. I know you think it terribly romantic, but it's not."

She shrugged. "And what would you know of such things? I figure my sister and your brother are old enough to know their own hearts. Who am I to say otherwise? Who are you?"

"I'm the man who doesn't want to have to shun his brother," Dante replied in a matter-of-fact manner. "My father has already made it clear that he will have nothing to do with Orlando if he marries your sister. If he disowns him, we will all have to follow suit, or Father won't have anything to do with any of us."

"But in time, perhaps your father will see reason."

"What my father sees is his son dishonoring him by disobeying. I would think even
the Panetta family could understand that.
The Bible does say that children are to honor
their mothers and fathers. Orlando is clearly
dishonoring our father."

"But he's no longer a child," Chantel countered. She took the cloth from Dante's face
and rinsed it in the basin. "He's a man full
grown, and as such, he must decide for himself what is right and wrong." Placing the cloth
on his face again, she added, "And even so,
his love for my sister does not equal dishonor
toward his papa."

"Tell that to our father," Dante said, meeting her studious gaze. "You don't know how
this has hurt him."

"I'm sorry that anyone should be hurt because two people hold a deep love for each
other. I'm even sorry your brother hit you,
although I can definitely understand why he
did it." A small smile grazed her lips.

"Smile all you like, but if you won't listen
to reason regarding the problems between
our families," Dante said, trying to win her
support, "then at least consider the fact that
they are both very young. Too young to be
embarking on something as important as
marriage."

Chantel looked at him as if he'd spoken a

strange language. "People marry this young all the time. Most women are wed by the time they reach Isabella's age."

"Here's some ice," Mama declared as she returned to the room. "I tied it into a dishcloth so it shouldn't be so cold against your skin. You know, you will probably have bruising. Your papa will want to know what happened."

"I'll tell him I fell," Dante muttered and added, "against Orlando's fist."

Mrs. Panetta chuckled as if she were dealing with nothing more difficult than patching up one of her own boys. "Brothers will fight. Your father will understand that."

"Yes, but he won't understand our absence," Dante said. He pushed aside the ice and sat up. The entire room began to spin, but he fought the urge to lie back down. "My nonna had already begun to set the table for our noon meal when my father realized Orlando was gone. I think Father thought he had just gone off for a brief walk, but I knew in my heart that this was where he would come."

"And so he did," Mrs. Panetta replied. "You are a smart young man. Seems a pity that you can't use that intelligence to resolve this matter without it coming to blows."

"He's the one who struck first. Not me."

"Well, then, that makes it all right," Mrs.

Panetta said with a rather jolly expression on her face.

Dante knew she was being sarcastic. He might have smiled himself at one time, but he couldn't find the will within him. Struggling to his feet, Dante again had to wait for the room to stop tilting before he could find Orlando.

"Thank you for tending to me," he told Mrs. Panetta. He gave a quick, sidelong glance at Chantel. "You are both very gracious, Christian women. I appreciate that you want peace between our families. I appreciate that you would feed and care for your enemy . . . that you are willing to forgive."

"You are not my enemy," Mrs. Panetta replied, sounding almost miffed. "And neither is your father. The devil alone is my enemy." She moved to the door. "Chantel, if he passes out, let him fall to the ground. Maybe he'll hit his head again and knock some sense into it this time."

Chantel chuckled, and Dante fixed her with a frown. "So you find that amusing."

She got to her feet and shrugged. "I've simply never met a more stubborn, senseless person in my twenty-two years."

Dante's head was already throbbing from the added pressure of standing. There was no chance he was going to stand by and let this young woman berate him, however. He pointed a finger at her and narrowed his eyes. "Then you should take a good long look in the mirror—and at your family."

He went to the open bedroom door and took hold of the jamb just before another wave of dizziness washed over him. *Orlando should take up boxing,* he thought, but said nothing. When the wave calmed once again, he stepped into the hallway and went in search of his brother.

Orlando looked up rather sheepishly when Dante entered the front sitting room. "You doing all right?" he asked.

"No thanks to you." Dante took hold of the chair back and steadied himself. The pain in his face made him wish he could go and lie back down. "Let's go home."

To his surprise Orlando still seemed disinclined. "Dante, I do love her. We will marry. Father might not approve, but I don't care. I will always care deeply about him—you and Nonna, too—but I can't walk away from what I know is right."

Dante got a horrible feeling in the pit of his stomach. "You haven't . . . you didn't take advantage of her . . . did you?"

Orlando jumped to his feet. "No! I would never do something like that!"

This time it was a wave of relief that washed over Dante's worried mind. "Good. For a second there I thought you were implying you had to marry her."

"Hardly that. I would never feel that I had to marry Isabella. I only know that I want to marry her—that without her I'm nothing."

"Stop it. You sound like one of those silly play actors on the stage. In time you'll find someone appropriate and forget about her."

This only served to anger his brother more, and when Orlando charged at him, Dante was pretty confident another blow was coming his way. This time he was ready and blocked Orlando's advance.

"Get out of my way," his brother declared. He moved past Dante and into the foyer, where Isabella Panetta now stood.

"I'm sorry to be the cause of problems between you," Isabella told Orlando.

"My brother is the cause of problems. My father is the cause of problems. You are not." He reached out and touched her cheek in a tender manner. "You are my heart."

Dante came to where they stood. "This has to end," he said, looking first at Orlando and then to Isabella. "You have to know that our father will never allow for this. He will move his entire family as far away as is necessary before he will allow you to marry her."

"Then I won't go with him—with any of you," Orlando replied. "Isabella will be my family. I don't need anyone else." His anger grew more apparent with each word. "If my family cannot love and accept the woman I love—then they are not my family." He looked to Isabella. "I'm sorry. I have to go deal with my father, but I will return." He left the Panetta house without another word to his brother.

Dante looked at Isabella. "This is your fault. If you weren't enticing him, demanding he forget his name and family, none of this would be happening. I hope you're happy."

To his surprise, the young woman burst into tears and fled the foyer.

Stepping outside before any of the Panettas could come to take issue with his comments, Dante scanned the street but saw nothing of Orlando. The dismal gray skies had begun to unleash snow, however.

"You are such a bully."

Dante cringed at the sound of Chantel Panetta's voice. He truly had no desire to deal with her just now. His head hurt, and he was already angry at himself for having made Isabella cry. He turned to face her, nevertheless.

"I only said what had to be said," he replied. "I am sorry for having hurt your sister's feelings, but she needs to see reason. You all need to see reason."

"And you think you're the one to show us?"

she questioned. "Why, I seriously doubt you know anything about love."

Dante bristled. "And I suppose you think you can teach me all about it?"

To his surprise Chantel gave a harsh laugh. "Mr. Calarco, I'm only a woman—not a miracle worker."

Chantel returned to the house and slammed the door closed behind her. Something had happened to her while tending Dante's unconscious form, and she couldn't yet reconcile it in her mind. The frustration and anger she felt toward him now was much easier to understand than the tenderness she had felt for him then.

She tried hard to put those thoughts from her mind. Dante Calarco was an ill-tempered bully whose only purpose in life was to cause others misery. Her sister's sobbing was proof enough.

Gathering up the dinner platters and empty bowls, Chantel sighed. The joy of Christmas that had filled their home earlier had disappeared. The thought of a father disowning his son at any time was heartbreaking, but at Christmas it was even worse.

Father, Chantel silently prayed as she moved

around the table, *this seems so impossible, yet I know that you are God over all things. You set the world into motion. You can change the heart of one man—or of many.*

She thought of her sister and continued. *Isabella is young, but, Father, I think she knows her heart. I think she truly loves Orlando, and that he, in turn, loves her. Please guide them, Father. Show me what I can do to help them.*

Chantel had the table cleared and dishes washed before her mother reappeared. "Oh, Chantelly, what a blessing you are to me," her mama declared, coming to give her a hug. "Thank you for seeing to this."

"Is Isabella better now?"

Mama shrugged. "It's hard to love someone so dearly and have so many troubles follow."

"Do you suppose Mr. Calarco will ever allow for their marriage?"

"Anything is possible with God."

Chantel nodded. "I was just thinking that a minute ago. God can do anything, but it's hard to trust that He'll see things our way."

"But our way is not what is important," Mama chided. She picked up a clean bowl. "God has His plans and ways. We have to trust Him for guidance. He will not forget our needs."

"I just want good things for Issy—for all of us," Chantel replied. "I hate seeing her so heartbroken. I worry about her."

Mama took a sack of almonds out from one of the lower cabinets. "Isabella is strong. She will survive this. And most likely they will soon be together."

Chantel looked at her mother in confusion. "Did she say that? Are they going to elope right away?"

"I would not be surprised by such a thing. If they have enough money to buy train tickets, I believe they will go to Duluth soon. I told them they could no doubt stay with Marilla."

Chantel's Aunt Marilla would be the perfect solution. She would enjoy the company of the young couple and could well afford to help them.

"I have some money from selling my tatting," Chantel murmured. "I had already thought to give it to Isabella as a wedding gift for their new start. Maybe I could send some additional lace with them to sell in Duluth." Her mind began to churn with thoughts. "Aunt Marilla said she could take all the lace we could send."

"Do not be thinking that this is a problem for you to fix." Mama waggled her finger at Chantel. "This is for them to figure out. You can help—but you cannot make their decisions for them."

She was right, of course. Orlando and Isabella must choose what their next steps would be.

Her mother sat at the kitchen table and began shelling almonds. "I promised Marco I would make more Torrone."

"I'm glad. I hardly got to have any," Chantel said, pulling the last of the oranges from the back of the cabinet. "I've been saving this in case we needed more zest."

"And you never found out who your secret admirer was?"

"I figure it was Leo Fortino," Chantel replied. "He didn't say so, but he's the only one I know with enough money to send off and have a dozen large oranges delivered to Ely."

"It's too bad he's . . ." Her mother fell silent.

Chantel took down the zester. "His affection is not something I desire, Mama, so it's not too bad as far as I'm concerned."

"If only he owned a grocery store or a dry goods. Even a restaurant would be acceptable. But he has all that drinking and gambling." Mama narrowed her eyes. "And then there are the women." She made a *tsk*ing sound and turned her attention back to the almonds.

"It is of no matter to me," Chantel said, taking a seat beside her mother. "I'm not even sure God has someone for me. Maybe I'm supposed to just stay here and take care of you and Papa. That wouldn't be such a bad life."

Her mother shook her head. "No. God has a husband for you. I know this."

Chantel could see the confidence in her mother's expression. "And just how do you know this?"

"Because God, He tell me in the quiet of my heart."

Chantel gave a sigh. "I wish He'd tell me. Did He by any chance mention who it might be?"

Her mother laughed. "No. So you will just have to wait for His time, Chantelly."

"I was afraid you'd say that."

An hour later Papa and the boys returned. They came in the back door, snow covering their hats and coats. Chantel jumped up to help them with their coats. She shook off the excess snow outside, then hung the coats close to the stove to dry.

"Where have you been so long?" Mama asked. "I thought you were just going to go chop wood for Mrs. Conti."

"We did that, and then we went over to the Calarco house," Papa replied. His stern expression and sober tone told Chantel the encounter had not been pleasant.

Mama couldn't contain her surprise. "I santi ci preservi!"

"I had hoped to talk again to Vittorio, but he wouldn't allow for it. Even his mother-in-law tried to reason with him to make the peace, but he said no. He said he would never be at peace with us."

"I am sorry to hear that." Mama shook her head.

"Mrs. Barbato told him that God blessed the peacemakers and that because he refused my gesture, he risked making God angry. He said he didn't care."

Mama grasped Papa's hand. "We must pray for his soul. That poor man—his anger and pride will destroy him."

Papa nodded and pulled off his boots, setting them beside his sons' on a special set of posts situated near the stove.

"What about Orlando?"

Chantel looked up to find Isabella standing just inside the kitchen. She could see her sister's swollen eyes and reddened nose. She'd been crying again.

"I don't know where he is," Papa admitted. "I didn't see him or his brother. Just Mrs. Barbato and Vittorio." He went to his youngest and put his arm around her shoulders. "I am sorry, Issy. I tried."

She burst into tears and buried her face against Papa's chest. Chantel also longed to offer her sister comfort, but the anger that stirred inside her wouldn't have been a comfort to anyone. Those Calarcos were causing her family more pain and grief than was fair. If only there was something she could do to put an end to it.

She remembered her mother's admonition. This wasn't something she could fix, and even if she could, it certainly wasn't her responsibility. But that didn't stop Chantel from trying to figure out how she might help her sister. After all, the Bible said they should help one another—bear one another's burdens. It seemed only right that she should find a way to help Isabella bear this one.

Chapter 12

For the next few weeks things seemed to calm down. Chantel figured the bitter cold had much to do with it. Orlando and Isabella weren't inclined to plan clandestine meetings in the sub-zero temperatures, and the single time Orlando had come to see Isabella at the house, the couple had made it clear to the Panettas that they were going to forego seeing each other to ease the vigilant watch of the Calarco men. Orlando felt confident that if they gave it a little time and pretense, his brother and father would assume he was giving up on the idea of marrying Isabella. Chantel's father hadn't encouraged Orlando to be deceptive, but rather had told him to continue praying that God would change his father's heart. Orlando had rightly countered that he supposed a man would have to want to change his heart before God could work on it. Chantel had to agree.

The one place Orlando and Isabella saw each other was at church on Sunday. Mrs. Barbato insisted on attending services, and Orlando had taken to accompanying her because the ground was too icy and temperatures too bitter for her to go alone. Mrs. Barbato was also her grandson's advocate. She approved of his romance with Isabella Panetta, and even though the young lovers could hardly be seen together at church without word getting back to his father, they were at least able to slip notes to one another via their family members and exchange a glance or two.

It was through one of those notes that Chantel learned of Isabella's plans to leave with Orlando around the first of February.

"I don't understand why you're waiting," Chantel said in a whisper. She handed her sister back the folded note.

The priest was concluding the service with prayers, but Isabella leaned over to speak nevertheless. "He needed to wait until he had enough money set aside."

"But I already offered you money," Chantel replied.

The service ended just then and the congregation rose. Isabella held fast to Chantel's arm. "I told that to Orlando, but he wanted to do this himself. I will take a little of the money just in case, but I don't want to shame him, so I don't want you to say anything about it."

"Of course I won't," Chantel promised.

Mama left the family and made her way through the congregation to where Orlando and his grandmother sat. Chantel looked to her father, who since nearly dying at the mine had become a regular churchgoer.

"What is Mama off to do?"

He glanced in the direction his wife had gone. "She was concerned about Mrs. Barbato. She didn't think the old woman looked well."

Chantel frowned. "I think I'll go make sure everything is all right." She pressed past her father and slipped into the stream of people.

By the time she reached her mother and Mrs. Barbato, it was evident that something wasn't right. The old woman looked quite pale and didn't seem to be feeling at all well.

"Mama, what can I do to help?"

"I don't want to make a scene," Mrs. Barbato whispered. "Orlando, help me to my feet, and we will go home."

"Nonna, I don't think you're strong enough to walk that far," he said, looking to Mrs. Panetta as if for instruction. "I think I should take you to Dr. Shipman's hospital."

"No. I won't go there," Mrs. Barbato said in a tone that made it clear the matter was not up for discussion. "Hospitals are where people go to die."

"Our house is just a block away," Mama

reminded him. "We will take her there and send for the doctor."

This seemed acceptable to the older woman, who by now was struggling to get to her feet. Orlando put his arm around her to offer his support. "I should carry you," he whispered.

"No!" Mrs. Barbato declared. "Just help me, and I will walk. I don't want everyone knowing." She gave a quiet cough into her handkerchief, then nodded that she was ready.

Chantel followed them from the church. "I'll go ahead and open the door," she told Orlando. She glanced back to see her mother explaining the matter to Papa and Isabella.

Hurrying ahead, Chantel made it to the house well ahead of Orlando and his grandmother. Marco was sitting at the table drinking coffee when she burst into the house. He looked at her oddly for a moment.

"Something on fire?" He yawned, and she could tell he hadn't been awake all that long.

Just then Alfredo came in from the back door with an armful of cut wood. Chantel motioned to him. "Put the wood down and come assist Orlando. His nonna is sick, and Mama is having her come here."

Alfredo stacked the wood and asked, "How do you want me to help?"

"Orlando may need you to help carry his nonna—she's quite weak. If not, Mama may want you to go for the doctor, since you already have your coat and boots on."

He nodded and headed to the front door. "I see them coming." He went to meet them while Chantel hurried to her bedroom. She pulled down the covers to her bed, deciding it would be best to let Mrs. Barbato rest here while awaiting the doctor's arrival.

She bustled back to the foyer just as Orlando and Alfredo came up the steps. They were on either side of Mrs. Barbato, who looked as if she'd fainted. Once they stepped into the house, however, she opened her eyes.

"Take her to my bed," she instructed Alfredo. "I've already pulled down the covers."

The men delivered the old woman to the room, and once she was seated on the bedside, Chantel dismissed them. Mama came into the room just as the boys were exiting.

"Someone needs to go for the doctor," she told them.

"I'll go, Mama," Alfredo replied.

Mama pulled off her gloves and coat. "Orlando, tell Isabella to put some hot water on to steam. We need to help your nonna breathe easier." Next, she turned to Chantel. "Go take off your things and go to the pantry for the vaporizing lamp. You'll find the eucalyptus oil in the medicine box."

"Yes, Mama." Chantel hurried to do as

directed. Pulling off her coat, she tossed it and her woolen scarf and bonnet aside.

The pantry was hardly big enough to turn around in, but Papa had made shelves to the ceiling. Thankfully, the vaporizing lamp wasn't too high up. Chantel pulled it from the shelf, careful not to disturb the glass shade. Next she located the medicine box and rummaged through it to find the oil.

By the time she returned to her bedroom, Mama had Mrs. Barbato partly undressed and resting against a stack of pillows.

"Where should I put this, Mama?"

"On the dresser will be fine. Go ahead and leave it there. I can manage," she told Chantel. "Why don't you keep watch for the doctor? Hopefully he'll be here soon," she said, speaking more to Mrs. Barbato than to Chantel. "Is it any easier to breathe propped up like this?"

Mrs. Barbato gave a weak nod. Mama smoothed back the older woman's hair. "Good. You just rest."

Chantel could see the look of worry that crossed her mother's face. Nonna Barbato's condition must be quite grave, she feared. She left the room and waited by the frosted front window for the doctor to arrive. Blowing hot breath onto the glass, Chantel cleared away a little circle from which to watch. After what seemed an eternity, a one-horse sleigh arrived with Alfredo and Dr. Shipman.

Chantel ushered the doctor into the house just as Orlando and Mama entered the foyer.

"Dr. Shipman, she's right this way," Mama declared, not worrying about any social greetings or formal proprieties. "She has a high fever and is struggling to breathe." Chantel heard her continue down a list of what had already been done on the woman's behalf. She could see the worried look on Orlando's face.

Chantel gestured toward the front room. "We can wait in here for the doctor."

Isabella came up from behind her fiancé and took his arm. "Will it take long for the doctor to tend her?" she asked her sister.

"I'm not certain."

"I knew she shouldn't have gone to services this morning," Orlando said, shaking his head. He went to the fireplace and leaned against the mantel. "She just didn't seem herself."

Isabella joined him and touched his arm. "You aren't to blame. Like you told me earlier, she would have gone with or without you. Thankfully you were with her."

"Father will wonder where we are. We always come right home after services. I suppose I should go and let him know what's happened, but . . ." His brow furrowed as his voice trailed off.

"Why don't you wait until you know what's wrong with her," Chantel suggested. "After all, there's really nothing to tell him other than she got sick and we brought her here."

Orlando's frown deepened. "And he's not going to like that one bit."

"I would think it more important that she get proper care," Isabella said softly.

He placed his hand atop Isabella's. "Most folks would, but not my father, Issy. His desire to continue this feud between our families keeps him from rational thought."

Chantel tried to think of comforting words she might offer, but in truth, she was equally frustrated. No doubt Orlando was right. His father would be livid when he learned the truth. A Calarco in the care of a Panetta was unthinkable to him.

The minutes ticked by in silence as the trio waited for news from the doctor. Chantel had no idea where her father or brothers had gone. She hoped they hadn't taken it upon themselves to inform the Calarco men of Nonna Barbato's situation. She doubted that Dante's father would even hear them out.

Finally Mama emerged. She came to where Orlando stood by the hearth. "Your nonna has pneumonia. She's quite ill."

His jaw clenched. Chantel had seen Dante do the same when vexed with her. Orlando looked past the women toward the foyer. "I suppose I should go tell my father. He'll wonder why we haven't yet returned from church. Maybe I could get the doctor to drive Nonna home."

Mama shook her head. "Dr. Shipman says she isn't to be moved. He doesn't even want to take her to the hospital. He fears such a disruption would end her life. We are perfectly happy to care for her here, however."

"My father . . . my father will never allow for it," Orlando said, meeting the woman's look of concern.

Chantel saw her mother give a slight nod. "He won't like it, but he will tolerate it. He must. Otherwise he would be responsible for her death. If you explain it to him that way, he'll have to accept the situation."

"You don't know my father," Orlando said, pulling away from Isabella. "I want to see Nonna, and then I'll go. I don't know what else I can do."

Mama patted his shoulder. "You can pray. We can always do that. Our Father in heaven hears our prayers. He will not forget such a faithful woman as your nonna."

Orlando nodded and hurried from the room. Chantel got to her feet. "Will she recover, Mama?"

"Her fever is high and her breathing is very

labored." Mama shook her head. "I fear for her. I sent your papa for Father Buh."

"Is it truly that bad?" Isabella said, taking hold of her mother's sleeve. "Oh, this is terrible. Poor Nonna Barbato. She's such a dear. She's the only one in Orlando's family who wants to see us married."

"She is a dear woman," Mama agreed, "but she's also quite old. A sickness such as this can easily take her life. Only time will tell. We will keep her here and do for her what we can."

"We'll pray for her recovery," Isabella said, casting a fearful glance at Chantel. "And that she doesn't pass away in our care . . . or it will no doubt go down in history as a Panetta killing a Calarco."

"Yes," Chantel said, nervous about that very thing. "We will pray."

"Where have you been?" Father bellowed as a snow-covered Orlando burst through the door.

Dante knew his father presumed the worst, although he had suggested that perhaps Orlando and Nonna had taken lunch with friends after church. Father had spent much of the afternoon pacing back and forth to stare out the window at the near-blizzard conditions, watching and grumbling about the duo's absence.

When it became apparent that Nonna was not with Orlando, Dante knew there must be a problem. The look on Orlando's face made him even more certain.

"What's wrong?" Dante asked.

Orlando unwrapped his scarf, sending snow scattering. "Nonna took sick," he declared. "The doctor says it's quite serious."

Father's dark brows knit together. "What has made her ill?"

"While at church she became weak, pale . . . she could barely breathe. The doctor says it's pneumonia. She may . . . she might not make it."

"We will go to the hospital and speak to the doctor," Father said. "Whatever she needs, we will see that she has it."

"She isn't at the hospital," Orlando said.

"Then where is she?" Dante couldn't help but question.

Orlando hesitated, and Dante could tell by the look on his face that the news wasn't going to be to their liking. "She's at the Panettas' house."

"What!" Their father pushed one of the kitchen chairs, sending it to the floor. "Why would she be there?"

"She fell ill in church and refused to let me

take her to the hospital. The Panetta house was the closest place to take her. Mrs. Panetta insisted. We sent for the doctor, and he came there to see her."

"You boys go and fetch your nonna home! She should not be in the house of our enemy."

"Dr. Shipman says she can't be moved," Orlando countered. "She's not strong enough, Papa. Her condition is very fragile right now, and the doctor said such a move would probably kill her. He didn't even want to risk taking her to the hospital."

"It's a risk we must take," their father replied. "It is worth it if we get her away from the Panettas."

Dante was appalled. "Father, listen to yourself. I can hardly believe you would suggest such a thing. If the doctor believes it too grave a danger, then we must respect that. Nonna will have good care there, and if the Panetta women are willing to see to her needs, we should be grateful."

Their father scowled. "I will not have Panettas caring for her. It would be better she die in her own bed than to be poisoned by the likes of that family."

Dante could hardly believe his father's ranting. "They would never hurt her, and you know it."

"This is where your ridiculous feud has

taken you, Papa!" Orlando accused. "You have no trust in anyone if they have the last name of Panetta. Well, frankly, I'm in agreement with Mr. Panetta. This feud is over. I refuse to carry it on."

Orlando took up his scarf and headed for the back door. "I only came here to tell you the news. I'm going back to be with Nonna."

"If you go, you will be a traitor to this family!" their father called out after his youngest son.

Turning, Orlando looked at him for a moment, but it was Dante who interceded. "Father, stop for a moment to think about this situation. Nonna needs special care and can't be moved. Even if she could be moved, we can't care for her here. We'll be at the mine for twelve hours of every day. We can't take time away without losing our jobs. And when we aren't working, we'll need to sleep. How can we possibly take care of a sick woman? Especially one so close to death? Will you deny her proper care?"

"I would deny her nothing," his father said, sounding less angry and more resigned.

"Would you deny us the right to see her and ensure that her care is acceptable?" Dante further questioned.

"Of course not." Father folded his arms against his chest. It was clear that the fight was going out of him.

Dante took advantage of the moment. "Nonna gave up her life after Mama died to come and see to our care. It's only right that we see to hers now. Orlando did the right thing by getting her help. Had someone else been closer, they might have suggested a different home, but this is what we are left with. Whether or not we can forget the past and forgive, we must at least care for Nonna's present needs."

Orlando stood silent while their father wrestled with the matter. Both sons waited for the man to recant his declaration or to offer his acceptance, but when he turned away and said nothing, neither were quite sure what to do.

Finally, Dante moved to retrieve his coat. "I'll come with you."

Later, as Dante sat beside his nonna, he was glad he had chosen to come. She was so very weak and sick that she hardly recognized him. From time to time she grew restless and agitated, then would once again fall silent. There were long periods when she struggled so hard to breathe that Dante found himself inhaling and exhaling with her—willing her to continue to draw air.

Dante had been impressed by the constant

care she received from the Panetta women during this time. When he'd first arrived, Mrs. Panetta had been wiping Nonna's brow with a damp cloth. Later, Isabella had come to help the old woman drink a bit of medicinal tea. But it wasn't until Chantel came to take her turn that he found himself completely taken in.

Dante couldn't help but watch the young woman as she tenderly cared for his grandmother. Her gentle hands and soft-spoken voice seemed to comfort Nonna. He marveled as Chantel talked to the old woman as if she were awake and fully capable of carrying on a conversation.

"Nonna Barbato, I remembered what you said about the candied melon rind," Chantel stated, taking up the wet cloth and water bowl. She began again to wash Nonna's face and neck, working tirelessly to bring down her fever. "Mama said they never used melon rind when she was a girl. I told her how Nonna Panetta did and that you agreed it was the recipe you followed. So we tried it and Mama thought it quite good. My brothers did, too."

She smiled at Dante and the gesture momentarily startled him. He tried to regain his composure as Chantel continued her chat. "Of course, my brothers will eat just about anything that isn't nailed down. Mama used to say it was because they were growing boys, but now they are full grown and still eat like horses."

"They work like horses, too," Dante threw in. "Mine work takes a great deal of energy and strength."

Chantel nodded. "Your grandson makes a good point, Nonna Barbato."

At that the old woman opened her eyes. It seemed for a moment there was clarity in her expression. "Dante?"

"I'm here, Nonna," he said, leaning forward to take hold of her hand.

"Sí, *che fa bene.*" That's good.

She closed her eyes, satisfied that all was well. Chantel smiled again and looked at Dante. "She's comforted that you're here."

"She hardly knows that anyone is here," he said, trying not to let his heart feel anything but concern for his nonna. It was funny how easily this Panetta woman maneuvered her way into his thoughts.

"You'd be surprised just how much she knows," Chantel said, returning her attention to her patient. "Mama says that it's good to just talk to the sick, even the unconscious, as if they were able to talk right back. She said sometimes it's just hearing the voice of loved ones that gives them the will to go on living."

She took up the cloth and bowl and moved

away from the bed. "You should try it. Just tell her what you're thinking. Talk to her as you would any other time. You might be surprised at how much it affects her recovery."

Dante watched her leave the room. When she turned in the hall to pull the door closed, he was more than a little bit aware of her bright eyes and full lips. Her oval face seemed as perfect as a china doll, and the rich plum color of her gown complemented her olive complexion.

When she didn't move, Dante felt uncomfortably self-conscious. She was studying him with as much intensity as he studied her. Their eyes locked, and he felt suspended—caught. When at last she closed the door and broke the spell, Dante didn't feel the relief he'd hoped for. Instead, there was a strange sense of loss.

Chapter 13

The deadly cold of winter increased as January moved into February. Nonna Barbato, however, was on the mend, and Chantel used every opportunity to take advantage of her presence. She loved talking with the older woman and often brought her sewing and tatting into the bedroom to do while keeping Nonna company. They spoke exclusively in Italian, and it reminded Chantel of her year in Italy.

"I've really enjoyed hearing your stories about my nonna," Chantel said, taking up one of her brother's shirts to mend. "I love knowing more about the family. I asked my nonna and nonno for stories, but they were less inclined to speak on certain subjects."

"Such as the feud?" Nonna asked, seeming to understand.

Chantel nodded and gave the woman a smile. "As you know quite well."

Nonna settled comfortably against the pillows propped behind her. Though she'd lost weight from her illness, her color had returned and she no longer struggled as much to breathe. "I suppose," she began, "the important thing to know is that it was not always so."

"I just can't imagine how two families who were once friends came to such a parting over a mule," Chantel said, paying close attention to the tiny stitches needed to repair the armhole of Marco's shirt. "It makes the people involved seem petty, don't you think?" She looked up rather abruptly. "Not that I mean any insult."

"No, of course you don't," Nonna replied with a smile. "And you should know the truth, even though the few who know it will rarely speak of it. It was not only about the mule, as you have guessed. The mule was simply the final blow, you might say."

Chantel shook her head. "Then what really happened?"

"The entire matter started between best friends—your great-grandfather Franco Panetta and Dante and Orlando's great-grandfather, Paulo Calarco. It was a matter of too many roosters interested in the same hen."

"This was about a woman?"

Nonna gazed toward the ceiling. "That should not surprise you. We have been causing problems for men since the beginning of time."

"But to put two families at odds over that . . .

well . . . it just seems uncalled for. There are so many other things that matter more."

"Ah, but not when the heart is involved," Nonna declared, looking back at Chantel. "Look no further than my Orlando and your sister. They are willing to risk everything to be together, and it was just that way with your great-grandfather Franco and his friend. He was in love with a beautiful young woman named Sophia. Paulo was also in love with her. Of course, this was before he married the boy's great-grandmother. He wasn't an improper man, you understand."

Chantel nodded and continued her work. "So what happened?"

"Well, you cannot hope things will go well when two men love the same woman. Sophia, she rather liked the attention and let both men pay her court. She teased and flirted with both, accepting their gifts and attention. That was her mistake. It only served to cause bitterness and hatred. The men, they did not like that she would not choose just one. But Sophia, she told them that she wanted her heart to choose and that she could not do so until she got to know each man."

"That seems perfectly reasonable to me," Chantel replied.

"Ah, but in the old country, it was not done in such a fashion. The mama and the papa, they would choose a suitor for their daughter. And that is what happened. Seeing that their daughter was gaining a reputation as a tease, they demanded that Sophia court and marry your great-grandfather. But it was as if by doing so, they made Sophia only want more to marry Paulo.

"They ran away together . . . to marry, you understand . . . but the priest he would not perform the ceremony. So they were forced to return in shame to the village. Her reputation was ruined. They walked for a week in torrential rains, and when they finally made it back, Sophia had taken ill. She died less than a week later."

"How awful and sad." Chantel thought of her sister. The loss would be impossible to bear.

"The families, they blamed each other, and your great-grandfather's family blamed the Calarcos most of all. The two men called each other out and would have murdered each other but for the priest. He came and told them that he would not allow either of them a proper church burial if they killed the other. That, you must understand, was a very strong threat. No one wanted to be without the church's blessing, so they did not fight. Instead, they began to cause each other problems in ways that could not be traced back." Nonna pointed her finger at Chantel. "But each one knew it was the other."

"Of course," Chantel replied. "There would be no reason to think otherwise. What did they do to each other?"

Nonna lowered her arm and clasped her hands together. "Well, as I am told, there were years and years of retribution. Paulo married and the children began to arrive, and your great-grandfather, he married and started his own family. And during all that time there were animals that went missing from each man's land. There were crops that were destroyed and property damaged. Ill will was spread throughout the village and people began to choose sides. By the time the mule was killed, it was clear that you were either a supporter of the Calarcos or the Panettas. No one was allowed to be neutral."

"How . . . well . . . childish," Chantel said. She hesitated. "I'm sorry if that was disrespectful to my ancestors, but to cause such trouble that an entire town had to choose sides seems not only a childish act, but a very unchristian one, as well."

"Sí. It wasn't at all Christian. The priest tried to intercede, but to no avail."

"How was it that you became friends with my nonna?"

Mrs. Barbato smiled. "We were quite young.

We met one day when she had fallen and skinned her knee. I helped her to sit and used some water and a handkerchief to treat her knee." She shrugged. "We became good friends and for years we were inseparable. After all, she had not yet married into the Panetta family."

Chantel considered that for a moment. "So you became friends and had that friendship for many years, and then she married my nonno and it all ended?"

"When I heard she was to marry Carlo Panetta, I was already wed to Leonardo Calarco's best friend, Daniel Barbato. We knew our families would never allow for our friendship to continue, but we weren't of a mind to stop being friends. We met in secret sometimes and shared news and other things."

"Like recipes?" Chantel asked, smiling.

"Recipes, books, gossip, secrets." Nonna Barbato closed her eyes. "As the years passed, we saw each other less and less, and when my sweet Gia died and left Dante and Orlando without a mama, I came to America. It was the end for our friendship. We could not write to each other. Not without someone finding out. We met one last time before I left for America. We promised we would always be friends, and we always will be. I miss her more than words can say." The pain of such a loss was evident in her expression.

Chantel felt a terrible sadness for the woman. Isabella had always been her best friend. She knew that when her sister left Ely with Orlando, she would bear a terrible emptiness.

"It's not fair that they should keep you from writing to each other." Chantel had a sudden thought. "What if you wrote to her through me? I could put your letter in with mine, and she could do likewise for you?"

Nonna Barbato considered this for a moment. "Do you really think it could work?"

"I do." Chantel couldn't see any obstacle to it. "If it should prove a problem, all Nonna would have to do is burn the letter or not write back. I think it's worth a try."

"I think so, too." The woman's entire face lit up. "I will send a letter right away."

Chantel put aside her sewing. "I'll go get you some paper and a pen."

Marco had tried hard to stay away from the lure of the Fortune Hole, but his old ways were seemingly impossible to overcome. Entering the saloon, Marco reasoned with himself that a few drinks would be all right. It wasn't like he was coming to Leo's with the thought of getting drunk. He just wanted two or three beers and some time at the gaming tables.

And, of course, seeing Bianca wouldn't be a bad idea, either. He knew it would displease his parents, but he was a man full grown with a right to do as he wanted. After all, he contributed to the household in every way they asked and then some. It was only right that he spend the rest of his money as he saw fit.

"It's good to see you here again, my friend," Leo said, slapping Marco on the back. "I was beginning to think you'd joined the Finnish Temperance Society." He motioned to the back door. "Come on back with me. We're going to have quite the time tonight."

Marco nodded. "Bianca around?"

Leo shook his head. "She up and left me. Owes me fifty dollars, too."

"Where did she go?"

Shrugging, Leo handed Marco a tall mug of beer. "Who can say? If I knew, I would have one of my men go bring her back. She met someone who apparently had enough money to get them both on the train out of town. Someone saw her at the station, and after that she was gone."

The idea that she'd left without so much as a good-bye caused Marco a moment of anger. He'd known she was a working girl—a woman just looking for her next best customer—but it irritated him nevertheless. He had thought they were friends . . . at least friends enough that she could have sent a note to say she was leaving.

"Well, if I ever find her again, I'll fix her good for leaving me without paying up," Leo said matter-of-factly. He led the way to the back hall door. "But it's not important tonight. That we have a lot of money changing hands is what's important—so some of it might as well belong to you."

Marco followed Leo to the gaming room. The Snake Room was full to capacity, and thick cigar and cigarette smoke made it hard to even see who else was there. Smoking was one vice Marco hadn't picked up, and the stench burned his throat. He took a long gulp of the amber ale in his glass, hoping it might reduce the smoke's effect.

"Come on over here," Leo said. "I'm just now relieving Clark." He leaned closer to Marco. "I'll see that you win a few hands."

Leo tapped the man called Clark on the shoulder. The man nodded and got to his feet. "I'll be taking a break now, gentlemen. Good luck."

The four other men looked up from the table to where Leo and Marco stood. Leo lost no time. "Well, let's see if we can make those stacks of chips get even higher." He motioned Marco to the table. "Find a chair and join us."

It wasn't easy, but Marco finally located a vacated seat and brought it to Leo's table. Leo had already dealt a hand of poker to the men and was awaiting their decision on additional cards. Two of the men folded and opted for more liquor, while the other two were battling it out with Leo. Marco knew Leo would string them along until they ended up losing everything they'd come with, but it didn't matter. It was a game, and no one was forcing them to play.

The night wore on and the men came and went. Marco was rather intrigued by one of the players who stayed on at Leo's table, however. The man had introduced himself, but Marco couldn't remember his name. Leo just called him the Finn, because the man was one of the many Finnish immigrants who'd settled into Ely.

The Finn seemed quite adept at playing cards and had won a good amount from Leo. It wasn't until he stood to leave, however, that Leo suggested they raise the stakes and play for some real money.

The Finn seemed torn. He'd already explained that he was saving up money to send for family in the homeland. His forehead wrinkled as he weighed his options. "I should go," he said, his accent thick. It was obvious that the temptation was great.

"Just a few hands and you might double your money," Leo said with a smile. "Unless of course, you're afraid."

"I'm not afraid of playing cards," the man protested. "I know my way around a deck. You can see that." He sat back down. "I play."

Marco won several hands himself—enough anyway that he felt safe to participate in a few rounds of Leo's high-stake madness. The man sitting to the Finn's right, however, was losing fast, and when he put his revolver on the table as part of his final bid, Leo took a moment to examine it. "I suppose I can give you two dollars for it," he told the man. "But nothing more. I've already got quite a collection of pistols."

"Two? You gotta be joking. That's a Smith & Wesson barely three weeks outta the store. I paid twelve for it."

"Then you were taken advantage of," Leo said, shrugging.

The man stared hard at Leo for several seconds, then heaved a heavy sigh. "All right, two."

Marco looked at the man. He could see he was intoxicated. "You sure you want to do that, mister? You've had quite a bit to drink and tomorrow you may regret this."

Leo frowned. "You're putting a damper on business. Why not let the man decide for himself. Looks to me he's looking for a good time."

"Yeah, but you and I both know he's had too much to drink."

The Finn exchanged a look with Marco that suggested he was in agreement with him, but said nothing. Leo, however, didn't care. "That's his problem, not mine. I'm running a business."

"Gimme the two dollars in chips," the man demanded. He looked at Marco with a snarled expression. "You mind your own business."

Marco decided it was best to let the man have his way. He wasn't the type who would usually say anything about another man's desire to play, but for some reason it really bothered him that Leo would take advantage of him in this manner. In another two rounds of cards, the man had lost everything. Marco fully expected him to start a fight, but instead he wobbled to his feet and gave Leo a salute.

"I'll be back on payday," he declared. "You keep my gun for me."

Leo nodded and the man staggered off across the room. "You two still in?"

The Finn checked the time. "Maybe one more."

Marco nodded and leaned back in his chair. He thought about ordering another beer, but decided against it. He already felt guilty for the three he'd had; no sense in making matters worse.

The Finn won the next hand, which only served to egg him on to play another and then another. Leo kept the man too busy with the cards to consider leaving, and nearly an hour later, they were still playing. Only now, the Finn was down considerably more than when he'd first planned to leave. Marco had won just enough to keep the game interesting, but now he was done. He was about to close out and head home when the Finn protested Leo's dealing.

"I saw you deal off the bottom," he accused. "I'm not going to stand for that."

"You callin' me a cheater?" Leo asked, his dark eyes narrowing. "I don't take that from any man."

"Then you ought not deal from the bottom."

Leo's arm shot out so quickly that his fist made contact with the Finn's nose before Marco even knew what was happening. The Finn was sober enough to protest his treatment by fighting back. He jumped to his feet and threw a punch at Leo.

Dodging the attack, Leo picked up the Smith & Wesson he'd acquired earlier. Marco feared he'd shoot the Finn, but instead he used the piece to hit him in the head. The blow sent the Finn backward, and Leo jumped around the table and was on him in a flash. Marco watched in horror as Leo pummeled the man's head several times with the butt of the pistol. When the Finn finally fell unconscious to the ground, Leo further stunned Marco by squatting down to go through his pockets.

"What are you doing?" Marco asked.

"He owes me for drinks."

Marco shook his head as Leo cleaned the man out. He looked around at the others in the room, but no one seemed to even care. Leo rose and stared down at the man on the floor. "He's probably dead." He gave the man's body a kick. "Yeah, he's dead."

Leo glanced around the room, then signaled one of his men. "Fred, get rid of this for me. Throw him on the tracks and leave him for the marshal or the train."

"You can't do that, Leo," Marco protested. "The man might not even be dead."

"If not, he soon will be. Nobody, and I mean nobody, calls me a cheat, Marco. You know that." He fixed Marco with a threatening look. "And you know better than to say anything about this to anyone."

Fred had already hoisted the Finn over his shoulder. Leo gathered the rest of the man's chips from the table. Marco could hardly believe that Leo had sunk to such lows.

"I'm going home," Marco said, feeling

sick. He had to figure out what to do, and he couldn't do it here.

"Good to have you back, Marco," Leo said. He motioned to Marco's winnings. "Don't forget these."

Marco looked at the chips. There were spatters of blood on them and the table. He felt his stomach turn. "Keep it," he told Leo. "I don't want it."

He left the Fortune Hole, barely taking the time to pull on his coat. Marco couldn't stop thinking of the Finnish man. Was he dead? Had Leo killed another man?

Guilt ate at Marco as he thought of Lamb. How many others had been killed? Leo didn't seem to mind having blood on his hands, and no one else seemed inclined to care. Sure, it was reported in the paper and talked about around town, but no one made too much fuss about it.

He pulled up the collar on his coat and trudged through the snow toward home. He wanted desperately to forget about everything he'd seen and heard, but the sight of the Finn on Leo's floor was more than he could ignore.

At home Marco found his father sitting at the table drinking a cup of coffee. Marco slumped into the chair opposite his father and put his head in his hands.

"What's wrong with you, son? You drink too much? I've got some coffee on the stove."

Marco shook his head, surprised at just how sober he was. "I'm not drunk."

"Then what's the problem?"

He met his father's gaze. "I . . . well . . ." He knew Leo had demanded his silence, but Marco found he couldn't live with his conscience and remain quiet. "I saw a man get beat up and left for dead," he finally said. He explained in brief, and by the time he got to the place where Fred was to dispose of the body on the tracks, his father was up and putting on his coat.

"We have to go find out if the man is dead," his father declared. "If he is, he doesn't deserve to be left on the tracks, and if he's alive, he'll freeze to death. We need to get him to the doctor."

Marco nodded. "I don't know exactly where they would have dumped him."

"It's no matter. We'll wake up Alfredo and take the lanterns. If he's on the tracks, one of us is bound to find him."

Chapter 14

The Monday day shift was just ending when Marco and Alfredo saw the marshal approaching. The man motioned Marco to join him; no doubt this was about the Finn. The Panettas had found him near death and half frozen shortly after they'd begun their search in the wee hours of Sunday morning. The Panetta men had managed to get the man over to Dr. Shipman's, but the doctor feared the man wouldn't survive. All day Sunday they had waited for word that the Finn had passed on, but it never came. Now the marshal was here, and Marco knew that couldn't bode well.

"I wanted to talk to you about what happened to Mr. Gadd."

"Was that the Finn's name?" Marco asked.

The marshal nodded. "Still is. I understand you were there when he was beaten up at the Fortune Hole."

Marco looked to his brother for a moment, uncertain how he should respond. If he told the truth, Leo would be implicated and possibly arrested. And Marco feared Leo's wrath.

But if he didn't tell the truth, it would be the same as approving of what had happened.

Turning back to the marshal, Marco nodded. "I was there."

"Want to tell me what happened? Gadd can't tell me much of anything just yet. Doc thinks he'll recover, but it may be slow going for a while."

"I'm glad to hear he didn't die," Marco said. He couldn't help but feel self-conscious as his fellow miners shuffled by on their way home. "You think we could talk somewhere else? Maybe you could come to the house later?"

The marshal's eyes narrowed. "You afraid of something?"

Alfredo jumped in. "It's freezing out here and looks like it's gonna snow. At home, Mama will have hot coffee and food. You'd be welcome to join us for supper."

Marco felt a sense of relief that his brother seemed to understand his apprehension. The marshal grinned. "Guess I have to eat, and I happen to know that folks highly regard your mama's and sisters' cooking. I suppose I could follow you over."

"Why don't you just meet us at the house," Alfredo said. "Marco and me gotta make a stop first, and then we'll be there."

The marshal nodded. "I'll be by in about twenty minutes, then."

Marco and Alfredo took off before the man could change his mind. Marco threw his brother a sidelong glance. "Thanks."

"I figure you don't need word getting back to Leo that you're talking to the law."

"I don't, but this is a small town. It's bound to."

Alfredo shook his head. "Leo deserves to go to prison for what he did to that poor man."

"It seems apparent that Leo is quite comfortable in ending lives." Marco couldn't help but shudder. It didn't sit well with him to know that he'd been rather blind to his friend's true nature.

Alfredo pointed to the general store. "Let's stop here and get Mama some peppermints. That way we won't have been lying when I told the marshal we had to make a stop."

Marco followed Alfredo into the store. A few of the other miners were already inside purchasing a variety of things. Marco waited just inside the front door as Alfredo made his way to the counter. He couldn't shake the sense of dread that washed over him. Leo seemed more than happy to put an end to his problems, even when those problems came in the form of people. What would he do to Marco . . . to his family . . . should he find out that Marco told the marshal the truth?

He'll know it was me. Whether anyone sees

me talking to the marshal or not . . . he'll know.
Maybe it would be better to say nothing at all.

Alfredo returned with a small sack of candy.
"This ought to make Mama happy."

"But having the marshal there won't," Marco
muttered as they exited the store. "She's going
to be all worried about what's going on."

"She'll be all right," Alfredo assured him.
"Papa probably already told her what happened. You know they don't keep secrets."

Marco nodded, knowing his brother was
right. The thought of his mother knowing
the truth, however, left him feeling deeply
ashamed. Their walk home was made in silence. The cold wind stung Marco's eyes and
burned his lungs. He ducked his face into
his coat, glad for the little warmth it offered.
Neither he nor Alfredo said another word on
the matter of the marshal or Leo.

At home, Alfredo gave Mama the peppermints and told her the marshal would be joining them for dinner. Chantel and Isabella
looked at Alfredo and then to Marco as if
for an explanation, but neither man accom-
modated. Mama seemed to understand and
instructed Isabella to set another place.

She knows, Marco thought. Papa had no
doubt told her what had taken place that night.
Marco also hoped his father had kept back
some of the details, but it wasn't likely. She

didn't seem at all surprised by the news about the marshal, but her face bore an expression that suggested worry. It only made Marco's shame increase.

Marshal Garrison arrived and chatted about the town as if he were there for the sole purpose of visiting. Marco, however, shifted uncomfortably and tried to focus on the meal set before him, but found it impossible.

"Ladies, this has been quite a delightful meal. I appreciate your taking me in like this."

"It's no problem," Mama said with a smile. "You are always welcome here."

"If you don't mind, I'd like to have a word with your menfolk," the marshal said, getting up from the table. "Could we perhaps adjourn to the sitting room?"

Marco saw his father nod. Standing, he motioned for Marco and Alfredo to follow. Reluctantly, Marco got up from his chair. He still wasn't exactly sure what he was going to say. He didn't want to lie; after all, he had told his father the truth. Maybe it would have been easier if he'd just talked to the marshal out on the street. At least then he wouldn't be so hard-pressed to be honest.

They took seats in the front room and waited while Papa added wood to the fire. The marshal looked quite intent on getting on with the matter, however. He fixed Marco with a look that suggested he would brook no nonsense.

"Now, why don't you tell me what happened at the Fortune Hole?"

Marco looked at the ground. "Not much to tell. There was a game of cards and a misunderstanding. Gadd and Leo Fortino got into it. Gadd thought Leo was dealing off the bottom."

"And was he?" the marshal asked.

Marco shrugged. "Could have been. I didn't notice."

"Were you in the game?"

"Yeah, but I wasn't paying too much attention. I'd had a few beers."

Marshal Garrison nodded again. "Go on."

"I don't know what else to say. Gadd accused Leo of cheating, and Leo took offense."

"So he dealt the first blow?"

Marco squirmed in his seat like a ten-year-old. "He pretty much dealt the only blows. Gadd fought him—don't get me wrong—but you know Leo. He's fast."

"Did he only use his fists?"

Marco looked at his father. He knew he had to tell the truth, but oh, how he wanted to avoid it. He didn't want to get on Leo's bad side.

"Tell him, son."

"He hit him with a pistol butt." Marco stopped and shook his head. "Look, I don't want Leo mad at me. He has to keep peace in his establishment. He just did what he thought he had to do. Gadd did fight back."

"But not well," the marshal replied.

"No, not well. Leo is wiry and fast."

"So what happened after that, Marco?"

Again Marco looked to his father. He could see that he expected nothing but the absolute truth. With a sigh, Marco resigned himself to the situation. "Leo knocked Gadd out. He figured he was dead and . . . and . . . told one of his men to get him out of there."

"Where was he supposed to take him?"

Marco dug his fingers into his legs. "He . . . Leo told him to dump the body on the railroad tracks." There, he'd said it. He'd left no doubt as to Leo's intention to see the man dead.

The marshal nodded. "I guess he figured if Gadd wasn't already dead, he would be when the train came through. I suppose I need to go have a talk with Mr. Fortino. Attempted murder can't be tolerated."

"Look, he's not going to like it that I said anything," Marco declared without thinking. "I don't want to see harm come to my family."

"Son, you don't need to worry about that," Papa interjected. "It's important that you told the truth and that the marshal can get justice for Mr. Gadd. That man did not deserve to be dealt with in such a manner."

"No, he certainly didn't," Marshal Garrison agreed. He got to his feet. "I'm not sure how much justice we can get, but I intend to do what I can. Given there's only a mandatory ninety-day sentence for murder, however, I'm not sure that Mr. Fortino will face anything more than a dressing down." He shook his head. "It isn't right, but until we have better laws, I doubt we can expect much more. I want to thank you again for supper, Mr. Panetta. Now I'll make my way over to the Fortune Hole and see what I can find out there."

Marco didn't bother to see the marshal to the door. He sat staring at the flames of the fire, wondering if he'd done the right thing.

Chantel felt her heart skip a beat when Dante and Orlando Calarco stepped into her bedroom to see their grandmother. She had been reading from the Bible to Nonna Barbato when they arrived. She glanced up to find Dante watching her with decided interest and couldn't help but feel all aquiver. The man's dark eyes connected with her own, and she felt a tug low in her belly.

"You have visitors," Chantel said, getting to her feet.

Nonna Barbato smiled and welcomed her grandsons. "You boys look tired. Was it a hard day at the mine?"

"Every day is hard there, Nonna," Orlando declared. He kissed her forehead. "That's why I don't intend to make it my living."

His grandmother eyed him with amusement. "Oh? And what do you suppose you'll do instead?"

Orlando slipped into the chair vacated by Chantel. "I don't know. Maybe I'll learn to bake bread like you make. I think I could be a good baker, don't you?"

Chantel heard the older woman laugh, but her gaze was fixed on Dante. He stepped forward and kissed his grandmother's forehead. "Orlando wouldn't make a good baker at all. He has no patience for it," Dante declared.

This brought a smile to Chantel's lips, and she seriously wondered what Dante knew about the patience needed for baking. Nonna, however, thoroughly enjoyed seeing her grandsons and didn't seem to care at all what the topic of conversation might be. She let the boys ramble on about their day and about the neighbors, all while Chantel stood near the door. She hadn't meant to eavesdrop, but for some reason she hadn't thought to leave. When Nonna asked her a question, however, Chantel realized she had been deep in thought.

"I'm sorry, Nonna, what did you say?"

"I asked if you had some dessert left over for my boys. You know they are at each other's mercy for food these days. Soon I will be well enough to return home, but I think they would very much like some of your *Pesche Ripiene*."

"Stuffed peaches at this time of year?" Orlando asked. "What a treat."

"We used peaches we canned last fall," Chantel replied. "It's not exactly the same, but they come out pretty good, if I do say so myself." She smiled.

"It sounds wonderful," Orlando replied.

"Then if you like, I'll bring you each a portion." She looked to Dante, and to her surprise he gave her an almost boyish grin of delight.

"It's one of my favorites, I have to admit."

She liked seeing the pleasure in his expression. Chantel hurried to the kitchen where her mother and Isabella were just putting away the last of the dishes.

"Mrs. Barbato asked me to give Orlando and . . . Dante some dessert. I hope you don't mind."

Mama pulled down two dessert plates. "Of course not. Take them coffee, too. It was probably a cold walk to come see their nonna."

Chantel nodded, but Isabella was the one to take the plates. "I'll help you. After all, it will give me an excuse to spend time with

Orlando." She lowered her voice. "We're trying so hard to keep our distance and not appear overly eager to be alone." She moved to where the glass dish of stuffed peaches sat and began to dish up portions for each man.

"You can't really imagine that the Calarcos have just forgotten about Orlando's plans to marry you," Chantel chided. She went to the cupboard and took down two cups and saucers.

"I don't know if they've forgotten or not, but Orlando said we should give them no reason to do anything rash. He said if his nonna hadn't gotten sick, his father might have insisted they move south. He's fearful of what his father might do if he perceives a real threat to his family."

"But what about your elopement? Won't that cause problems anyway?" Chantel asked.

Isabella shrugged. "By the time he could confront us, we would be legally married. There would be nothing more he could say or do."

"Except disown his son." Chantel noted her mother's frown. "I would hate to think of such a joyous occasion separating a family."

"It would only be separated at Mr. Calarco's choosing," Isabella replied.

Chantel knew her sister was right. She had the feeling that even Dante wouldn't protest overmuch should the young couple marry. He seemed more accepting of her family since they'd taken over care for his grandmother. It wouldn't be long, however, before Nonna Barbato could return to her home.

The sisters served the Calarco brothers their dessert and coffee in the bedroom. Nonna seemed delighted to have the foursome around her and insisted the girls remain. Sitting on the edge of Isabella's bed, Chantel and her sister did as she asked.

Sampling the dessert, Orlando threw them an ear-to-ear grin. "This is good. Nonna, it tastes just like yours."

"It's not hard to make," Isabella declared. "Chantel taught me just this morning. In fact, I ground the almonds and peach pulp. Chantel took care of crushing the lady fingers, and then we blended it with sugar and candied fruit. That makes the stuffing."

"Well, it's delicious," Dante said, his gaze traveling to Chantel's face.

She felt her cheeks grow hot under his scrutiny. Why should he have such an effect on her? Goodness, but the man made her feel most uncomfortable. She looked to Nonna, who had closed her eyes. "Do you need anything, Nonna Barbato? Some tea perhaps?"

"No," the older woman said, shaking her head. She opened her eyes and looked up with an expression of contentment. "I'm just fine. I'm very happy."

"What's got you so happy, Nonna?" Orlando asked. "You like watching Dante and me eat?"

Their grandmother nodded and gave a chuckle. "Sí. I very much like that. It means all is well. It means you are healthy and safe. It means we live another day."

When it was clear that Nonna Barbato was ready to sleep, the foursome exited the room. Chantel offered to take the plates and suggested Orlando and Dante warm up by the fire before heading home. When she returned to the front room, she was surprised to find Isabella and Orlando gone and Dante talking with her brother Marco. Chantel paused outside of the room to overhear what was being said.

"I think so long as my grandmother is under your roof," Dante declared, "it is my business."

"I suppose you're right," Marco replied. "The truth is, the marshal was here because of something I saw. A man took a beating and was left for dead the other night. It happened at the Fortune Hole. I was there. My father and brother and I rescued the man from the railroad tracks and took him to Dr. Shipman."

"I see. And who was responsible for leaving him to die?"

"Leo Fortino."

Chantel put her hand to her mouth to suppress a gasp. She had never thought Leo a reputable man, but she'd never considered him to be a killer.

"I'm afraid he might become vindictive," Marco added. "I know he's capable of most anything."

"He wouldn't hurt the women, would he?" Dante asked. "I recall him being rather heavy-handed with your sister Chantel one evening not so long ago."

"He fancies himself in love with her," Marco said with a near snarl.

Chantel pressed closer to better hear the conversation. She was surprised at the concern and interest that Dante seemed to have for their safety.

"Is there anything I can do to help you in this matter?" Dante asked.

"Why would you help?"

Chantel hadn't expected this bluntness from her brother. "I suppose you mean because of the feud," Dante replied. "Even so, as I said before, my nonna is here. If Fortino means to do you or your family harm—it might involve her. And . . . well . . . I wouldn't want to see harm come to any of the ladies here."

"Nor would I," Marco replied. "It isn't their fight and not their fault. I put myself in a dishonorable place—they didn't." He sounded so downcast that Chantel could no longer stand it.

"I hope I'm not interrupting," she said, entering the room.

Marco got to his feet. "No. I was just headed to bed. Feeling kind of spent. Might be catching a cold."

Chantel put her hand to his brow. It was cool. "I can make you some tea with herbs."

"No, I'll just go to bed. Thanks anyway." He turned back and nodded at Dante. "Evening."

Chantel hadn't expected to be left alone with Dante. She wondered if she should try to start a conversation or if it would be best to remain silent. She didn't wonder long.

"Did you manage to hear everything?" he asked, looking amused.

She startled at the question and was unable to hide her surprise. "I . . . what do you . . . mean?"

He laughed. "I saw your shadow on the foyer floor. You were listening just outside the door to our conversation."

Chantel let out a breath and tried to hide her embarrassment. "Guilty as charged. I suppose I was just surprised that you and Marco would have anything to talk about in a civil manner."

Dante shrugged. "I know how to keep my temper and mind my manners. So what do you know about this problem with Fortino?"

"Very little until tonight. Though the marshal was here, he spoke privately with the men. Marco has been quiet. Papa and Alfredo aren't talking about it, either."

"I can't say that I blame them. You should know about it, however, so that you can be more careful. If Fortino is of a mind to harm this family, any of you could be at risk."

Dante's tone had grown very serious, and he'd moved a step closer to her. "I'll keep that in mind." Not knowing what else to say, she remained quiet.

A silence hung between them, heavy with unspoken words. At last Dante reached for his coat, then turned and looked intently at her face. "I couldn't bear to see you hurt," he said quietly. Then he stepped out the door.

Chapter 15

"I feel confident that you can safely return home," Dr. Shipman told Mrs. Barbato. "I think the excellent care you've received these last few weeks saved your life. Perhaps that will give your son-in-law cause to forego the ill will between your families." He put his stethoscope away and closed his medical bag.

Mrs. Barbato looked at Chantel, then spoke in her broken English. "I prayed to God . . . He would . . . make soft Vittorio's heart. He no come here to see me, but did talk to me . . . ah . . . he talk with the boys." She smiled. "I sorry, my English is no good."

"I understand perfectly, Mrs. Barbato." Dr. Shipman patted the old woman's shoulder. "Now, I want you to take it easy. I don't want you walking home in the cold. If need be, I'll drive you in my carriage."

Nonna seemed confused by the rapid-fire English, so Chantel quickly interpreted. She gave a nod and a smile. "Thank you, Doctor. I will be . . . good."

Chantel assured the doctor that they would see to Mrs. Barbato's safe delivery. "My mama has already arranged to borrow a cart," she assured him. "We'll wrap her up and keep her warm for the journey home."

"Good. I'll trust you to see to it," the doctor replied. "In the meanwhile, please let your brother and father know that Mr. Gadd would like to see them."

"Mr. Gadd? Is he the man they brought in—the one who was beaten up?"

The doctor nodded. "He would have died if your menfolk hadn't found him. Mr. Gadd would like to express his thanks."

"When they return from work," Chantel told him, "I'll see to it that they get the message."

Just then Mama appeared in the open doorway. "Dr. Shipman, can I offer you some coffee and pastry?"

The man smiled. "No. I'm afraid I must get back to the hospital. But thank you all the same."

"Then let me get your coat," Mama declared. She escorted the doctor out of the room while Chantel went to help Nonna Barbato with her heavy wool shawl.

"I'll bet you'll be glad to have your bed back," Nonna said, moving to the small rocker Chantel had brought for her comfort.

"I have slept perfectly well. I'm just delighted that you have made a full recovery. I know your grandsons were quite worried . . . as were we."

"God isn't finished with me yet," the older woman replied. "He wants me to help make peace between our families, I think. I must have a long talk with Vittorio. It's time he better understood the truth about the past."

"Do you think it will make a difference?"

The older woman shrugged. "Who can say? I pray that it might be so. You should pray, too. With the way you girls feel about my boys, you would benefit from the peace, no?"

Chantel was momentarily flustered. "I . . . ah . . . well . . . it would make it easier for Orlando and Isabella, if that's what you mean."

Nonna laughed and shook her finger at Chantel. "You cannot fool me. I know you like my Dante. He likes you, too, I think."

Momentarily speechless, Chantel felt herself go hot from the tip of her head to the bottom of her feet. *Good grief, have I been that obvious?*

"You two are good together. You don't allow my Dante to push you around. You are strong . . . like him. You would make him a good wife."

"Oh, Nonna Barbato, I think you have the wrong idea," Chantel said, going to the bed. She began to smooth out the bedding and plump the pillows. "Isabella is the one with marriage on her mind."

"Sí, I know this. But I think you could love, as well."

Chantel didn't know what to say. It was true that Dante stirred up feelings in her that she didn't really understand. However, the man could make her mad just as easily as he could make her weak-kneed.

"I think you must be mistaken, Nonna Barbato."

Nonna's expression, however, suggested she felt differently.

Dante glanced out the door of their small house and saw the reason for the knock on their door. Nonna had been brought home by the Panettas. Mr. Panetta and Marco pulled a small two-wheeled cart in which Nonna rode. She was bundled under many layers of blankets and waved at him from where she sat.

Looking over his shoulder with uncertainty, Dante stepped out to greet them. "You should have let us know she was ready to return home. Orlando and I could have come for her."

As if on cue, Orlando appeared at the door to join his brother. "Nonna! You've finally come home." He disappeared just as quickly.

"If you'll give us just a minute," Dante

interjected. "We need to get our boots on. Then we can bring her into the house."

"We can wait," Mr. Panetta said, nodding. "We have to keep the cart balanced anyway."

Dante headed to the back of the house for his boots and found Orlando had already grabbed them. "Here." He handed the boots to Dante, then pulled on his own. Without bothering to tie them, he bounded out the door.

Dante, too, slipped his boots on and didn't worry with the laces. He followed Orlando outside and found him already at the cart. "Nonna, are you really in there under all these covers?" Orlando asked.

She chuckled. "I am, but I cannot move. Mrs. Panetta didn't want me to take a chill, so she made certain I would stay nice and toasty."

Mr. Panetta spoke up. "You might want to lift her out while we continue to hold up the cart. Once we let go, the cart will tilt backwards and your nonna will spill out the back."

Dante and Orlando quickly went to work removing some of the blankets. Dante lifted the old woman in his arms. She couldn't have weighed even one hundred pounds. He carried her easily into the house, but not before overhearing Marco tell Orlando that his sister would like to see him.

He delivered Nonna to the front room,

where a fire was already burning in the little cast-iron stove. "You sit right here while I take back the rest of these blankets," he instructed. "I'll fetch you a quilt in just a minute. Oh, and I'll clean up the melted snow, too. Sorry about the boots."

"Don't worry about a quilt," Nonna said. "The fire will keep me warm enough." She smiled and looked around the room. "It's so good to be home."

Dante headed out to the cart with the blankets in arms. He hoped he could get the Panettas to leave before his father realized who had come calling.

"Thanks again for bringing her home. It hasn't seemed right without her here."

Mr. Panetta nodded. "Is your father home?"

Dante glanced over his shoulder. "He is, but . . . well . . . I don't think it would be such a good idea to confront him just now."

Panetta shook his head. "I wasn't of a mind to confront him. I just wanted to make sure he knew how much we enjoyed caring for Mrs. Barbato."

Orlando had taken up his grandmother's suitcase, the one he and Dante had delivered right after her collapse at the church. "We enjoyed a reason to get out of the house and come visiting," Orlando declared. "I don't know about Dante, but I'm gonna miss all the nice treats and great coffee." He motioned toward the house. "Nonna makes wonderful food, but her coffee is nowhere near as good as Mrs. Panetta's."

Mr. Panetta laughed. "I'll tell my wife you said as much."

Dante grimaced. His father would be outraged if he found Panettas on his property. "We don't want to keep you out here in the cold," he said. He motioned to the house with his head. "Come on, Orlando, we need to see to Nonna."

Dante thought to thank Mr. Panetta again, but when he turned to meet the man's gaze, he could tell they'd run out of time. Looking back over his shoulder, Dante found his father standing at the door.

"What do you think you're doing here?" he asked, stepping out without his boots.

"Evening, Vittorio," Mr. Panetta said, giving the bill of his cap a slight lift. "Dr. Shipman has allowed your mother-in-law to return home. We were just delivering her."

Dante's father narrowed his eyes. "Get off my property."

Panetta frowned. "I kind of thought, given the fact that we took care of your mother-in-law, you would find it in your heart to see our goodwill. We mean to put the past aside and be your friend."

Vittorio Calarco spit on the ground. "That is what I think of friendship with a Panetta. Now go, or I'll get the marshal."

It was an empty threat. All of the men knew there was little the marshal could do in this matter. Dante feared, however, if he didn't get his father back inside, he might well start something more than an exchange of words.

"Nonna's in the front room. I'm sure she wants to see you," Dante told his father. "Come on, I'll take you to her."

His father looked at him as if he'd lost his mind. "I know my way." The older man turned and stormed into the house. Dante followed after him with Orlando bringing up the rear. He knew there would be a price to pay for his father's anger. No doubt the man would rant and rave about the injustice of it all—of the disrespect they'd shown their ancestors and how disappointing they were to the Calarco name for having allowed an enemy to care for one of their own family members.

To Dante's surprise, however, his father went into the kitchen without a word. Orlando delivered his grandmother's suitcase to her bedroom, then rejoined Dante in the front room.

He knelt down to tie his boots. "Sorry about the boots, Nonna. I'm going to . . . town."

"Do you think that wise?" Dante asked. "Nonna just returned and Papa . . . we . . ."

"Bah, you needn't worry about me," Nonna said. "Let the boy go."

"Go where?" their father asked.

Dante looked to Orlando and shrugged. He wasn't about to get in the middle of this battle.

Orlando didn't seem to care. He stood and met his father's fixed gaze. "I'm going to town."

"To do what? You just got home, and now your nonna has returned. You should stay here."

"I have something I want to do," Orlando insisted. He headed for the door.

"You're going to go see that Panetta girl, aren't you?" his father countered.

The ire in his tone caused Orlando to stop and turn. "I am."

"I forbid it!" His father crossed the room in two long strides. He took hold of Orlando's shoulders. "Do you hear me? I forbid it."

"Vittorio," Nonna Barbato interrupted. "You should not be so angry. The Panettas took good care of me. They treated me as one of their own family. They blessed you by blessing me. They even offered up prayers for your safety and that of your sons. You should be ashamed that you refuse their friendship."

Dante's father let go of his son and looked hard at his mother-in-law. "You can go and live with them for all I care. If you want to betray this family in such a manner, then I say good riddance."

"Papa!" Dante let the word slip without thinking. He'd never heard his father be so disrespectful toward an elder. To cover his own embarrassment at rebuking his father, Dante quickly added, "Nonna is still quite weak, I'm sure. We should probably see to getting her to bed rather than stand here arguing."

"Your nonna is strong enough to chastise me," his father replied. He narrowed his eyes. "None of you seem to understand."

"It's you who do not understand, Vittorio." Nonna's gentle tone did nothing to soothe her son-in-law's anger. "God does not wish for this ugliness to continue."

"I am the head of this household. I am the papa," he declared, slapping the flats of his hands against his chest. "I am the man. You do not show me respect. You do not show me love."

Dante could see Orlando was torn over what he should do. To his surprise, however, Orlando began to unbutton his coat. "Papa, if the only way I can prove my love and respect is to stay here and discuss this matter with you, then I am willing."

Their father shook his head. "You will stay this time, but not another. You will go and see that woman. You do not care about this family, and I am ashamed to call you son."

Orlando stopped undoing the buttons and met his father's enraged expression. "I am ashamed, as well. Ashamed that we should be such a people. People who hold on to grudges and hatred. Jesus forgave our sins on the cross, but you cannot forgive the sins of a family who were once called friends by our ancestors. Father Buh taught last week that if you will not forgive man their sins, the heavenly Father will not forgive you yours. Is that what you want?"

Dante knew his father would never stand for being spoken to in such a manner. In a flash, the older man had doubled his fist and punched Orlando square in the jaw. To Dante's surprise, his brother barely flinched. He stood silently, just staring at their father.

"You must not fight," Nonna said. "This is not what God would have you do."

"God is not the one in charge here," Vittorio countered.

"That much is certain," Nonna replied, looking at him and nodding. "You took God from His rightful place and replaced Him with yourself."

Vittorio Calarco said nothing in response. Dante could not understand his father's impassioned bitterness. All of his life, Dante had heard the stories of deceitful Panettas—of their wrongdoings and harm. But he'd only witnessed examples of their kindness and love. Now his father had shown yet another side of this longstanding feud. It was an ugly, hopeless side that left no room for God or mercy.

"You will make a choice," their father finally said, turning back to Orlando. "Choose this family or theirs, but you cannot have both. In two weeks' time, I am sending you to Italy. I planned it many weeks ago now."

"I won't go," Orlando said, narrowing his eyes. "I won't."

Dante could see the swelling already starting to discolor his brother's jawline, but if Orlando was in pain, he didn't show it. He had to admire his brother's willingness to stand up for what he believed.

"If you do not go as I have told you," their father said, "I will never see you again. I will no longer call you son. I will put you from this family and you will be my enemy." He turned to Dante and shook his fist. "And you . . . you keep him away from that Panetta woman or you'll answer to me!"

Chapter 16

"The message says it's urgent that we meet," Isabella told Chantel. "I can't imagine what's wrong. Orlando told me we shouldn't see each other, but now he says we must." She held the note out to Chantel. "What do you suppose has happened?"

Chantel read over the messy note. It looked to have been hastily written. "I can't imagine. What are you going to do?"

"Meet him, of course. But I'll need your help. If something is wrong, then most likely it will mean his father and brother will be on the lookout for him to do something rash." Isabella grabbed her wool bonnet. "There's no telling if he can slip away from them at noon, but I'm going to go to the place we used to meet and see if he shows up there. I want you to come with me and keep an eye out for Dante and his father."

"But, Isabella, they're going to know what I'm up to if they see me near the mine."

Isabella tied her bonnet in place. "Not if you take something for Papa and the boys for dinner."

"But they took their dinner pails with them," Chantel protested. She had a bad feeling about this entire matter.

"So you can take them some of those cookies you baked this morning. A nice big sack of cookies is always welcomed by men."

Chantel frowned. "And when did you become such an authority?"

Isabella shrugged. "I know my brothers and papa as well as you do. Now get your bonnet, and I'll fetch the cookies and tell Mama what's happened."

Chantel realized she had no choice in the matter. Isabella was determined to meet Orlando whether Chantel helped her or not. It would probably be best if Chantel went along.

They bundled up in layers of sweaters and wore old trousers under their skirts. They topped this with their heaviest coats and mittens and tied thickly knitted scarves around their faces. With any luck, Chantel thought, no one would have any idea of who they were. Of course, with the weight of the extra clothing, Chantel thought they'd be lucky to walk even half the distance to the mine.

And the miners will still know we are women. They'll know we have no purpose being there at the mine. Goodness, why do I let myself get talked into these things?

Trudging through the snowy roads, Chantel

couldn't help but feel oddly on display. She caught a few pedestrians staring after them from time to time and worried that someone would stop them. By the time they could see the depot, she breathed a little easier, but only marginally.

Isabella stopped her before they came to the crossroads that led to the mine. "Here, you take the cookies and see about finding the boys. But remember to keep an eye open for Dante and his father."

"I know what to do, but are you certain you'll be safe?"

Isabella gave a muffled laugh. "Of course. I did this all last year if you'll recall, and no harm came to me. Now I'm going to leave you here." The noon whistle blew and Chantel knew that soon the area would be filled with men.

"You go ahead." Isabella slipped off behind the depot before Chantel could say a word.

Chantel looked around at the men who were milling about. None of them looked familiar.

She waited a few moments, watching for any sign of the Calarco men. Overhead, the murky gray sky left her feeling as dismal as the day. She hated winter and fervently wished she could be back in the warmth of an Italian summer. How she had enjoyed her days there in the sun. Just thinking about it seemed to warm her a bit. She remembered long walks with her nonna and other relatives. She conjured up visions of food-laden tables and outdoor eating. Sometimes Nonno read to them from the Bible and encouraged them to do right in the eyes of the Lord. It was a joyous and peaceful place—a sort of heaven compared to this.

"Miss Panetta?"

She whirled around to face Dante Calarco. How in the world had he managed to sneak up on her? "How did you know it was me?" she asked without thinking.

He shrugged. "It wasn't easy. You must be wearing quite a few layers, because I know you aren't as plump as you appear. However, I recognized the coat and bonnet. What are you doing here?"

"I . . . ah . . . have cookies," she said, holding up the sack. "I wanted to bring some for Papa and the boys, but I haven't seen them anywhere."

"I could take them," he offered. "Of course, I would probably have to sample them on the way." A hint of a smile touched his lips.

He has such nice lips. I wouldn't mind at all. . . .

"Miss Panetta?"

She startled, glad that the scarf kept him from seeing her surprise. "I suppose . . . that would be acceptable." She opened the sack and drew a deep breath. This was just as good a way to occupy him as any. "Why don't you try one first and decide if it's worth the effort."

He didn't have to be asked twice. Reaching in, Dante pulled two cookies from the sack. "I might have trouble telling with just one."

She said nothing and waited for his opinion on her baking. Dante gave every pretense of thoroughly considering the cookies. He looked each one over, then sniffed them and finally bit into the first one. He chewed slowly and looked heavenward as if contemplating his evaluation. Without a word he finished that cookie and soon had the other one eaten, as well.

"So what is your decision?" Chantel asked.

"I believe they are quite tolerable. I will be happy to deliver them to your father and brothers."

"Thank you. I'm relieved to know they've passed your scrutiny."

He took the sack from her and gave a bit of a bow. "I'm always glad to help."

"Even when it's a Panetta you're helping?" she asked.

Dante shrugged. "So long as the cookies taste this good."

He started to go, but Chantel thought of Mrs. Barbato. "By the way, how is your nonna?"

"She's doing well," he replied. "She seems to be back to her old self—strong as a mule and twice as stubborn."

Chantel nodded. "I very much enjoyed her company. I miss her now. She reminds me a lot of my own nonna in Italy. Did you know they were good friends once?" She hadn't meant to share this information, so she hurried to cover up her indiscretion. "They knew each other when they were young."

"Yes, I knew that. Nonna told me something about it once when I was there to see her at your house."

"Pity they couldn't still be friends," Chantel said. She glanced around, hoping to see if there was any sign of Isabella.

"Who are you looking for?" Dante asked.

She felt her face grow hot beneath the scarf. Had she really been that obvious? "My . . . ah . . . brothers . . . and Papa, of course."

He started to nod, but then Dante looked at her as if seeing her for the first time. "Chantel . . . please tell me your sister isn't here seeing my brother."

She couldn't recall him ever calling her by her first name. It both startled and pleased her. "Why, Mr. Calarco, you are certainly suspicious—and after I let you sample the cookies."

"Our father is watching him like a hawk

seeking prey," he said, looking around the mining grounds. "He means to send Orlando to Italy in a little more than a week's time."

"What?" Chantel's scarf fell away from her face and the bitter cold nipped at her cheeks. "How can he force him to go?"

Dante continued to search the area. "He's threatened to disown him if Orlando doesn't do what he commands. I know my brother, however, and so does our father. I'm supposed to keep Orlando from seeing your sister or it's going to come down on me."

"I don't see why it matters. They plan to marry. I'm sure Orlando would rather be with Isabella than go to Italy. I can't see why your father thinks he can force him to go."

"You don't know our father. He can make life very bad for his enemies."

"But Orlando is his son."

"Not if he continues with your sister. Our father will make him an enemy and that will mean . . . well . . . it won't bode well. Orlando won't be able to get work at the mines because my father will see to it that he's refused. The owners respect my father. He's one of the best explosives experts in the business. In fact, they're sending him south for a few days to help with some problem areas at one of the Mesabi Range mines."

"I thought those were mostly open pit

mines," Chantel countered, hoping that if she kept him talking, Isabella and Orlando would have more time together.

"They are, but they want to start underground work. The ore is softer and more crumbly, however." He looked behind him and then at her again.

She hurried to question him more. "So your father is going to help them. I think that's nice."

He frowned. "Where are they, Chantel?"

"Who?" she asked innocently.

He all but growled. "You know very well. Where are they meeting?"

"I think I'd better take those cookies," she said, reaching out. "Papa and the boys will be finished with lunch by the time you get these to them."

Dante looked at her and shook his head. "You aren't helping anything. If my father finds out what's going on . . . he'll put Orlando on the next train out of here. Mark my words." He headed off in the direction of the shaft tower without bothering to give her back the sack of cookies.

Chantel didn't care. She hurried back to where she had parted company with Isabella. "Issy?" she called as quietly as possible.

It was only a matter of minutes before her sister appeared. She pulled at Chantel's coat sleeve. "We have to hurry."

"I was just about to say the same thing. Dante knows you were meeting Orlando. He says Orlando's father is watching him carefully and plans to send him to Italy."

"I know," Isabella said, all but pulling Chantel down the road. "That was why he had to meet me. He said his father is being very unreasonable. He has threatened to disown Orlando and make it impossible for him to get work."

"Yes, Dante said as much."

Isabella motioned to a side street. "Let's take the shortcut."

Chantel nodded and followed her sister down the narrow street. "Look, Dante said that his father is going south to the Mesabi Range to help them for a few days with their explosives."

Isabella nodded. "I know. That's why Orlando and I are going to take that opportunity to leave. I didn't want to take money from you, but now I will have to. Orlando said his father has confiscated most of his. He only managed to hide a little away from him."

"That's all right," Chantel said, feeling her heart rate accelerate. It was rather like they were racing against an unseen clock. "I have more than enough to help you get train tickets. You can get to Aunt Marilla's, and she will help you from there. I know she will.

She could probably even lend you money if necessary."

"I knew you'd understand, Chantel. I know Mama and Papa will, too."

Chantel glanced over her shoulder, worried that someone might have followed them. "Unfortunately I think they'll be the only ones."

On Saturday evening March seventh, the talk was all about Ely becoming a town in its own right. That week they had received approval and the incorporation was granted. "This was the best thing we could have done for the place," Papa told the family. Chantel worked on a long piece of tatted edging and listened as her father continued.

"They now can tax the mines, and that will bring in funds to clean up this town and make it better."

"It'd look a sight better if they were to pull those tree stumps just beyond the town limits," Marco threw in. Chantel had noticed he'd been sticking close to home lately—especially since word had come that Leo Fortino had not been jailed while waiting to have his case reviewed by the judge.

Chantel knew he worried what Leo's retribution might be. She worried about it herself. "I suppose," she said, hoping to keep her brother's mind occupied, "that the tax money would allow the city to pay for their removal."

"Yes," her father agreed. "In fact, someone could start up a new business to do just that. If a fella had a couple of good draft horses, he could pull those stumps out easily."

"I just hope that the incorporation will allow for more law and order," Mama declared. The bobbins fairly flew through her fingers as she worked to complete a piece of lace she'd promised to the wife of a mine owner. She'd been working on it for more than a month.

"I wouldn't count on things changing right away," Papa replied, putting his newspaper aside. "Although I did hear them say that an election would be held on the seventh of April. They plan to vote for a mayor instead of a village president."

"Do you suppose Dr. Shipman will run?" Mama asked.

"I don't think so." Papa shook his head. "I heard he wanted to focus on his plans to build a new hospital. Not only that, but he has his hands full now as it is. I was glad to hear we are getting a new doctor to help him. With the mines expanding, there are more and more accidents."

"Well, the Finnish Temperance Society plans to use this occasion to see that alcohol is eliminated from town," Mama said with a nod toward Marco and Alfredo. "I'm so glad that our boys have decided to turn away from such things."

Chantel knew her mother was delighted at the change in her son's entertainment habits. Drinking was bad enough, but gambling had led to the ruin of many a man in Ely. It seemed there was nothing that could not be wagered on. Dog fights, cock fights, cards, and so much more were ready and waiting to steal a man's hard-earned money. In fact, there were even bets on when the ice would be off the lake. It was a yearly event of which even the staunchest non-gamblers often partook.

As the hour grew late, Chantel suppressed a yawn and put aside her tatting. "I believe I am going to bed. I want to be fresh for morning services." She got to her feet and stretched. "Good night." She walked to her mother and kissed her on the cheek.

"You are in my prayers," Mama said, giving her a smile. *"Dio sia con voi."*

"And God be with you, Mama." Chantel kissed Papa's cheek and repeated the blessing.

She made her way to the bedroom and was surprised to find Isabella still awake. In fact, she was not only awake, but was rather busy folding clothes. All at once it dawned on Chantel what was happening.

"You're preparing to leave."

"Yes," Isabella replied, flipping her long, unbound hair over one shoulder. "Orlando's father is going south tomorrow. He'll take the afternoon train and be gone for the week. We figure to leave on Monday. That way we'll have plenty of time to get away before he even knows what has happened."

"And Orlando is ready to be disowned?"

Isabella straightened. "He feels he has no alternative. He won't give me up, nor I him."

"And what of his father's threat to see him ruined in mining?"

"That's the least of Orlando's worries. He hates mining work. He has always planned to take on a different trade."

Chantel sat down on the edge of her bed. "It won't be easy. Without references or knowing someone in the trade he chooses, he might well find it impossible."

"I think Aunt Marilla will have friends who can help us."

"So you'll remain in Duluth?"

Isabella shook her head. "Not necessarily. I'm hopeful that our aunt can put us in touch with someone in Chicago."

"Why there?"

"It's far enough away and bigger. Far bigger than Duluth. I believe we can move there and lose ourselves among the population. At least that's what we hope for. I also figure I'll have a better chance at getting a job."

Chantel tried to imagine her sister employed and smiled. "I don't suppose Orlando will want his wife working . . . at least not for long."

Isabella crossed the room to take more clothes from the wardrobe. "He doesn't mind . . . at least not until I find myself with child."

"It's hard to imagine you married and gone from here, much less a mother," Chantel said. A wave of sadness swept over her. "I shall miss you more than I can say."

"I will miss you, too. I missed you when you left for Italy, and I suppose that's why I started having such an interest in Orlando." She smiled. "Maybe you will find a man to keep your mind preoccupied as he did for me."

Chantel immediately thought of Dante and shook her head. "I don't know that there is anyone here for me. In fact, I might well return to Italy."

Isabella stopped her folding and looked to her sister. "You could come with Orlando and me. We could work together, and then I wouldn't feel so bad about taking your money."

She smiled and shook her head again. "No, you and Orlando must make a life together.

Besides, Mama will be far too lonely if I go, as well."

Shrugging, Isabella returned to the task at hand. "I suppose you're right. But you know you will always be welcome in my house. I do hope you'll come to visit me."

"I will," Chantel promised. But even as she made the pledge, she couldn't help but wonder if that would even be possible. It was hard to think of the family going their separate ways. They had always been so close. Family was everything. Perhaps with Papa getting older, she could convince her parents to join her in returning to the land of their birth. Maybe in Italy she could forget about Dante Calarco.

Chantel began to undress for bed, still pondering that idea. She thought of Orlando and Isabella and how their marriage would come as a shock to her relatives in Italy. Would it do what Issy hoped and bring the two families together? Or would it only serve to further tear them apart? Her thoughts came in flurries as she realized she would only have this night and one more with her sister.

I won't be sad. I won't make Issy question her decision. She and Orlando were meant to be together. Hopefully in a very short time, even the Calarcos will be able to realize that.

"Is there anything I can do to help?" Chantel asked after pulling on her nightgown. She pulled the pins from her hair and let the long coil of brown hair swirl around her shoulders and down her back.

"No, I'm nearly done." Isabella paused a moment. "I take that back. You can do one thing—pray. Pray that this will go well. Pray that we can get away without trouble following."

Chantel took hold of Isabella's hands. "I will pray . . . just as I have been praying all along since you first told me of your love for Orlando. I know God will guide you. I believe that with all of my heart."

"I do, too," Isabella replied. "And so does Orlando. We truly believe that in time, this will unite our families. Of course, we aren't marrying for that alone." She smiled in a dreamy sort of way that Chantel couldn't help but envy. "We are definitely a love match," Isabella added.

"I hope you're right . . . about the uniting of the families," Chantel said.

"Remember when we were little and first learned of Jesus' death on the cross? Mama told me that it was like there was a huge canyon between us and our Father in heaven. Jesus was like a bridge between sinners and God. He put himself between His Father and us so that we could have a way to reach God. I remember telling Mama that I thought it very unfair that anyone should have to sacrifice so much for us."

"I remember thinking something similar," Chantel replied. "It didn't seem right that someone else should have to pay for my sins."

Isabella nodded. "But Mama said that without Jesus's offering for us, we would forever be at odds with our heavenly Father."

Chantel nodded. "I remember that, too."

"Well, I am taking up the example Jesus gave," Isabella declared, striking a stance that took on the appearance of a fierce female warrior. "I am going to be that bridge for our families. With God's help, of course."

Chantel hugged her sister close and murmured a silent prayer. *Oh, Father God, please protect them from harm. Please lead them onto the right path—the choice you have made for them. Let them seek you and listen for your voice. Help Isabella to be the bridge to peace that she feels directed to be. Amen.*

Chapter 17

"I wish you didn't have to leave," Mama told Isabella. They were awaiting Orlando's arrival that early Monday morning, and emotions were high.

"I know, Mama, but it must be this way. Hopefully everything will be worked out soon and God will help Mr. Calarco to put aside his anger and forgive us."

Chantel finished packing a basket the young couple would take with them on the train. "There's enough food here for a small army," she told her sister.

"That's good," Isabella countered. "Orlando can eat like a small army." She hurried to the window for the sixth time in as many minutes. "Where is he? The train will be here soon, and we must be on it."

"Don't worry," Chantel said, coming up behind her. Mama joined them at the window to keep vigil.

"But there is no other way to get to Duluth," Isabella fretted, "other than sleigh or dog sled—and we have access to neither. We have to make the train and do it today. We need as much time as possible to distance ourselves from Ely before his father returns."

"You know we will do what we can to keep him from discovering where you've gone," Chantel said, taking hold of Isabella's shoulders from behind. Isabella reached up to clasp Chantel's right hand. Her fingers felt icy.

Finally the women wearied of standing at the frosty window and made their way into the front sitting room, where Isabella's suitcase awaited.

"I wish I could have taken a trunk," she said, looking sadly at the single case, "but Orlando said we needed to be able to move quickly."

"We can send you whatever you leave behind," Mama promised, her accent thick with emotion. "When you get settled, we will ship all your things."

Isabella nodded and paced in front of the fireplace. "He should be here by now. Something must have happened. Maybe Dante wouldn't let him leave."

"I thought you said he was going to go to work with Dante as if nothing was amiss, and then slip away," Chantel said.

"Yes, but they work together so much of the time—as a team," Isabella added. "He might have found it difficult to get away from him."

"I suppose that is possible. It would explain the delay. But maybe he wanted to wait until the last minute so that Dante wouldn't have time to realize he was gone. With the depot so close to the mine, it might be difficult for Orlando to time things properly."

"He still needs to get back to the house and get his things. Then he will come here for me and—"

A knock sounded against the front door. Isabella rushed for the foyer. "He's here!"

Chantel and her mother followed and were relieved to find Isabella had been right. The couple embraced for just a moment before Orlando put Isabella aside.

"We need to go quickly. The captain put me to work in one of the other shafts, so Dante won't miss me for a while. But the train will depart soon."

"I'm ready," Isabella said, hurrying into her coat. She pulled on her gloves and looked to her sister. "Chantel, would you get my bonnet and suitcase?"

Chantel nodded and went to retrieve the things. She tried not to feel overly anxious for the young couple. It would be difficult for them to make their escape, but not impossible. Especially if God was truly in this, as Chantel believed He was.

"Here you are," Chantel said, handing her

sister the bonnet. She held on to the suitcase and waited for Isabella to secure her hat. To her surprise, Orlando took the case and then hugged her.

"Thank you for your help. I will repay you as soon as I can."

"It's a wedding gift," Chantel declared. "No need to repay anything."

Orlando shook his head. "I can't let you do that. It wouldn't be right to start my married life that way." He looked to Mama. "I intend to do right by Isabella. I told your husband the same thing when he gave me his blessing to marry her. I will work hard, and I will love her forever."

"That is all any mama could hope for," she said, giving Orlando a kiss on the cheek. "Stay close to God, Orlando. If you draw near to Him and Issy does likewise, you will find that you draw closer to each other, as well."

He nodded and turned to his wife-to-be. "Come on. We need to go."

"Oh, the basket of food!" Chantel said and hurried to the table. She brought back the goodies, and Orlando took those, as well. He smiled and nodded his appreciation.

"I'll be outside," he told Isabella.

Chantel kissed her sister and whispered against her bonneted head, "I love you, and

I will do what I can to make things work out here."

Isabella pulled away and smiled. "If anyone can find a way to fix things, it's you, Chantel. Just don't worry for us. We'll be fine."

She hugged her mother and then hurried out the door after Orlando. Without another word or look, the couple disappeared around the corner. Chantel stood in the open doorway with her mother and watched the empty street for a moment longer. When the cold finally forced them back inside, the house seemed very empty.

Chantel looked at her mother and saw that she was crying. "Oh, Mama, they will be all right," she said, hugging her mother close.

Her mother reverted to Italian once again. "I know, but I wish they didn't have to run away like this. Isabella could have married in the church with a fine wedding. It's a mama's heart to desire such things for her children."

"Maybe one day Mr. Calarco will realize that this is a good thing, and we can at least have a party for them."

Mama nodded. "Maybe."

Evening came and with it the men returned from their hard labors. They had taken time to clean their hands and faces at the company washhouse, but their clothes were still filthy.

Chantel didn't cherish the thought of having to do all the laundry without her sister's help. Winter always made such chores much harder, although the heat from the cauldron fire was far more welcomed. Mama would offer to help, but Chantel knew she would have enough of her own work to tend to, what with the ironing and mending that would need to be done.

"Have they gone?" Papa asked.

Mama gave a sad smile. "Yes. They left in time to catch the train. Since I've not heard anything to the contrary, I believe they must have made it."

Papa nodded. "I hope they will be careful."

"Come, we will have supper," Mama said. "Chantel, she made a wonderful meal for us. Let's eat it now."

They made their way to the table, where Chantel had already placed a massive serving bowl of meatballs. Another large dish of baked pasta and vegetables sat at the opposite end of the table with two large loaves of bread gracing either side. It looked like more food than the small family could possibly need, but Chantel knew her brothers and father would most likely eat every last morsel and still have room for dessert.

Papa offered a prayer, and then the five of them dug into the meal. They all seemed painfully aware of the empty sixth chair at the table. Isabella's vivacious spirit was hard not to miss.

Don't be such a ninny. She's not dead and gone forever. We will see her again.

They were nearly ready for dessert when a loud banging sounded on the front door. Mama and Papa exchanged a look. They all knew that this moment would come. Dante Calarco would know to look for his missing brother here.

Chantel was surprised it had taken this long. She rose to answer the door, but her father shook his head. "Marco will get it."

Marco nodded and went to the door. Chantel could hear Dante rage at her brother, demanding to know where Orlando was. It was only a matter of minutes before he stormed into the room searching the table for Orlando.

"Welcome back, Dante," Mama said as sweetly as if he were there for a Sunday visit. "We were about to have dessert, but if you haven't eaten supper yet, you're welcome to join us."

Dante calmed at her words. "No thank you. Nonna has a meal waiting for me. I came for my brother."

"As you can see," Papa said, "he isn't here."

That seemed to momentarily stupefy Dante.

He seemed to consider the situation before posing his next question. "Where are they?"

"I presume you mean your brother and Isabella," Papa replied. "Have a seat, and I will try to explain."

Dante shook his head. "I don't want to sit down. Just tell me where they are so I can fetch him home. My father gave me charge to keep Orlando in line. I was afraid something like this might happen. I knew I couldn't trust him to stay away from here."

"Be that as it may," Papa said in a collected manner, "I have not yet had my dessert and would very much like to enjoy it before speaking further on this." He looked to Chantel. "Will you serve us?"

"Sí, Papa," she said, getting to her feet. She looked to Dante. "Are you sure you won't join us? I've made stuffed peaches again, and there is more than enough."

Dante looked at her for a long moment. "I can't. I need to get back. When Orlando shows up, tell him to come home straightaway."

"We will," Papa replied.

Chantel knew it wasn't an outright lie, but it almost felt like one. She couldn't help but feel sorry for Dante. He walked from the room in such a dejected manner that she very nearly ran after him to explain. Instead, she went to retrieve the peaches.

The evening wore on, but instead of feeling any better about the situation, Chantel only felt the tension build. She could imagine Dante sitting in his house, watching and waiting for a brother who would never show up. She hoped that Orlando had explained the situation to Nonna Barbato. The old woman would be supportive of the elopement, Chantel knew, and perhaps in time she could even help Dante and his father to understand.

Eventually, her father and brothers took themselves to bed and Mama kissed Chantel on the forehead. "I believe I will retire, as well. We've a busy day tomorrow."

"I won't be long," Chantel said. "I just want to finish this handkerchief." She had been sewing tatted lace to the edges of a linen cloth. She wanted to send more to Aunt Marilla to sell in Duluth.

"Just don't strain your eyes," Mama implored. "The light is not very good."

"It's enough for this. I won't be very much longer, anyway." Mama nodded and left without another word.

The house settled into silence, with only the crackling of the logs on the fire echoing through the room. Chantel didn't bother to hurry her stitches, though she knew the next morning would come far too soon. She dreaded going to her empty bedroom. Without Isabella there, it would seem so lonely.

Chantel thought of her sister embarking on a new life. Isabella had found a mate, a partner with whom she could share the joys and burdens of this world. Chantel, in comparison, now found her own life rather empty. She had no one but Mama and Papa . . . and they wouldn't live forever.

Tears began to stream down Chantel's cheeks and a sob broke from her throat. She put aside the handkerchief for fear of marring it with her tears. Burying her face in her hands, she began to cry in earnest. Loneliness gripped her heart.

When the knock sounded this time on the front door, it wasn't as heavy- handed as before. Chantel couldn't imagine who it might be. It was well past time for visitors, and her family had already gone to bed. Nevertheless, she did her best to stifle her emotions and went to see who it was. She dried her eyes on the hem of her apron, but knew she couldn't hide her red eyes.

When she opened the door to find Dante Calarco standing silently on the other side, Chantel could no longer contain her feelings. *He looks just as miserable as I feel. Like he's lost something valuable—something precious.* Without thinking of the repercussions, she burst into tears once again and fell into his arms.

Dante stood holding the sobbing woman—his enemy—his heart. He couldn't bear that she was so upset, and yet he didn't know what he could say that wouldn't add to her pain. He'd come here looking for answers. Looking for his brother. Instead he found his mixed emotions only further complicated by Chantel's heartbreak.

For several minutes he did nothing but hold her, cherishing the feel of her warm body next to his. The cold of the Minnesota winter was at his back, but the heat of the woman he'd come to love was making him forget who he was and why he was there.

Without meaning to, Dante buried his fingers in her hair and raised her damp face to meet his. Then, knowing he shouldn't, Dante lowered his mouth to hers and kissed her with all the pent-up longing he felt. She didn't resist, but returned the kiss with an ardor to match his own. Then, without a word, they broke apart and stood staring at each other.

Chantel had stopped crying, but now looked terrified at what they'd just done. She touched her fingers to her lips, which only served to make Dante want to kiss her again. He stood his ground, however, and did nothing.

"I thought I heard a knock," Papa said, coming up behind Chantel.

Dante forced himself to look away from her and greet Mr. Panetta instead. "Sorry to bother you again, but Orlando hasn't returned. I can see he isn't here."

"Son, I think you know that they're gone," Papa declared. "They've gone to get married and leave this place for good. I'm sorry if that causes you grief or makes it difficult for your papa, but that's just the way it is."

He put his arm around Chantel's shoulders. "Go on to bed, daughter."

"Sí, Papa," she murmured, leaving the two men alone.

Dante shook his head. "My father will disown him and make it impossible for him to get work around here."

"I wouldn't worry about that. I don't think they will stay anywhere near here," Papa replied. "And who would want them to under the circumstances? It's never easy to live with bitterness and hatred."

Dante considered Panetta's words for a moment, then shook his head again. "My father is a hard man, and he won't easily let this matter go unpunished—even if he has to seek out Orlando in order to deliver his retribution.

I need to find my brother before my father returns."

"Son, I don't know if you're a God-fearing young man, but I have to believe you are. Your nonna would not have let such matters be void in your life."

"I believe in God," Dante replied, not at all certain why he felt the need to answer.

"Good. Because I want to share something with you that I've only told a couple of people. One was Father Buh, and the other was my dear wife." He motioned to the front room. "Come. I want to tell you about what happened to me when the mine collapsed and trapped me."

Dante followed, but he had no interest in the older man's story. "Just tell me where they've gone . . . please."

Mr. Panetta turned. "I don't honestly know exactly where they've gone. What I do know is that you cannot stop them from marrying, and once they are man and wife, you cannot interfere with what God has joined."

Dante felt the hopelessness of the situation. "Then I suppose I should go."

"Go where, son?"

"To search for my brother. I'll have just a few days before my father returns. I have to find him before then."

"But I've already told you—you cannot stop this marriage."

Dante nodded. "But if my father learns the truth, I'm afraid he will."

"He cannot. The priest would not allow it. Your papa won't be able to annul it."

"I'm afraid you don't understand, Mr. Panetta. If my father finds out about this marriage, he will put an end to it—because he will put an end to Orlando's life."

Chapter 18

Dante slept very little that night, and the next day at the mine he looked around in hopes that his brother might appear as usual. When the hours wore on and there was no sign of Orlando, Dante knew Mr. Panetta had been right. The fool had run off to marry Isabella. Dante was hard-pressed to know what he should do. No doubt the couple had taken the train, but to where? They could have gone to any of the small towns along the rail line or even on to one of the bigger cities. He thought perhaps he could ask at the train depot, but even if the stationmaster could tell him, there was no way to know if the couple would remain in one place.

"How are you doing, son?" Mr. Panetta asked.

Dante looked up at the older man and his sons. Panetta motioned his boys to go about their business before turning back to Dante. "I don't imagine you slept very well last night."

"I didn't," Dante admitted. "I spent most of it trying to figure out how to hunt down my brother and get him back here before our father returns."

"Don't you think it would be better to just let him go?"

"You don't know my father."

Mr. Panetta gave him a sympathetic nod. "I suppose you are probably right, but maybe God will change his heart. God changed mine, after all."

Dante narrowed his eyes. "My father is a hard man."

"So was I," Mr. Panetta admitted. "Until the accident. Remember last night I told you that I wanted to share something with you about that?"

"I remember."

"Well, when I was buried under that rock, God spoke to me as if He were right there beside me."

Dante frowned. He had long ago given up on the idea that God might communicate with His people. God seemed like a distant onlooker—nothing more. Nonna would have boxed his ears for such thinking, but Dante couldn't pretend to feel otherwise.

"Now, I know that may sound farfetched," Mr. Panetta continued, "but I swear to you it's true."

"And what was it God had to say?" Dante asked, unable to keep the sarcasm from his tone.

"He told me to make peace with all men. He told me to forgive my enemies and make a better life for my loved ones."

"God told you that? He just appeared and spoke to you like we're talking just now?"

Panetta shrugged. "Not so much like us. I didn't see His face, but I heard His voice in my heart and soul. It was so clear and distinct, it seemed audible. I'd lost consciousness from my injuries, but I felt at peace. My initial fear was gone. It was as if I knew that because of God's words to me, I would live to fulfill His commands."

"And that was why you told my father you wanted an end to the feud?"

"In part." He smiled. "Obedience to God is something I think we should definitely pay heed to, but I have long seen the futility in this war between our families. The problems of the past should remain in the past. There is far too much at stake for the future to continue in bitterness and revenge. Your father's desire for these things will only hurt him in the long run."

"I don't know that Papa had in mind for any particular revenge," Dante replied. "He simply feels it's unnecessary for our families to be friends. Family is everything to him—it's the reason he will be so angry, so betrayed if he returns to find Orlando has disobeyed him."

"If family is truly everything to him, then he will set aside his pride. You feared last night he might well end your brother's life. But to a man who loves his family and values them above all, this would be impossible."

Dante knew it sounded contradictory, but it wasn't. In his father's way of thinking, better a child should die than betray and dishonor his people. "Do you know where they've gone?"

"I do," Panetta replied. "But I cannot tell you. I promised that I wouldn't, and I am a man of my word."

"As am I," Dante said, letting out a heavy breath. "I presume they went by train, so I will start there. I've already spoken to the mine's captain. I'm taking the rest of this week off to find him."

"And when you find him," Mr. Panetta said, looking Dante in the eye, "what will you do when he refuses to give up the woman he loves and return to Ely?"

Dante shook his head. "I don't know. I guess I'll have to cross that bridge when I get there."

"And then he left," Papa said, explaining the entire scene with Dante to his family. "I don't know if the stationmaster will tell him that they went to Duluth or not."

"Oh, this is terrible," Mama declared. She closed her eyes, and Chantel knew she was praying.

"I could go and warn them," Chantel interjected. "If I sneak out and catch the train before Dante learns where they went, I could get to them and warn them what has happened."

"Yes," Mama agreed. "She could go and warn them. Marilla will know what is to be done after that."

"We would have to use some of the money we've been saving for a better house," Papa said, considering the matter. "And I don't like that she would travel alone."

"But if more than one of us goes, we will be easier for Dante to spot and follow," Chantel replied. "I can be quite secretive—I could even dress in some of Mama's old things and cover my head like an old woman. No one would suspect it was me . . . and looking as such, I would probably go unnoticed and unbothered."

Papa nodded. "Then go. I will send Marco to get you a ticket for the train."

The next evening, Chantel arrived at her aunt's house on East First Street in Duluth. The hired carriage drove up the circled drive, but because of the darkness, Chantel couldn't make out much of the Gothic Revival stylings of the large house her aunt called her "little nest." Light shone from only a couple of the windows, but Chantel felt certain she would be warmly welcomed.

As soon as the driver pulled to a stop, Chantel jumped from the carriage without his help. She hurried up the steps to the front door and pounded the brass knocker several times against the wood. In only a few moments a well-dressed man appeared, and Chantel instantly recognized him as Mr. Bartell, her aunt's butler.

"Mr. Bartell," she said, pulling the shawl from her head, "it's me, Chantel Panetta."

The older man smiled. "Welcome, Miss Panetta. I could not imagine who would be coming to visit us this evening."

The driver came up from behind with Chantel's bag. She hurried to pay the man and thanked him for his help before turning back to Mr. Bartell. "I wonder if my sister and her . . . husband are here?"

"Why, yes, they are. Your aunt, however, is out for an evening affair. She'll be late getting back."

"I see." Chantel reached for her bag, but Mr. Bartell took it up instead.

"I'll have this delivered to your room after

I take you to your sister and Mr. Calarco. They are in the music room."

"Thank you," Chantel said, breathing a sigh of relief. "It's most urgent that I speak with them."

The older man nodded and led the way. Chantel never failed to marvel at the beautiful home. Her uncle had made a fortune from his early involvement with iron speculation and freighting. He had quickly become one of Duluth's many millionaires, and this house was his opulent proof.

Mr. Bartell led her past the first large parlor, which displayed her aunt's decided taste. The beautiful damask draperies of pale gold perfectly matched the striped wallpaper of the same hue. The furnishings here were lavish and pristine, in rich mahogany and burgundy velvet. It was clearly a parlor used only for visitors. Bartell quickly slid open the pocket doors that separated this room from the next.

They made their way into yet another room of plush furniture and bric-a-brac. Here the gold colors were continued, but this time they were contrasted with powdery blues and coral. Opening yet another set of pocket doors, Mr. Bartell announced her arrival.

"Miss Panetta."

Isabella looked up from where she sat near the fire. "Chantel! What are you doing here?" She frowned at her sister's appearance. "Goodness, and why are you dressed like that? Isn't that Mama's old garden dress?"

Chantel nodded. "It's a long story, but I came to warn you. Dante knows you and Orlando have run away to get married." She paused and looked at her sister quite seriously. "You are already married, aren't you?"

Isabella laughed. "Yes, and happily so. Aunt Marilla saw to it first thing. Orlando has just gone to the kitchen to sneak some additional dessert. I told you he has a great appetite." She sobered again. "But why this warning? We knew Dante would learn that we'd gone, and we knew he would suppose that we had married."

Chantel nodded. "I know, but Dante is determined to hunt you down and bring Orlando back."

"He'd have a hard time doing that," Orlando declared, coming into the room.

Seeing the younger man, Chantel felt almost a sense of relief. "I'm so glad you are here and safe. Even so, Dante said your father would just as soon see you dead as to see you betray the family this way. He intends to find you and bring you back before your father returns from the Mesabi Range."

"I'm not going anywhere without my wife," he said with conviction, moving to

Isabella's side and putting his arm around her shoulder.

"I can definitely appreciate that," Chantel replied. "But frankly, I'm terrified by Dante's claims. He truly seemed to believe your father would act in such a way. Could he be exaggerating?"

"I wish that were the case, but I doubt it seriously," Orlando replied. "My father commands obedience, and he takes loyalty very seriously. He'll be angry that I defied his plan to send me to Italy, but he'll be absolutely irate when he learns that I married against his wishes."

Isabella looked at him, her expression betraying her fear. "Will he really try to kill you? His own son? How could a man murder his own child?"

Orlando shook his head. "My father has never been the same after losing our mother. That, along with the bitterness between our families, has caused anger to fester within him. It controls him, and makes him react poorly and often without any thought to the consequences. I'm not at all certain he can control his temper, given the situation."

"That's why I had to come and warn you. You must get away from here, hide. With Aunt Marilla's help, we can get you on your way to Chicago or elsewhere. But we'll have to hurry. You will need to leave no later than tomorrow."

"I'm afraid there won't be a chance of that happening."

Chantel felt her blood run cold at the sound of Dante Calarco's voice. She whirled to find him crossing the room as if he owned the place.

"How . . . how . . . did you . . ." She shook her head in stunned amazement.

"I followed you." He narrowed his eyes and fixed his brother with a hard look. "You're coming with me."

"I won't," Orlando said. "I'm sorry, Dante, but I'm married to Isabella, and I won't let Father take that from me."

"I'm not suggesting you do. I'm suggesting you come back long enough to explain it to him yourself and face the consequences."

Orlando shook his head. "We both know that could turn out bad for the both of us."

"Be that as it may," Dante said, speaking as if he and Orlando were the only ones in the room, "you made this bed and now you must lie in it. Marrying a Panetta against his wishes was foolish, and you know it. On the other hand, I promised our father I would keep you in Ely. Now get your things; you're coming with me."

Orlando took a step forward. "I'm telling you that I won't."

"And I'm telling you that if you love this woman as you say you do, you'll come back with me and settle up with our father. If we leave in the morning, we can beat him back."

"And then what?" Orlando asked.

Chantel watched the two men in a mesmerized fog. Dante being here in her aunt's house was the last thing she had ever expected. She had been so careful and thought herself quite sly. Now she realized that this man had easily outfoxed her.

"I can have the butler send someone for the police," Chantel said in a barely audible voice.

Dante turned a hard glare on her. "You stay out of this. You've caused enough trouble already."

"Me?" Chantel felt her fear ebb and anger rise. "You accuse me? You and your father treated Orlando like a prisoner. He's a man full grown and now married with a wife! And who knows . . . perhaps even a child is on the way."

Dante's face paled at this. "Tell me that isn't possible."

"I can't," Orlando declared. "We are, after all, married."

Exhaling a heavy breath, Dante squared his shoulders. "All the more reason to come back with me. If you don't return, I fear he will hunt you down—act without hearing you out. If you come back and explain that the deed is done—that there might be a baby on the way—perhaps he will just disown you and let you go on your way. With Nonna's help we can surely convince Papa to see reason."

"You can't make him return," Isabella interjected. She clung tightly to Orlando's arm. "Don't let him do this."

"He has no choice," Dante reiterated. "He's either coming with me peacefully, or I'll hogtie him and take him back by force." He looked at his brother. "What's it to be? Shall we tear into each other and this place?" He motioned to their beautiful surroundings. "Shall we destroy this fine house just so you can prove you're a man?"

Orlando didn't speak for several minutes, and when he did, Chantel was surprised. "All right. I'll go with you to your hotel. We can talk about this further . . . in private." Isabella started to cry, and he pulled her close. "Don't worry, sweetheart. Wild horses couldn't keep me away from you."

But a bullet through the head will. Chantel looked to Dante. He met her eyes and held her gaze for a long moment. He didn't seem at all happy about any of this.

Chapter 19

Aunt Marilla arrived home to find Chantel and her sister in quite a dither. Isabella hadn't stopped crying since Dante had forced Orlando to accompany him back to the hotel. Orlando had told Isabella that he wanted to keep her safe and that she needed to remain in Duluth with her aunt while he went back to face his father. He had promised to return within a week's time, but Isabella and Chantel knew he might not keep that promise if his father had his way.

Chantel explained the events of the evening as quickly as possible. Her aunt listened sympathetically, pausing from time to time to comfort Isabella.

"I hope you don't mind, but I had your stableboy follow after Dante's hired carriage. He followed them to a hotel not far from the train station. I believe they plan to leave first thing tomorrow."

"Oh my." Aunt Marilla pulled off her gloves and set them aside on a small table. "Whatever are we to do?"

"Well, I have an idea that I've discussed with Isabella, but it will involve you helping us."

"But of course," the older woman replied. "What are aunties for, after all?" She leaned in conspiratorially. "What must I do?"

Chantel smiled in return. "Well, this will involve quite a bit on your part. Our actions will be most inappropriate for our gender and your station."

Marilla's laughter filled the air. She seemed so genuinely amused by this that Chantel was momentarily uncertain of what to say next. Marilla quickly explained.

"My dears! My station, as you call it, will survive. I'm well known for my eccentric behavior. Most of my friends simply accept my peculiarities. Some because they truly hold affection for me, while others respect me for the sake of my money. So you see, I shan't be worried about what will be said if I am found out."

Chantel loved her aunt all the more for her enthusiasm and began to outline her ideas. Marilla called for several of her servants in order to get their help with the details. With a plan in place, Isabella was able to dry her tears and find the strength to do her part.

"Isabella, I'm going to need you to pack all of your things and anything that Orlando has left behind. We'll send the groomsman to load it in the carriage."

"We'll take my larger coach," Marilla declared. "It will accommodate all of us and has plenty of room for luggage."

"And you honestly think this will work, Chantel?" Isabella asked, sounding hopeful for the first time since Dante had taken Orlando away. "I mean, Orlando did go willingly."

"He went willingly to avoid causing a scene that would have been harmful to this property. I think if he's given a chance to flee with you, then that's what he will do. After all, that was the original plan. So in answer to your question, yes. I do believe this will work. It must."

Half an hour later, after engaging Mr. Bartell and the stableboy in a variety of duties, the three women made their way to the hotel where the Calarco men were seen registering. They rode in Aunt Marilla's enclosed brougham with the shades pulled down. She assured the girls that no one would recognize her coach from any other as they had the cover of night and there were a bevy of wealthy folks who drove the same type of vehicle. The driver pulled to the side of the street nearly a block from the hotel. He reluctantly left the carriage and the women long enough to do as Chantel had instructed. After nearly fifteen minutes, he made his way back to the carriage.

"There is a back exit for freight and workers, as well as a fire escape," he told Chantel.

He explained the exact location, and Chantel made certain she understood before climbing down from the coach.

"You wait here, Aunt Marilla. Isabella and I will go to the hotel. If everything goes as planned, Issy and Orlando will join you shortly."

"Be careful," their aunt instructed as Isabella departed the brougham with the driver's help.

"We will. Please pray for us," Chantel replied.

She and Isabella hurried up the walkway to the hotel. Though her heart was racing like a steam locomotive, Chantel wasn't about to give in to her fear. She would have only one chance.

Before reaching the registration desk, Chantel looked around the lobby for a place Isabella could hide. "That area over there by the large potted plant would afford some coverage," she whispered. "Maybe you could wait there until I can get Dante to meet me. Hopefully, I'll be able to get his room number and let you know what it is before he arrives. Then, while I have him occupied, you go upstairs and get Orlando. Sneak out the back, and Aunt Marilla will take you to her friends."

"What of you?"

"Don't worry about me. I'll be fine. Can you hide here?"

"I suppose so," Isabella said, looking the area over. "I can squeeze in behind the larger chairs and duck down if I need to."

Chantel nodded. "Let's first see if we have the right hotel."

She went to the registration desk and asked the clerk if she might see Mr. Dante Calarco. "I'm . . . family . . . and need to speak to him immediately. If you could send someone to his room and ask him to come down to the lobby, I'd be most grateful." She pushed a coin across the desktop as her aunt had instructed her.

The clerk smiled and took the coin. "Mr. Dante Calarco has stepped out for a short time. If you would care to wait for him here, I don't imagine he should be long."

Chantel frowned. "And what of his brother?"

"He's here in room 204. Should I send for him instead?"

"No, I'm here with his wife. We'll go to meet him. Room 204, you said?"

The clerk nodded. "Just up the stairs and down the hall to the right."

Chantel gave him a warm smile. "Please don't say anything to Mr. Calarco when he returns. We want this to be a surprise."

The clerk grinned. "I wouldn't dream of it.

Besides, the night man will be taking over, and I won't even be here. Your secret is safe."

She hurried to where Isabella waited and motioned her to follow. "We haven't much time, but the plan has changed. Come on."

They hurried up the stairs and made their way to room 204. Chantel didn't even pause before pounding on the hotel door.

"What are you doing here?" Orlando asked as he opened the door. Isabella threw herself into his arms.

"We have a plan," Chantel declared. "I got you into this mess when I decided I needed to warn you, and now I'm going to help you fix it. In fact, with Dante gone, it makes this all the easier."

Orlando gave her a look of disbelief. "And how do you plan to do it?"

She came into the room and noted the two small beds, the nightstands, and dresser. "Aunt Marilla has the coach waiting at the end of the street. We'll go out the back way."

"But my brother already knows where your aunt lives. He'll just follow us there."

"Ah, but we accounted for that. The coach is not going to take you back to the house; instead, Aunt Marilla arranged with friends to have you put aboard a freighter that's heading out in just a matter of hours."

"But Dante will be back any minute. There isn't time for this."

Chantel considered the matter. "Of course there is. I'll go downstairs and stall Dante."

Orlando looked at her with the most hopeless expression she'd ever seen on any man's face. "It won't work. The minute he sees you, he'll be suspicious. If he sees that I'm missing, he'll call in the police and anyone else he needs to hunt me down."

Chantel wrung her hands and paced the few feet of hardwood floor between the two beds. Her gaze stopped on the rumpled covers; obviously Orlando had been stretched out atop them. An idea came to mind. It was risky, but it just might work.

"Then we won't let him see that you're missing."

"What are you talking about, Chantel? We have to get away from here," Isabella declared in a frantic tone.

"And so you shall. You and Orlando will go out the back way as we planned. I will take Orlando's place here. If I climb in bed and cover myself from head to toe and pretend to be asleep when Dante returns, hopefully he won't bother to check that it's really Orlando."

For the first time since they arrived, Orlando's expression changed. "Maybe it will give us some additional time. Especially if you were to snore a bit. Dante says I often snore."

Chantel laughed. "I can do that. I'll imitate my father." She gave a little snorting sound, and even Isabella smiled. "Just go. Go now." She pushed them toward the door.

Orlando started to gather his few things, then stopped. "If I take my things he'll know I'm gone."

"Never mind that. You can buy what you need once you get to Chicago."

"But I can't. Dante took all of my money. All of the money you gave us."

Chantel was undeterred. "Aunt Marilla has money for you. Don't worry about it, just go."

"Please, Orlando!" Isabella pled. "Please, let's go now."

With nothing more to stop them, Orlando took what little he felt he could get away with and kissed Chantel on the cheek. "Thank you. I promise to take good care of Isabella. We'll get word to you somehow."

"Just write to Aunt Marilla. She can forward any letter to our mother." Chantel pushed them from the room. "Now go. There isn't much time."

With the couple on their way, Chantel gave a quick look around the room. The little bed she would use was set up against the far wall. With any luck at all she could hide until Dante fell asleep and then sneak out of the room. She hadn't really considered how she might get back to her aunt's house after that, but she was certain the clerk could help her arrange for a carriage.

In quick order Chantel discarded her coat and bonnet and shoved them under the blanket of the bed. Leaving one small lamp lit in the opposite corner, she slipped in between the sheets fully dressed and pulled the bedding up over her head. She carefully pulled her skirts in close around her legs so that there would be no chance of them spilling out from beneath the covers, then turned on her side and faced the wall.

No sooner had Chantel settled down, feeling rather confident that nothing was amiss, than she heard someone at the door. Her heart skipped a beat and she fought to slow her breathing. Remembering what Orlando had said about snoring, Chantel tried to give a little muffled sound as the door opened.

"I see you decided to go to bed," Dante said.

Chantel said nothing as fearful realization crept over her. What if Dante planned to talk to Orlando? What if he refused to let him sleep?

"I know you're angry at me," Dante continued. Chantel could hear him moving around the room and figured he was most likely getting ready for bed. The thought of Dante stripping down for bed made her feel even more uncomfortable. What had she gotten herself into?

"It doesn't matter how mad you are," Dante said. "It's not my fault that our father can't see his way through this. You and I both know, however, if he came back to find you gone, it would go much worse for you. For me, as well, since I had charge of keeping you under control."

She heard the springs of the other bed groan. Apparently Dante had gotten into bed or at least was sitting on the side. She clenched her jaw to keep her teeth from chattering.

Lord, she prayed, *I know this is a game of deception, but even Rahab hid the Hebrew spies for the greater good. Lord, I truly believe this is the greater good. After all, Issy and Orlando are married, and no man should try to separate what you have joined. Please help me.*

A moment later when the light went out, Chantel felt as if God himself were reassuring her. In the dark it would be even easier for Chantel to maintain the charade. Dante would go to sleep, and that would be that. But that wasn't Dante's idea.

"You know, since you aren't talking, it gives me a chance to say a few things that have been on my mind. Mr. Panetta talked to me long and hard the other day about the foolishness of this feud. I'm beginning to see what he means. I told Nonna about what he said and how he's determined to make peace with our father, and she said it was the right thing to do.

"I suppose that's why she was so supportive of you marrying Isabella. But honestly, Orlando, you're just nineteen. There's no need to marry so young." He paused and sighed. "I know the deed is done, however. Hopefully she doesn't yet carry your child. That would be a terrible conflict." He fell silent for a few moments, and Chantel bit her tongue to keep from commenting about children being a blessing and not a conflict.

"I truly feel that in time, we might be able to convince Papa to let go of his anger—at least where it has to do with you and Isabella. If you both return to Ely as if nothing has happened and live apart while we work on him, then perhaps in time he will accept the marriage. Or at least stop his threats of harm."

Chantel wished Dante would stop talking and go to sleep. She was so weary from her own travels that she feared if she wasn't careful, the comfort and warmth of the bed would lure her into an unconscious state. She couldn't let that happen. Not only would Dante find out his brother was gone, but her reputation would be ruined.

Of course, if anyone finds out about this, it will be ruined anyway. She supposed she should have given her impetuous actions more thought. But now it was too late to worry about it. *Thankfully, few people know me in this part of town.*

"I don't want you to think I don't care about you, Orlando." Dante's voice sounded less angry, more brotherly. "You're all I have left of Mama. I don't think I ever told you that, but it's true.

"When Mama died giving birth to you, I wanted to hate you, but I couldn't. Mama had told me that you were a gift from God for all of us. Before you were born, she charged me to always look after you and see to your welfare. I suppose that's why it was so important I find you. I know you think I'm against you, but really I'm not. I can see that you love Isabella. I can understand that you don't care what anyone else thinks. Believe me, I understand."

Chantel suppressed a yawn. She couldn't help but feel a bit of tenderness for him as he spoke on and on of their childhood. *It would have been so hard to grow up without Mama.* Their mother was the very heart of their family. It had probably been the same for Dante's family. No wonder Mr. Calarco was such a disagreeable man. Why, Papa himself might not be the same man without Mama. They might all be difficult and displeasing without Mama's gentle spirit to guide them.

Dante woke to a bright stream of light flooding the room. He startled and jumped up from the bed, worried that he'd overslept. They had a train to catch. He checked his watch. There was still plenty of time.

"Orlando, wake up," he called as he pulled on his trousers.

When there wasn't even so much as a grunt from the bed, he shook his head. "Look, I don't care if you talk to me or not, but get up. We have to make that train, and I'd like to have some breakfast first. If you don't get up, I'm not going to feed you."

Still his brother said nothing. Dante pulled his shirt on before going to his brother's bed. "I'll turn this mattress upside down on the floor and dump you out if need be." He yanked back the covers and froze.

Beautiful black lashes fluttered open to reveal dark brown eyes—eyes that clearly did not belong to his brother.

Chapter 20

Marco Panetta sat listening as Judge Van Blarcom reiterated the details of what had happened to Jalo Gadd at the Fortune Hole. Marco had taken time off from the mine that morning in order to testify as to what had happened the night Leo had beaten the Finn and left him for dead. He'd come with the certainty that justice would prevail. Judge Van Blarcom was a good man and well liked in the community. But as the short hearing continued, Marco became less convinced of the outcome.

The situation soon felt hopeless. Marco was the only one who would step forward on behalf of the Finn. Gadd could remember very little of the night's events, thanks to his head injuries. Marco was able to tell what he'd seen happen, but he, too, had to admit to having had several drinks. He related how he and his father and brother had gone searching for the Finn and found him deposited on the railroad tracks just as Fortino had ordered. His father and brother could attest to that, as well, if needed.

Leo, always two steps ahead of the law, had brought in at least a dozen witnesses who either stated that Marco was lying or that he had been too drunk to know what had actually happened. His reputation of drinking preceded him.

"I only had three drinks!" he declared at one point, jumping to his feet.

The judge pounded his gavel and demanded order. Marco had no choice but to sit back down or face contempt of court. Leo gave him a sneering smile, then turned back to his lawyer to whisper something. Afterward his lawyer rose.

"Your honor, I move that the charges be dismissed against my client." A hush fell over the room and Marco was again tempted to shout out his protest. He held his tongue, however.

"It seems to me that the preponderance of evidence suggests a misunderstanding brought on by the heavy imbibing of liquor," the judge declared. "Additionally, it seems there is no one who can attest to actually seeing Mr. Gadd taken from the saloon and deposited on the railroad tracks, and without a witness, I see no reason to take the charges of attempted murder any further. We could perhaps further review the assault charges; however, by the testimony given, we know that both men were involved in fighting. Since Mr. Gadd has recovered from his injuries and Mr. Fortino from his, and with a lack of evidence to support anything further, I am inclined to agree. I am dismissing this case." He pounded his gavel.

Marco felt a tightening in the pit of his stomach. Leo would have it out for him now. Deciding not to risk any possible encounter with his old friend, Marco slipped through the crowd and hurried back to the mine. He knew that work would be the only way to get his mind off his anger and fears. He spotted his father and Alfredo loading ore. He pulled on his gloves and joined them.

"So did they finally put Leo in jail?" Alfredo asked in a low voice so that the other men wouldn't overhear.

"No. The case was dismissed. Fortino brought in a dozen witnesses who swore under oath that he had done nothing wrong. They even swore that Mr. Gadd had left the Fortune Hole under his own strength, and that if he had ended up on the railroad tracks as we said, it was because of his own drunkenness."

"I feared that might be the case," Papa replied. "The judge, he is a good man, but he must rule on the evidence brought forward."

Marco shook his head. "Even if the evidence has been contrived by less than honorable men?" He didn't bother to bring up the fact that his own reputation had been questioned.

"Nevertheless, you did the right thing," Papa told him. "I am proud that you stood up for Mr. Gadd."

Marco reached for a pick. "Knowing Leo, this won't be the end of it."

He worked alongside his father and brother in silence. There was no use explaining his fears of what Leo might do for retribution. His father and brother already knew of Leo's reputation for getting back at folks who crossed him.

What really worried him was how Leo might try to harm the rest of his family. Marco didn't trust that the man would limit his revenge to him alone. Leo was crafty, and Marco knew better than to discount any possibility. He would have to talk to his father about what they should do to ensure the women's safety. At least for now, Isabella and Chantel were out of harm's way in Duluth. Of course, that left Mama alone during the day.

He raised his face and saw his father's worried expression beneath the glow of his mining candle. No doubt he had been pondering the same things as Marco.

Mia colpa. This is all my fault. I brought this upon my family because of my drinking and being unwilling to heed the advice of my parents.

Marco clenched his jaw and slammed the pick into a large chunk of rock. *I have to make this right so that no one else pays the price.*

Chantel came fully awake at the sight of Dante Calarco standing over her. Her stomach clenched. She'd made a grave mistake in falling asleep the night before.

"I . . . ah . . . I can explain," she said, trying not to sound as terrified as she felt.

With catlike reflexes, Dante snatched her from the bed and placed her on her feet. "You bet you will."

Chantel squinted against the brilliance of the sunlight and tried hard to think of what to say next. Anger emanated from Dante.

"Start talking," he said, folding his arms against his chest.

"Well . . . you see . . . that is . . ." She knew she was rambling. "Could I have a drink of water?"

He frowned. "Not until you tell me where my brother is! You have no trouble speaking your mind any other time—so talk."

Chantel nervously put her hand to her hair and realized she must be quite the sight. Feeling for her hairpins, she pulled them loose and let her hair fall around her shoulders. "I'm sorry, I realize finding me must be a shock." She used her fingers to brush through the tangles of her hair before wrapping it into a knot and repinning it.

"You have to understand"—she fought to keep her words soft and even—"my sister and your brother are very much in love. Orlando knew the risk when he left home to marry her, and it seems to me that . . ." She paused to put a couple of the pins in place. "Well, it seems to me that you are more concerned about yourself than him."

Dante's expression never changed. He continued staring at her with those same intense eyes that Chantel had come to see in her dreams. She couldn't help but notice his lips and remember the night he had kissed her. Could it really have been just a few days ago?

She forced such thoughts aside. "I know your father will be angry about Orlando marrying Isabella, but if family truly means all that you say it does to him, then what you really need to consider is this: The baby that results from this marriage will be a Panetta and a Calarco."

Chantel felt herself blush before continuing. "That's the future we should all be focused on." She looked away from Dante. "Look, I know it was wrong of us to dupe you this way, but we felt we had no choice. I love my sister, and I promised to help her in any way I could."

"So you would ruin your own reputation by spending the night in a man's hotel room—a man to whom you aren't related—all for the sake of your sister's desires?"

"Isabella and Orlando deserve to be happy. I would do it all again. That and much more," Chantel said, feeling confidence overtake her fear.

"Oh, really," Dante said rather casually. He stepped toward her. "Like what?"

"I . . . uh . . . don't know what you mean," she said. What strength and determination she'd felt was fading quickly at his nearness.

"To exactly what length would you go to see your sister happy?" he asked, his gaze settling on her face.

Chantel could barely breathe. "I would do anything."

He touched her cheek. "Anything?"

She didn't know what to say. Her tongue all but stuck to the roof of her mouth, and though she swallowed hard, she couldn't clear the lump that had formed in her throat. Her mind felt foggy, but her heart warned her that she was in danger. Gathering what little remained of her wits, Chantel pushed against Dante's steel-like chest.

"Anything within reason," she finally

managed to say. "Anything necessary to see to her safety and well-being. Now she and your brother are safely away, and I don't have to worry about them anymore."

Dante refused to move. "No, but you do have to worry about me."

She shook her head. "No, I don't. I'm leaving."

He pulled her into his arms and kissed her roughly. Chantel didn't so much as move. She didn't want to encourage his behavior, and yet as his kiss became less demanding and more passionate, she felt herself giving in to her own desires.

Without warning, Dante dropped his hold on her. He walked away to where his things were and started to gather them. "If I were a less than honorable man, I wouldn't have stopped at stealing a kiss. You were a fool to put yourself into such a situation."

Chantel felt so weak in the knees that she had to sit on the side of the bed to regain her composure. How was it that he had such power over her emotions?

"You would risk everything—your innocence, your very life—for the sake of your little sister having her own way?"

"No," Chantel said, her voice weak. "I risked it . . . for love. For their love." She straightened. "Orlando loved my sister enough to lose everything dear to him. He loved her so much that he was willing to die for her. That's a powerful love, one that I might never know." She felt her throat grow tight and feared she might start to cry. "But whether anyone ever loves me that way, I rejoice that Isabella has found such happiness and loyalty. I might have been foolish to come here—to risk my reputation—but my own welfare seems unimportant when I look at what we've gained. Isabella and Orlando are now safely away." She sniffed back tears and stood. "Now, if you don't mind, I would like to go home. My aunt is probably half sick with worry, and I need to let her know that I am all right."

"We'll have a message delivered to her. I have tickets to board a train that leaves in less than forty minutes. You can use the ticket I purchased for Orlando, but we need to go now."

Chantel didn't argue with him. There was no point in it. After all, he was doing exactly what she asked. He was taking her home. They paused by the front desk, and Chantel penned a brief message to her aunt. She knew Marilla would be curious as to how everything had worked out but relieved to know that Chantel was on her way back to her parents.

"I hope you and the missus enjoyed your

stay with us," the clerk said, handing Dante a bill.

Chantel grimaced at the comment, wondering if Dante would correct the man. When he didn't, she felt a sense of relief. He was doing his best to protect her reputation, she supposed.

"I'm sure my aunt will post the few items I left at her house," Chantel said, after handing the clerk her note and the address.

Dante paid for his room, then gave the man additional coins. "Please see that this note gets delivered right away." The man nodded and assured Dante it would be sent immediately.

On the way to the train station, Dante purchased a sack of roasted peanuts and two apples. "This will have to suffice for breakfast," he said, handing her one of the apples. "We can share the peanuts on the train. We'll buy something else along the way."

She still didn't know quite what to say. The memory of his kiss kept invading her thoughts. Though he could have acted differently, he had cared too much for her reputation and well-being to hurt or take advantage of her.

"Thank you," she murmured, looking up at him.

He seemed to understand, but said nothing. It only served to confuse Chantel's heart all the more. She couldn't deny that she cared for him. And to her surprise, she found that she wanted to stand beside him and help him when he faced his father.

Dante allowed the rhythmic sway of the train to lull him to sleep. His dreams, however, were filled with thoughts of the woman who traveled at his side—who'd spent the night in his room only a few feet away from where he slept.

His mind conjured up visions of her smiling and welcoming him into her arms. He found himself longing to hold her—to kiss her again. And in the fogginess of his mind, he did just that. It felt so real that he awoke with a start at one point, only to find Chantel dozing, her head now on his shoulder.

Nonna Barbato had always told him that when his heart was confused on doing the right thing or the wrong thing, he should pray. But Dante had given up such things long ago. He couldn't help but think about Mr. Panetta and what he'd said about God speaking to him in the mine. Had God really talked to him?

Dante felt the last speck of his resolve crumble at the sight of the woman now so close to him. They looked like a comfortably married couple for all intents and purposes, he thought. And for the first time in his life, Dante found himself wishing they were.

What was he to do? How could he fight the growing feelings he held for this woman? And why should he have to? Perhaps Orlando was right. It made no sense to continue calling the Panettas their enemy. Especially the women of the family—they'd clearly done nothing to deserve such a title. His father would never agree, but Dante could at least now understand why Orlando had been willing to risk his relationship with his family . . . and even his own life.

When Chantel snuggled up against him, Dante put his arm around her and held her close. He knew that it went against social etiquette, but he didn't care. There were very few people in their train car and all of them were men. If anything, they would only envy him.

Chantel slept on. *She feels safe with me.* Dante shook his head. Somehow he was going to have to explain to his father that not only had his brother married a Panetta, but Dante planned to do likewise. The thought startled him. *I want to marry her. I want to spend the rest of my life with this woman.* He smiled. Of course, he would still have to convince Chantel, but somehow he didn't think it would be all that hard.

Dante closed his eyes. It should seem wrong

to contemplate marriage, but it didn't. It felt like the missing piece to a puzzle had finally been found. He was in love with Chantel Panetta and intended to marry her.

Dwelling again on what Mr. Panetta had told him about God speaking on peace and reconciliation, Dante thought of how hard he had fought to ignore God over the last half of his life. He supposed his father's negative outlook on God had something to do with it, but Dante also knew he was responsible for his own relationship with the Almighty.

I have to start somewhere. The train continued to rumble along, swaying him as gently as a mother would her babe. For reasons Dante couldn't explain, he felt a great sense of peace.

God, I know it's been a long time since I listened for your voice, but I want to hear you like Mr. Panetta did. I want to know that you really care—that you are there. He rethought his words and started again.

I'm sorry, Father. I came with demands when I should have come pleading and begging for forgiveness. Help me, because I have a feeling that if left to myself, I'm just going to make a bigger mess of things than I've already made. My heart is taking me in a direction I never expected, and my father is going to be livid. I'm going to need your help on this, God. But first I want to make things right between us.

He thought of what Nonna had taught him and of the Scriptures he had once committed to memory. Choosing to accept Jesus for his Savior involved repentance and a willingness to turn away from sin.

I accepted you a long time ago as my Savior, Lord, but I know I've been living wrong for some time. I want to make a change. I want to do right in your eyes, but I'm going to need more than my own strength to see it through. Please forgive my abandonment of your teachings. Forgive my arrogance and pride. And please, help my father to understand and let go of his hatred and anger.

Chapter 21

The following Sunday, Dante sat at the break-fast table. His father had returned late the night before, and now as they sat across from each other, he explained all that had transpired in his absence. It hadn't been easy, but Nonna had assured him it was the right thing to do.

"I thought I had convinced Orlando to at least come home and tell you in person what he had done, but he changed his mind." The last words were given in the form of an apology.

Dante could see that the older man was carefully considering what was to be done. Nonna served them a platter of sausages to go with their steaming cups of coffee. Italian breakfasts were traditionally laden with sweets, but the Calarco men worked much too hard to survive on such things alone. She gave Dante the slightest nod of her head. She approved of what he'd done, but she could never save him from his father's wrath.

Spearing one of the sausages, Dante continued to wait, knowing further words would serve no purpose. The silence might seem welcome to some, but Dante knew it was just the calm before the storm.

Nonna, too, held her tongue. She joined them at the table with a plate of *bomboloni*—fried pastries filled with custard. They were one of Vittorio Calarco's favorites, and Dante knew his nonna had made them to assuage her son-in-law's anger.

Dante was on his second cup of coffee when his father finally spoke. "You will go after him."

"I did, Papa. I went to Duluth and tried to bring him back. I told you that already."

His father slammed his open palms onto the table. "I said you will go after him."

"And where would I even begin to look? There were trains and ships, carriages and freighters. How am I supposed to find them now? It's been days, and they could be almost anywhere."

His father's face reddened. "I won't tolerate your disrespect. I don't care where you look or how you do it, but you will find him."

Dante wiped his mouth with a napkin and set it aside. "No, Papa. I won't."

"Vittorio . . . your boy, he is married," Nonna said, joining their English conversation. "You cannot interfere with this thing God has done."

"God?" Dante's father questioned. "It seems

God has been taking things away from me all of my life. My parents, my home in Italy, my wife, my brothers . . . and now He demands my sons? Well, He cannot have them."

"You blaspheme," Nonna declared in Italian. "You talk about God as if He should follow your directives, rather than the other way around. Vittorio, God did not rob you of your family, nor has He taken your sons. You have pushed them away and put a mountain of hate between you."

"Be quiet, woman," he snapped. "I won't hear anything more from you. From either of you."

"I'm afraid you're going to have to listen to me, Papa," Dante said, trying his best to sound respectful. "Orlando and Isabella have been married for nearly a week. She soon could be expecting a child. That baby will be flesh of your flesh, as well as that of the Panettas. It is time to put aside the past and look to the future."

His father said nothing for several moments, and Dante thought perhaps he'd actually gotten through to him. When his father stood, however, Dante realized just how wrong he had been.

"Get out. You are no longer my son. If you seek a peace with the Panettas, then go. Go live with the Panettas if that is your desire, but

I never want to see you again. I will see to it that you never work in the iron mines. I will declare you to be worthless and deceptive—as you are." He tore his shirt in a bellowing rage. "I have no sons! I have no family!"

Dante said nothing as his father stormed from the room. Nonna was beside him almost immediately. She put her hand upon Dante's shoulder. "He doesn't mean it. He's just upset. Once he takes time to think it all through, he will change his mind."

"I don't think so, Nonna. Especially when he learns that I, too, am in love with a Panetta."

A smile spread across her lips. "I knew it would be so. Chantel is a beautiful girl, and she loves God very much."

"I know. She loves her family, as well. She risked everything to help her sister and Orlando get away from me. She doesn't love lightly, to be sure."

"That is a good kind of woman to have for a wife. She will be good for you and to you."

"But at the cost of my father." He shook his head.

Dante's father came back into the room, but he said nothing to either one of them. He went to the back porch and retrieved his boots. Dante waited as his father laced up his boots, wondering what he might say to him.

To his surprise, however, his father marched

back into the kitchen and pointed his finger at Dante. "You be gone by the time I return." With that he turned and, without bothering to close the door between the kitchen and porch, opened the outside door and allowed a blast of cold March air to fill the room. He left the house without another word.

Nonna padded over to the open doors and closed them one by one. "He is being unreasonable."

"It is his home and right," Dante said, getting to his feet. "And well past time for me to go."

"Mrs. Merritt has rooms to let," Nonna told him. "She's a good woman. You should go there."

Dante nodded. "I guess I will." He looked around the room, wondering if this was how Orlando had felt. "Will you be all right?" he asked Nonna.

"I will talk to him when he comes home. He might not listen, but I will speak my mind," Nonna replied. "And if need be, I will return to Italy."

Dante knew that such an arduous trip would most likely cost his grandmother her life. "No, don't go. Find me, and I will locate a house where we can both live."

She smiled. "And Chantel?"

He nodded. "If she'll have me."

Mrs. Merritt showed Dante to a very small room with a single twin bed. It looked hardly big enough for a child, much less a man. "If you are sure you can't share with the others, this is what I can offer you. I have a bigger room with two beds, but the price is greater and frankly it seems imprudent to waste the space. Bath is at the end of the hall and you share it with everyone on this floor."

Dante liked the no-nonsense woman and smiled. "This will be fine. I'm not sure how long I'll need to stay anyway."

"Well, you pay a week in advance. Price includes all your meals. If you leave your lunch pail in the kitchen each night, I'll have it packed for you to take to the mine. You won't go hungry," she said with a nod. "Not in this house."

Dante paid her the week's rent and waited until she had gone before he explored the room more thoroughly. There was a small dresser for his clothes and a nightstand by the bed with a single lamp and nothing more. There was one small window that allowed in the light. The shade had been raised by Mrs. Merritt when they'd arrived to review the room, and now Dante went to gaze out it and contemplate his future.

He had money enough of his own to take care of his needs, but only if he were allowed to keep his job. As he had mentioned to Nonna, he could probably afford to rent them a little house, but if his father got him fired, there would be no sense remaining in the area.

Maybe I should have a talk with the mine captain, he thought. *Maybe I should just go to him now and explain the situation and see if we can't work something out whereby I can stay on. Maybe even just be a mucker.* He considered the backbreaking labor of loading ore all day. At least it was a job, and the mines always seemed to need the common laborers. The pay would be far less, he knew, but even the offered $1.50 a day would be better than most other jobs.

He should probably seek work in one of the other mines. That way he wouldn't have to encounter his father at all. He looked at the clock. Most of the mining officials would be headed to church with their families. Perhaps he should join them. *With any luck at all,* Dante thought, *I might be able to talk to someone today.*

Chantel couldn't hide her surprise at the sight of Dante Calarco at the morning services. He wore the same clothes he'd had on in Duluth, probably his only good clothes, she mused. But today he was clean-shaven—she hadn't seen him this way since returning from Italy. She had rather liked his beard and mustache, but she had to admit their loss was a vast improvement.

After services, Chantel found herself caught up in a conversation with several ladies about a fundraiser for St. Anthony's, and after that she lost track of where Dante had gone. Even so, from time to time she searched the crowd for some sign of him. She longed to be near him again, to feel his arm drawing her close.

I hope his father didn't get too angry with him. I would hate to think of them coming to blows. Papa said that he'd seen many a man handle his sons with his fist. The very thought caused her to shudder.

"Do you think you could manage that?" Mama asked her.

Chantel nodded, not having any idea what it was she was supposed to manage. She looked at her mother in confusion. "I'm sorry. What is it you need me to do?"

"We were talking about the bake sale," one of the other women said. "We need a pledge of food from each family. We will hold the sale near the mine and are sure to sell out quickly. We'll have a large tent put up for the occasion and several families are donating tables for us to use. Since many of the miners are single, this will be a great way to raise money."

"I'd be happy to do whatever I can to help," Chantel replied.

"Your mother has the list of all the baked goods we'll need from each family," the woman continued. "And we'll need you to take a shift at the tent, as well."

"We can do that," Mama replied. "If it raises money to help the church, it will be worth the time and effort."

"Yes," Chantel said in agreement. She again let her gaze travel the room in search of Dante. She soon spied Nonna Barbato.

"Excuse me," she told the ladies and hurried to where Dante's grandmother stood talking to old Mrs. Nardozzi.

The women smiled at her approach and welcomed her to join them. "We were just talking about news from the old country," Nonna Barbato told Chantel. She hugged her close. "Mrs. Nardozzi has a new great-grandson."

Chantel could see the delight on the old woman's face. "Congratulations. May he live a hundred years."

"Grazie," the woman said, nodding. "My friend tells me that your sister has married her grandson Orlando."

"Sí." Chantel looked to Nonna and smiled. "They are quite happy together."

"But his papa is not so happy," Mrs. Nardozzi interjected.

"I'm sure that's true. In fact, that's why I came to speak with you, Nonna." She hoped Mrs. Nardozzi wouldn't be offended. "I wondered if when you finished here, could I see you . . . alone?"

"You go ahead," Mrs. Nardozzi said, patting Nonna's hand. "I must find my son and daughter-in-law." She smiled again at Chantel. "You tell your mama to come see me soon."

"I will," she promised. Once Mrs. Nardozzi left them, Chantel guided Nonna to the far side of the church where no one stood. "Is everything all right? I mean, I know that Dante's father was to return late last night. Did he?"

"Sí, he came home very late. Dante went to bed early so he wouldn't have to give his father the bad news until today. Dante told him about Orlando and Isabella this morning."

Chantel nodded, knowing it wouldn't have gone well. "I prayed for him, for you—even for Mr. Calarco. I know that God can change his heart."

"He alone has the power to do that. My son-in-law, he is very angry. I should probably not tell you this, but he has put Dante from the house. He has disowned him and said he wants never to see him again."

"What! That's terrible. Dante was only trying to do what he knew his father would want. Did he explain that he came all the way to Duluth and tried to get Orlando to return with him?"

"Sí, but that doesn't matter to Vittorio. He raged and blasphemed. He needs God to change him, but he doesn't want to have anything to do with God."

Chantel's mind was still on Dante. "Where will Dante go?"

"He has taken a room at Mrs. Merritt's, and I think I will join him there. He came here today now that he's made peace with God." She smiled at Chantel. "You have been a good influence on my Dante."

Her face grew hot. "He . . . he's a good man."

"He is. He cares enough to take care of his nonna, so I must say so," she replied with a chuckle. "But I would say so anyway."

"Would you both like to come have dinner with us today?" she asked, knowing her mother wouldn't mind.

Mrs. Barbato's eyes lit up. "I think that would be wonderful. I will tell Dante, and we will come."

"Tell Dante what?" he asked, coming up from behind Chantel.

"We've been invited to eat with the Panettas. I told her we would."

Chantel turned to find Dante only inches away. Her gaze locked with his, and when he smiled she thought she might well lose all sense and throw herself into his arms.

"Your nonna told me . . . told me . . ." She looked away to regain her thoughts. "She said you moved into Mrs. Merritt's boardinghouse."

"Yes. It's a temporary solution for what will probably be a very permanent problem."

She nodded. "I'm sorry, Dante." She forced her gaze back to his. "I truly am. Would it help if Papa went to speak to your father?"

"I doubt anything will help at this point, except maybe prayer." He smiled. "It seems that between you and Nonna, I have come to realize that there is power in praying and making peace with God."

Chantel smiled in delight. "Indeed there is. If we pray in faith, we can move mountains."

"Or the heart of Calarcos," Nonna said with a grin.

Chapter 22

Dante felt a sense of relief after talking to the mining officials. He was assured he would continue to have work and in the days that followed, the same was impressed upon his father. The mining corporation had a contract with the two men, and the captain told Dante and his father that they expected the men to honor it to the letter. The mining captain further explained that the skills of both men were important, and with the mine ever expanding, they would need every man they could get.

When they were alone, the mine captain told Dante that his experience and knowledge of explosives was too valuable to lose. Dante had worked all of his adult life at his father's side, and because of that training knew more than most explosives workers. Not only that, but Dante was far more open to some of the new innovations. If his father insisted on making threats about the matter, they would find a way to employ Dante elsewhere. Ultimately, they planned to encourage Dante's father to let the matter drop. The two men had always worked well together and their abilities were needed.

Dante knew his father, however. Vittorio Calarco was a man bent on revenge—the feud was proof enough of that. Forcing Dante and his mother-in-law from the family house was equal proof.

Still, as the weeks slipped by and April was nearly finished, Dante knew two things with absolute certainty: Letting Orlando go was the right thing, and he was falling hopelessly in love with Chantel Panetta. He had seen her on several occasions at church and when he and Nonna had been invited to share meals with the Panettas. Their time alone had been very limited, however. That was a problem he intended to rectify.

"You are deep in thought," Dante's grand-mother said. "Are you thinking of that little house you went to see?"

He looked up from where he sat on the edge of his bed. "That and much more. Sorry for my silence."

She smiled. "You made it sound like a lovely little house. It sounds large enough for all of us."

All of us. He smiled at the statement. Nonna was quite impatient for him to propose mar-riage to Chantel. But instead of saying any-thing, she changed the subject.

"Will you work with your father today?"

Dante donned his jacket as they spoke. "If you can call it that. I don't know how much longer they'll have us in the same mine. The contract is up next month, so hopefully the officials will see fit to have us work apart. These past weeks have been difficult, and they know it. Papa has made it clear that he isn't happy working with me. He's threatened to quit several times, but they've always managed to smooth things over and remind him of his contract. Frankly, I don't know what they've been promising him.

"I know, too, that Papa's anger makes him unsafe. He spends too much time focused on our problems instead of keeping his mind on the job. That will get him or someone else killed. Separating us will be best for everyone."

"I wish only that he would make peace with you. He is a stubborn man, however. I have tried to speak to him, but he told me I was a traitor to side with you. So I am praying for him," Nonna said. She worked to make the two small beds before they headed downstairs for Mrs. Merritt's breakfast. It was a routine she and Dante had fallen into since Nonna had come to live with him at the boarding-house. Thankfully Mrs. Merritt still had the larger room available, suiting their temporary needs.

As they made their way downstairs, Dante took special care to help Nonna on the steps. She seemed so small and fragile since having suffered pneumonia, and Dante worried about her. Maybe it was for the best that they had come here. At least now Nonna's workload was cut considerably. She still handled their laundry, but she no longer had to worry about shopping for food and preparing it. She also wouldn't have to wear herself out with the cleanup of meals or of a large house.

Dante could only imagine how his father was faring. He'd tried to speak to him at work, but the man refused to communicate about anything. Dante was hard-pressed to even get information regarding the day's work. He would be very glad when the working arrangements were changed.

Mrs. Merritt bustled around the large dining room, making certain that everyone had a bowl of oatmeal and plenty of cream and sugar. She chatted with each of her boarders, offering bits of news she knew would be important to them. She had twelve men who rented rooms and two ladies. One, Mrs. Bramley, was the mother of one of the men, and then there was Nonna. Mrs. Merritt seemed happy to have other women in the house and showered Nonna and Mrs. Bramley with gossip from the neighborhood. Dante could only imagine how the trio spent the workday.

With the oatmeal in place, Mrs. Merritt then deposited platters heaping with hot sliced ham. The men deferred to the ladies and allowed them to take their portions first and then dug into the mounds, reducing the number of slices in quick order. Mrs. Merritt followed the ham with golden brown biscuits and two large bowls of gravy. It was a feast fit for a king.

When breakfast was over, Dante kissed Nonna good-bye and headed to the mine with the other men. No one seemed overly interested in conversation. A few of the men tucked plugs of chewing tobacco into their cheeks, knowing that smoking would be strictly forbidden in the shafts. Dante was glad he'd never taken up either habit.

Once he'd been delivered down the shaft to where they were working, Dante made his way to where he and his father had their supplies of explosives. He found his father already there, checking the inventory of dynamite.

"Morning, Papa," Dante greeted as he did every day since being put from the house. The older man didn't so much as grunt acknowledgment. Dante took it all in stride. He hoped that once the initial upheaval had settled, his father would see how ridiculous he'd been. At least that was Dante's prayer. *It will take an act of God to bring Papa around, but if God could get my attention, He can surely do the same for Papa.*

To his surprise and his father's disgust, the mine captain arrived with Mr. Panetta. "I'm glad you're both here," he told them. "I have a project that I need your thoughts on," he began. "I've asked Panetta to join us so that we can make certain to cover all the details."

Dante's father clenched his jaw and narrowed his eyes. Dante was surprised he said nothing, however.

"So this is the plan," the captain continued. "We've an area that has shown a vast wealth of ore. We're going to plan to cave it for direct loading into the trams. I want you, Calarco, and your son to make minimal charges for this. We'll position small charges six feet apart in a crossing fashion." He drew an *X* in the air. "They will be placed in the center of the area where we feel the ore is richest. We've had great results doing this in the past."

"And when are we going to do this?" Dante's father asked.

"At the end of the last shift tomorrow. If you need anything, let me know. I can always wire Duluth and get it on the next train."

"Why not just set the charge today?" Calarco asked.

"If we wait and do it Saturday night, it will give the dust a chance to clear. When we start loading and mining on Monday, the crew will be fresh. I want everyone good and rested. We have no room for error in this. That ore is greatly needed." He nodded toward Chantel's father. "Panetta still walks with a limp, and we can't afford additional accidents."

Dante's father muttered something under his breath, but Dante couldn't make it out. No doubt his father's words were just as well unheard.

"I want you to coordinate the explosion with Panetta and make certain the trams are in place. We want this as neat and orderly as possible. Saving lives and time is what we're about. We'll all benefit if we get the ore out in the fastest and safest possible manner. Any questions?"

When there were none, the captain bid everyone a good day and left to see to other matters. Dante thought his father might comment on the job, but instead he grabbed up some supplies and left without another word.

"I see he's still not speaking to you," Mr. Panetta said with a sympathetic smile.

"No. He's angry because I won't go after Orlando and bring him home." Dante shrugged, trying to make light of the sad facts. "I suppose it was time to leave . . . all birds must leave the nest sooner or later."

"True, but I just wanted to remind you that you are welcome at our house. You and Mrs. Barbato."

"Thank you, sir." Dante had to smile. He had never thought he'd be using such respect in speaking to a Panetta.

"We're family now, whether your father likes it or not. We heard from your brother, and he and Isabella are happily settled."

"I'm glad." He was happy to mean it. "I wonder if I might talk to you about something else. Not here, of course."

"Why don't you come to supper tonight and bring your nonna. The weather's warming and thawing the ice, but for now the roads shouldn't be too impassible."

"I'd like that and I'm certain Nonna would. Mrs. Merritt doesn't exactly prepare food to her liking."

"I can imagine," he said. "It's not Italian, eh?" Dante nodded and Panetta continued. "I'll expect you tonight. After supper, we can talk about your matter." He gave Dante a sly grin. "I have a feeling I already know what you want to talk about."

Dante felt a moment of embarrassment at this. He hadn't expected Chantel's father to be quite so open about Dante's relationship with his daughter. Dante hadn't even talked to Chantel, since they both seemed to find it easier to just accept that things had changed between them. He didn't want to jinx it with a discussion. At least that was how he saw it.

Chantel reread her sister's letter from Chicago and shook her head. "She's working for a sewing house. Can you imagine it? Issy was never that fond of sewing."

Mama smiled. "A woman has to do what she has to do when times are difficult. I'm glad they both found work." She folded a letter from her sister that had come with Isabella's missive. "Marilla said they sounded quite happy when they wrote to her, as well." She tucked her sister's letter back into the envelope. "You were smart to have Issy write to Marilla. That way no one can know where they are unless we tell them."

"It's a pity it has to be that way," Chantel replied, setting her sister's letter aside. "I keep asking God to intercede, but perhaps the time simply isn't right."

"God's timing is up to Him," Mama replied. "We cannot know why He says yes to one and no to another, or why the rains fall in one place but not another. Ours is not to understand, but to trust. That is where faith comes in. We must have faith."

"I know you're right." Chantel picked up her tatting. "It sounds like Issy and Orlando have made a nice little home together, but it also seems they will both be working very hard."

Isabella had explained that Orlando had found work helping to offload cargo at the docks. They had rented a small furnished apartment in a decidedly Irish neighborhood and, despite their cultural differences, had made a few friends.

"Hard work is not a bad thing," Mama countered. "It will do them good. Speaking of which, you and I must make plans for our garden. There is much to consider." She drew a piece of paper from her pocket and took the pencil that hung from her chatelaine. "I've been making a list of what we should plant."

Chantel listened halfheartedly as her mother outlined her ideas. Planting a garden was the least of Chantel's interests at the moment.

"Mama," she interrupted. "I wonder if I could talk to you about something else."

Her mother seemed confused. "Something else to plant?"

Chantel smiled and shook her head. "No. Something else altogether. Something about me."

"Of course. What is it?" her mother asked, still focused on her list.

"I'm in love."

Her mother immediately dropped the paper to her lap. "Love? You are in love?"

"Sí, Mama." Chantel drew a deep breath. "I know this may sound completely crazy, but I've fallen in love with Dante Calarco."

Her mother's expression took on a look of disbelief and then of amusement. "Goodness, Mr. Calarco will never recover from this."

"I don't know exactly how Dante feels about me, but I think he feels the same. We haven't talked about it, but we . . . well . . . on the train ride home from Duluth, it felt like everything somehow changed between us. Neither of us were interested in fighting anymore. We were . . . in fact . . . well . . . content in each other's company. Now I find he is all I can think of. I want to see him every day."

"Ah, *amore*," her mother declared, touching her hand to her breast. "The heart, it knows."

"What should I do?"

Mama smiled. "Give it time. If Dante feels as you say he does, he will not let you go. He will pursue you if it is God's will."

"But I thought he might have said something by now. It's been weeks since we returned. I know it's been difficult for him since he was forced to leave his father's house . . . but even so, he's been to supper here several times."

"Do not fret so, Chantel! Again, God's timing is not always what we think it should be. If He has made Dante for you—for your husband—He will bring it to be. Your job is to pray and stay out of God's way. If you try to force this before its time, you may lose everything."

Chantel knew her mother was right. She sighed and got to her feet. "I'd best get to the laundry. That will give me plenty of time to pray."

The prayer time did Chantel good, and before she knew it, the wash was done and hung to dry on the lines. She had paused only once to have a small lunch with Mama, and now she noted that the day was nearly at a close. With the laundry complete, she made her way into the house to help Mama prepare supper.

The women worked well together, but Isabella's absence settled over them once again. Chantel had always loved her sister's sense of humor and vivacious spirit. Isabella made their days joyful and light.

"I miss her," Chantel said aloud without thinking.

"I do, too," Mama replied, needing no explanation.

"Issy always makes it easier to work. I

suppose now I shall just have to learn to find ways to be joyful without her."

"It's the way of life. A mama cannot expect her children to remain at home forever. One day your brothers will marry, and if you wed Dante, then it will be just your papa and me."

"Will that make you sad?" Chantel had never really thought of what life would be for her mother once they all went their separate ways.

"It would make me sadder if you didn't find true love," Mama admitted. "But I will miss having my family all around me. Your papa and I, we have a special love, and I know I will never tire of his company. So I remind myself that when my children are gone, I will still have him. And then . . . one day . . . I hope to have grandchildren." She gave Chantel a broad smile. "A whole houseful to spoil and love."

Chantel liked the idea of that very much and found herself whispering a prayer that it might be so.

Chapter 23

Chantel had just finished setting the table when her father and brothers came in the front door. She was surprised by this as they usually came in through the back in order to leave their dirty work boots and coats. She started to comment, then realized why they'd chosen the front door. Dante Calarco was in their company.

Dante's eyes met hers, and Chantel couldn't help but feel a little shy in his presence. She couldn't keep the memory of his kiss from invading her mind, and she felt herself blush. Was he as tormented as she?

"I hope you don't mind," Papa told Mama, "but I invited Dante to supper."

"What about his nonna?" Mama asked.

"Nonna was teaching Mrs. Merritt how to make lasagna and told me to come without her," Dante said with a grin. "I think the boarders will be very happy about this change. Mrs. Merritt is a good woman, but she's not Italian."

Everyone chuckled at this, and Mama

motioned to the dining room. "Well, the supper is ready. You boys come and take your places."

"We aren't staying, Mama," Marco announced. "Alfredo's gal has invited us to a birthday celebration at her house."

Mama looked to Alfredo and admonished him in English. "You should have told me sooner. I could have sent her a gift." She brightened. "I know. I'll give you some preserves. I have that nice blueberry jam your sister made."

"I know she'd like that, Mama," Alfredo replied. He jabbed Marco. "We're gonna go get cleaned up and changed. I'll get the preserves before we head back out."

"Well, that just leaves the four of us," Papa declared. "A nice number for supper, don't you think?"

Chantel nodded and tried not to squirm under Dante's gaze. She could sense his eyes following her, and she longed to feel his touch once again. But she remembered what her mother had said about letting things take their course and giving God time to work.

Papa embraced Mama and walked with her into the dining room, leaving Chantel and Dante standing in the foyer.

"It's good to see you again," Chantel said softly.

"You too." He smiled, and her stomach fluttered in response.

"We had a letter from Issy and Orlando. They are doing well. I thought you might like to know."

Dante nodded. "Your father mentioned it. I'm glad they're happy. And though it was a difficult decision, I know now that their marriage was the right choice."

"I'm glad," Chantel said, folding her hands together. "I know Orlando . . . well, he loves you."

"Yes."

Dante's dark eyes bore into her own. Chantel felt as if he could read her thoughts—her heart. She wanted to move away, but her feet seemed nailed in place. She licked her lips in a nervous gesture and said the first thing that came to mind.

"Are you hungry?"

He took two steps to cross the distance between them, then pulled Chantel into his arms. "Hungry doesn't even begin to explain it." With that he kissed her with a deep intensity that left Chantel breathless. When he pulled away, he grinned in a self-assured manner and headed for the dining room.

For a moment Chantel couldn't even think clearly. He obviously had feelings for her, so why didn't he just tell her rather than kiss her? *Of course,* she touched her lips, *I rather like the way he explains himself.*

Dante sat across from Chantel at the supper table. Had her brothers been with them for the meal, it might not have seemed so intimate, but with just her parents and Dante, that wasn't the case.

"That new resort, Crossman's Park, is to open next month," Papa announced. "I read it in the paper. It sounds like it will be quite the place to enjoy the luxuries of life."

"Against the backdrop of a mining town hardly seems a fit setting," Mama said, passing Papa the bread. "Of course, I know that away from town there is great beauty, and the resort will be at the big lake. But I'm afraid when people arrive by train they may question their choice and turn back."

"Well, it isn't likely any of us will be using it," Papa replied. "I understand it will mainly be used to draw in tourists from the big cities. And don't you worry, dear. I heard talk of great plans to beautify this town—buildings to be painted, flower gardens planted. Pretty soon it will look mighty fine, I'm thinking."

The conversation soon turned to the upcoming summer and all that was planned for the town of Ely. Chantel tried to remain interested, though she wished she and Dante could talk again in private.

I wish I were better at waiting. Patience isn't exactly my best virtue, is it, Lord?

"Marshal—I mean Constable Garrison—said that he has begun to tighten control on the gaming houses and brothels," Papa added.

"And I heard it said that the city council is now holding meetings in the city hall," Dante threw in.

"It's quite the grand building, what with the fire department and courtroom there, as well. I do believe we are becoming a real town. Who knows, in time we might very well become a large city like Duluth," Papa said before cutting into his meat.

The mention of Duluth caused Chantel to think back to her trip, and she felt her cheeks grow hot at the memory of awaking to Dante standing over her. Her love of Isabella had given her courage, but now the entire matter seemed so foolish. She looked across the table to find Dante grinning at her as if he could read her mind.

"Dante, would you like more bread?" Mama asked.

Chantel was grateful his attention was placed elsewhere and lowered her gaze. *If I don't control my emotions, Mama and Papa are going to demand to know what's going on, and I can't tell them I spent the night with Dante.* She swallowed hard and bit her lower lip.

"The Pioneer Mine is expanding, and there has been some discussion about running three shifts at the Chandler," Dante declared.

Mama looked at him in disbelief. "Three shifts? Goodness, there will never be any quiet."

"That will cut the length of time we have to spend down in the mine," Dante added. "But it may also cut back our salaries."

"I heard the captain say that wages might well be increased to coordinate with the shortening of hours. I suppose all we can do is wait and see," Papa replied.

Chantel really didn't care about Ely or the mine at this point. Would this meal never end? *But once it's over, then what? Will Dante want to leave for the boardinghouse, or will he stay and talk with me? Maybe I should just ask him to stay for a time.*

After nearly twenty minutes of conversation about new mines and the price of iron ore, supper was finally concluded. Chantel was just about to ask if she could delay in helping with cleanup in order to spend time talking to Dante, when Papa cleared his throat.

"Dante and I will speak in private while you ladies clear the table."

Chantel hid her disappointment. "Would you like for me to bring you both coffee?"

"No," Papa replied with a shake of his head.

"In fact, I would rather you both let us alone. I will come for you when we are finished with our business." With that, he followed Dante from the room.

Puzzled by her father's comment, Chantel turned to her mother. "What kind of business does Papa have with Dante?"

Mama shrugged. "I suppose it has to do with the mine. He didn't say anything to me."

Chantel helped her mother wash and dry the supper dishes, but all the while she kept wondering what her father and Dante were up to. They seemed so secretive, and she was almost certain her father's eyes held the same devilish twinkle he got when he was preparing a surprise.

"What are you doing, Chantel? Where is your mind?" Mama asked.

Chantel looked down to find herself putting away the baking dish . . . in the oven. She straightened and shook her head. "I'm afraid my mind was elsewhere." She went to the cupboard and put the dish away properly.

It was only another ten minutes or so before Papa appeared with a smile. "I'll finish helping Mama. You might want to go to the sitting room and speak with Dante. He has something to say."

"To me?" she asked in surprise.

Her father chuckled. "Yes. We finished our

discussion and now I believe he prefers to speak with you."

Chantel untied her apron and hung it by the door. She trembled slightly as she made her way to the front room. Dante had leaned back against the sofa and looked for all the world as though this were his home. In all his visits before, Chantel had remembered him as quite tense—almost as if he might jump up at any given moment to run from the house. But not this time.

"Papa said you wanted to speak with me?"

Dante got to his feet and nodded. "I think it's about time, don't you?"

He could see that Chantel was hesitant. She looked past him at the window and bit her lower lip for a moment, an action he'd seen her do when her nerves got the best of her. "Why don't you come sit here," he said, directing her to a chair. "I want to make certain you are comfortable and can hear me out."

Chantel did as he suggested and perched on the edge of the chair. He couldn't help but smile as he drew up another chair to sit directly in front of her. "I had a long talk with your father," he said, meeting her questioning gaze.

"About the mine?"

He laughed. "No. About you."

"Me?" Her eyes widened. "What . . . what about me? You didn't tell him about . . . that . . . night. Did you?"

"You sound as nervous as a girl about to receive her first kiss, although I know quite well that isn't the case." He reached out and took hold of her hand. Her fingers were cold, and he did his best to warm them in his grip.

"Chantel, I think we both realize how we feel about each other." He shook his head. "I certainly never thought to follow in my brother's footsteps and fall for a Panetta woman, but it would seem I have." He smiled. "And quite happily, I might add—lest it sound like something I dread."

"Your father will certainly be unhappy to hear it," she said matter-of-factly.

"He's not speaking to me anyway," Dante replied. "So I'm not inclined to consider his feelings in the matter. Even so, I'm sure you're right. It will come as a shock to realize he has not one, but two sons, married to Panettas."

"Married?" She barely squeaked out the word.

Dante's eyes narrowed. "If you'll have me. After all, you have already spent the night with me."

She flushed a pretty red, making him smile all the more. He liked that she was embarrassed at the reminder. It spoke of her innocence and sensibility.

"If you're doing this because of that night . . . out of a sense of duty . . ." Chantel's words faded, and she seemed to struggle to find the right words.

Dante shook his head. "This doesn't have anything to do with a sense of duty. It has to do with . . . well, having lost my heart to you. I know neither of us set out to fall in love, but I have to believe you feel the same way about me."

She looked up and met his gaze. "I do feel the same way," she admitted.

"Good. So you'll marry me?"

Chantel nodded. "I will." Her expression filled with understanding. "So that's what you wanted to talk to my papa about?"

"Yes. I asked him for permission to marry you. I had thought only to ask for permission to court you, but I realized my intentions were far more serious than that. I want to spend my future with you by my side."

She smiled, and it warmed his heart. "There's no other place I want to be."

Dante got to his feet and pulled her up, as well. A wave of tenderness washed over him, and he put his finger under Chantel's chin and tipped her face upward. "I never intended to fall in love with a Panetta."

"I never figured to love a Calarco," she replied.

"I suppose my brother's bad influence has brought this about."

Chantel nodded. "I blame my sister."

"Nevertheless, I suppose we must make the best of it."

Her gaze never left him. "I suppose we must."

Gently Dante touched his lips to hers. Chantel in turn wrapped her arms around his neck and pulled him close. Dante's arms encircled her waist as the kiss deepened.

"I take it she said yes," Mr. Panetta said from the doorway.

Dante jumped back as if he'd been caught stealing eggs. "Yes, sir. Yes, she did."

The older man chuckled. "I'm glad. I think you two will be very happy together."

Dante left the Panetta house nearly an hour later. His spirits were high as he relived his time spent with Chantel. He had never expected to propose to her, but then, he'd never anticipated falling so deeply in love with any woman, much less her.

He couldn't help but grin. He was in love, and he would soon marry. But there was a great deal to accomplish in the meantime. He would need to secure a house and find furnishings. He knew Nonna would help. She had a good many friends who would probably be able to assist, as well.

The dark of evening surrounded him as he walked home, feeling like he had the world by the tail. But the thought of telling his father came to mind, and he shuddered. His father would likely punch him in the face when Dante shared the news. If he was even willing to hear Dante out.

Dante was nearly to Tenth Avenue when three men darted out from the alleyway to his left and came at him in a full run. He thought for a moment they meant to attack him, but when they flew on past, Dante could only turn and watch them flee. His heart raced, and Dante couldn't help but put his hand to his chest. He couldn't imagine what the trio had been up to, but so long as they weren't after him, Dante supposed he could relax.

He drew a deep breath and started on his way again. As he drew near the alley, however, he heard something. Pausing, he listened. Was that moaning? He glanced back over his shoulder, wondering if the three men had been the cause.

"Who's there?" he called out, stepping toward the darkened alley.

The moaning sounded once more, followed by silence. Dante stepped into the darkened area. "Is someone here?"

He could make out something on the ground directly in front of him. It looked like a pile of trash in the darkness, but as Dante knelt down, he made out the form of a man. Dante shook the man gently.

"Hey, buddy, you okay?"

He figured the man was probably some drunk who'd managed to get himself robbed. Dante reached up to pat the man's face and felt something sticky and wet. He held his hand up but couldn't really see anything in the dark. Nevertheless, Dante was pretty sure his hand was covered in blood.

There was nothing to do but get the man to the doctor. Dante hoisted the man up. He was quite heavy—at least Dante's own size. The man didn't so much as issue a grunt or groan, however, when Dante settled him on his shoulder.

Making his way back in the direction he'd come, Dante hurried to find help but remained watchful, lest the culprits return. When he reached Dr. Shipman's, he gave the door a pounding and waited.

The light came on and Dr. Shipman himself appeared. "What seems to be the problem?"

"I found this guy in the alley at Tenth Avenue. Three men were running away from the scene. I figure they beat him."

"Bring him right back to my examination room," the doctor instructed.

Dante did as he was told, grateful when the doctor helped ease the burden of the man. Together they laid him onto the examination table and stepped back. Dante gasped at the sight. The man had been pulverized, but Dante could still make out the features enough to know him.

"Marco Panetta," he whispered.

Dr. Shipman was already examining the bloodied body. "You'd better go for the family. He's in a bad way." He looked at Dante and shook his head. "I don't think he's going to make it."

Chapter 24

Chantel's mouth dropped open at the sight of Dante on the other side of her door. "Did you forget something?" she asked, then frowned as he came into the light. He had blood all over his shoulder and back.

"What happened? Are you hurt?" She pulled him into the house to further examine his wounds.

"I'm not hurt, but Marco was. He's at the doctor's and it . . . well . . . you need to come with me right away."

Chantel stepped back, shaking her head. She looked at Dante, hearing his words but not quite understanding the full meaning. "How? Where?" she finally was able to murmur.

"In the alley over by Tenth Avenue. Where are your folks? Dr. Shipman said to hurry."

"I'll get them," Chantel said. She moved through the house thinking this must be a nightmare. Marco and Alfredo had gone to a birthday party some hours earlier. How could it be that Marco was now lying bloodied at the doctor's office? Surely she would awaken soon.

"Mama? Papa?" Chantel called and knocked hard on their bedroom door.

Papa appeared in his nightshirt. "What is it? Is something wrong?"

Chantel nodded. "It's . . . Marco. Dante just came to say he's been hurt. He's at Dr. Shipman's—we must hurry."

Mama came to the door. "Marco is hurt?"

"Yes. Dante came to tell us. He said we need to hurry. Marco is hurt badly."

Papa nodded, and Mama began to weep. "We'll be there in a moment. First we must dress."

Chantel returned to where Dante stood by the front door. "Who would have done such a thing?"

"I saw three men flee, but I wouldn't be able to identify them."

"What about Alfredo?"

"He wasn't there." Dante shook his head. "At least not that I saw. I suppose I should return to the alley and check it more thoroughly. I'll do that after I see your family safely to Dr. Shipman's."

"We'll be fine," Chantel said, stepping forward to take hold of his arm. "Go now. It's only a short walk. Papa will see us there. You go and see if you can find Alfredo and bring him to the doctor's, as well."

"All right." Dante gave her a quick kiss,

then hurried from the house. Chantel took up her shawl and waited for her parents. The night air was heavy with dampness and the chill went through to her bones. She started to pull out her coat, but changed her mind when Papa and Mama appeared.

"Where's Dante?" Mama asked. Her eyes were red and puffy, but she'd managed to stop weeping.

"He's gone to find Alfredo," Chantel replied. *Please, God, let Dante find him quickly.* She draped her mother's woolen shawl around her shoulders while Papa pulled on his coat. They made their way into the darkened night and hurried up the street, grateful for the glow of lamplight. When they reached the doctor's office, Chantel stepped aside to allow her parents to go in before her. She wasn't sure what she would do at the sight of her brother's injured body, and she didn't want to be in the way should she faint.

The minute they stepped into the house, however, Dr. Shipman stood, apparently waiting for them. His expression was grave. Chantel reached for the wall to support herself.

"I'm sorry, Mr. and Mrs. Panetta. I did everything I could, but he was too badly wounded."

"What are you saying?" Mama questioned, shaking her head. "Let me see my boy." She started to move past the doctor, but he took hold of her instead.

"Mrs. Panetta, he was severely beaten. The culprits caved in the left side of his head, and it's quite gruesome."

Mama looked at him a moment, then turned to Papa. "Take me to him, please."

Papa nodded. "We will see him," he told the doctor.

I can't do this.

Chantel couldn't bear the thought of seeing her brother in the condition the doctor had just described. Her body refused to move.

I'm a coward. What if Mama needs me?

No one seemed to notice her. Instead, the doctor ushered her parents into the examination room while Chantel remained fixed in place. She leaned up against the wall, unable to comprehend the truth that her brother was dead.

I was just talking to him this morning. How can he be gone? Chantel tried to recall the last thing she'd said to him. *Why can't I remember?*

The front door opened, and Alfredo and Dante entered the room. Chantel met Dante's quizzical expression and shook her head. Tears came to her eyes as he drew near.

"He's dead," she was barely able to say before collapsing into his arms.

"Marco's dead?" Alfredo asked in disbelief.

"No. He was just with me at the party. He left to head home without me. No! He can't be dead!" He left them to go in search of answers.

Chantel sobbed against Dante's chest. "My mother wanted to see him, but . . . but . . . I couldn't. The doctor said . . . he told us . . ." She broke down and couldn't speak.

Dante stroked her hair and held her close. "Shh, you don't have to see him. I'm glad you didn't go."

"Are you sure you didn't recognize any of the men?" someone asked.

Chantel lifted her head. It was only then that she realized the constable had come with Dante and Alfredo. Dante pulled back to reply. "I can only say for certain that there were three of them."

The constable nodded. "It's going to be hard to find the responsible parties."

Alfredo returned from the back room. His face had taken on an ashen hue. "Leo Fortino was behind this," he declared. "I know he was."

The constable turned from Dante. "How do you know? Did you witness this?"

"No, but Leo's had it in for Marco ever since Marco testified against him. He's the only one who'd want to see Marco dead." Alfredo looked at Dante and Chantel. "You know full well he's behind it."

"That's probably a reasonable deduction," the constable declared, "but without proof, we'll be hard-pressed to make charges stick. When morning comes, I'll head over to that alleyway and see if they left any clues behind, but otherwise I'm not sure there's much I can do."

"And so Fortino gets away with yet another death?" Alfredo asked. "Is that it? Is that your idea of justice?" He pushed past the lawman. "I'll take care of this myself, then."

The constable reached out and took hold of Alfredo. "You don't want to do that, boy. Your mother has enough to deal with in losing one son."

"She's right," Chantel interjected. She left Dante's side to go to her brother. "Mama is devastated, and you need to be strong for her and Papa. We both need to be strong." But even as she said the words, Chantel didn't know where she'd find the strength.

God, please give me courage. Help me to be useful to Mama and Papa. And please, help Alfredo. She wanted to say something on Marco's behalf, but she had no idea what to pray. God had surely known what was to have taken place on this night. God must have allowed for this evil thing, even if He did not cause it. She shook her head and felt the tears come once more. *Help us, Lord. Help us to endure this tragedy.*

Mama and Papa emerged from the examination room. One look at Mama's face, and Chantel felt a helplessness she'd never experienced before. What could she possibly do to help at a time like this? She had no words to say that could ease her mother's loss.

"I'll arrange for the undertaker," Dr. Shipman told them. "You folks go on home now and try to get some rest." He looked to Chantel's father. "Give her two teaspoons of that medicine when you get home."

"I will," Papa assured the doctor and patted his pocket. "I will."

The constable seemed to consider the matter, then turned to the doctor. "I'd like to see the body."

Dr. Shipman nodded. "Come on back. I'll explain the cause of death."

Papa moved Mama toward the door. "Let's go home," he said in a barely audible voice. Alfredo joined them, leaving Dante and Chantel to follow. There was nothing to be said. Nothing that would allow them to awaken from this nightmare.

Chantel clasped Dante's hand and thought she might well drown in the rush of emotions that threatened to overtake her, had it not been for his support. What a joyous and tragic day. Dante had proposed, but Marco had been killed. It seemed impossible to comprehend.

Mama stumbled and her legs gave way. Alfredo and Papa kept her from falling to the ground, however. Papa, despite his injured hip, lifted Mama into his arms and carried her the rest of the way home.

At the house, Chantel helped ready her mother for bed while the men spoke in the other room. Mama sat with a blanket wrapped around her shoulders. She looked almost childlike. She was such a small woman—tiny but fierce, Papa would always say. Chantel couldn't help but wonder how she had ever given birth to four children, much less raised them to adulthood.

Chantel gently helped her mother into a warm flannel nightgown and then into bed. Mama gripped her hand tightly as Chantel finished drawing the covers up.

"I keep thinking I will awaken in the morning and this will be nothing more than a bad dream," she said, her voice hoarse. She met Chantel's eyes and shook her head. "He cannot be dead. He was a good boy—a good man. He stopped drinking. He told me that he was praying again."

Chantel simply nodded, knowing if she said much of anything, she'd burst into tears. She wanted to be strong for her mother. The door opened, and Papa entered without a word. He couldn't have timed it better.

"I have her medicine," Papa said in a far-off manner. "I just remembered it."

"I'll get you a spoon," she offered.

"I already have one." He held it up like some sort of award. He walked toward the bed in a stupor. "I have your medicine, Maria. I have your medicine."

Chantel hurried from the room, unable to witness her father in such a broken state. She found Dante waiting alone in the front room. When she saw him, Chantel could only collapse beside him on the sofa and find comfort in his arms. The entire world had fallen apart, and nothing made sense. Nothing at all.

Back at the boardinghouse, Dante told Nonna about the trouble. She listened silently, then ordered him to get out of his bloodied clothes. She left the room and was gone for quite a while before returning.

"I have a hot bath waiting for you. Go now, and I'll take care of these clothes." She gathered up his discarded garments. "Tomorrow I will go to help the Panettas."

Dante stood in his socks and trousers. The chilled air against his bare skin seemed only to remind him of Marco's cold, lifeless body. He made his way to the shared bathroom, grateful for his nonna's kindness and care. Inside, he stripped off his remaining clothes and climbed into the tub.

The hot water felt comforting, but the shock of the evening was finally settling over him. Dante felt his body tremble. He couldn't stop shaking for a good long time, and finally he sank down beneath the water to cover his entire head and body.

He stayed that way until his lungs hurt from holding his breath, then he pushed himself back up to exhale and gulp in air. The action seemed to settle his nerves just a bit. Closing his eyes, Dante leaned back against the tub and prayed for strength. What he'd seen that night had left him longing for a sense of well-being and family. He found himself longing for his father . . . to tell him about the matter and hear his thoughts on what had happened. Of course, that wasn't going to happen. His father wanted nothing to do with him, and even if he somehow came to terms with the fact that Orlando had married Isabella Panetta, Dante knew his father would never accept Dante betraying him by marrying Chantel. It would all be just too much of a slap in the face as far as his father would be concerned.

Lathering his body with the strong lye soap provided by Mrs. Merritt, Dante tried not to think about the night or the broken body of Marco Panetta. He did his best to forget his father's anger and Alfredo's longing for revenge. He thought instead of Chantel's soft hands in his. Her gentle touch and the way she looked to him for strength.

Dante prayed that he might be worthy of her newfound trust in him. He prayed, too, that he might help her family to learn the truth of what had happened to Marco. There were far too many unanswered questions to allow any of them a chance for rest.

"Help us, Father," he prayed aloud. "Help us to find the truth."

The next morning Chantel awoke to a silent house. The usual aroma of coffee and pastries was absent. Her mother had no doubt remained in bed, thanks to the medicine provided by the doctor.

Chantel got up and dressed, then made her way to the kitchen. She made a fire in the stove and watched it for a few moments to make sure it grew stronger. Poking at the pieces of wood, she watched the dancing flames.

By the time her father and Alfredo stumbled into the kitchen, she had a plate of fried bacon waiting, along with a pot of strong coffee. She poured them each a cup, but said nothing.

There didn't seem to be anything they could say. It was still impossible to believe that Marco was really gone.

Chantel pulled a pan of fruit pastries from the oven and set them to cool on the windowsill. She smiled. Marco and Alfredo used to sneak around the outside of the window to snag a pastry or two on their way to the mine. She would always chide them for their actions, then laugh at the game. *Will we ever laugh again?*

Papa and Alfredo finished eating while Chantel packed their lunch boxes with bread, cheese, and thick slabs of ham. This was their usual fare as it was easy to take to the mine. Chantel added a few of the extra pastries, hoping they might find comfort in the treat. How strange it seemed that they should head off to work as if nothing had happened, but Chantel knew they had no choice. The mine captain would expect them.

"You will take good care of your mama?" Papa asked her as he made his way to where Chantel stood in the kitchen.

"I will, Papa."

He handed her the bottle of medicine. "The doctor says if she needs this, she can have two teaspoons."

Chantel took the bottle and read the word *Laudanum* on the label. She looked back to her father and nodded. "I'll see to it."

Her father drew in a long breath, then let it go in one heavy sigh. "I think it will be the hardest day of my life."

Chantel hugged him tight. "I know, Papa. I was thinking the same thing."

He pulled away. "You will get word to your sister, won't you?"

She felt bad that she'd been so focused on her own grief that she hadn't even thought of Isabella. "I will, Papa. I'll get word to her immediately."

He looked at her for a good long moment. "Thank you, Chantel." There were tears in his eyes—something Chantel had never seen before this moment. "This is just so hard."

"I know, Papa. I know."

Alfredo looked into the room. "We'd better go, or we'll be late."

Chantel went to retrieve their lunch pails. "I've packed your lunch. It's ready to go." The two men took the pails without another word and walked from the house, shoulders bent as if the load were far too heavy to bear.

No one came to the window to steal a pastry.

Chapter 25

Dante saw his father, and for a moment he just watched him. *How would you feel if it had been me killed, instead of Marco Panetta? Would you regret disowning me? Would you even care?*

"Papa?" They were alone, and Dante hoped his father might talk to him about what had happened. Everyone in the mine knew by now. In fact, the captain had sent the Panetta men home, telling them they didn't need to be concerned with work that day or the next.

Dante's father refused to even look him in the eye. He felt his anger rising, and he quickly crossed the distance between them and took hold of his father's shoulders.

"I'm talking to you, Papa. The least you can do is acknowledge me."

The older man's eyes narrowed, and he pulled away from Dante's grasp and threw a punch. Dante ducked to the side. His father's fist made a whooshing sound as it narrowly missed his ear.

He'd rather hit me than speak to me. The truth of it only served to make Dante angrier.

"I found him, you know? Marco Panetta?

I found him bloodied and dying after three men beat him." His father said nothing, but neither did he look away. "His blood was all over me by the time I carried him to the doctor. It could have just as easily been my blood or Orlando's. Is that what you want?"

His father refused to reply, and Dante could only shake his head. "You shame our family name." The older man's eyes widened, but still he said nothing.

"Someday you'll regret not making peace with me . . . with Orlando. Someday you'll realize that you're all alone, and the sorrow will tear you apart." Dante started to walk away, then paused to look back. "I hope you know that I'll always love you, but I won't live a lie. Orlando was right to marry the woman he loved. I plan to do the same thing."

He walked away, unable to tell his father that the woman he loved was Chantel Panetta. *Let him think on what I've said, and then he can ask me what I meant.*

Reaching the work site, Dante scanned the area. The explosion that had been set late Saturday left loose ore scattered about, now ready to be loaded onto trams. Dante knew some minor charges would need to be set here and there as the debris was cleared away. It was his job to check the drift and see just where those charges should be placed to further the caving of ore. But his mind wasn't on work at all.

Marco Panetta wasn't even as old as I am, and now he's dead. Dante remembered the devastating wound and all that blood. *Jesus shed His blood for my sins.* Prayer wasn't so foreign to Dante these days, but he still felt awkward in his relationship with the almighty God of the universe.

I've long ignored you. Forgive me. Dante checked one of the charge sites and made a mental note to have the muckers clear some of the rock away so that he could better assess the situation.

God, I need you to help me in this . . . this . . . division between me and Papa. There has to be a way to make this right.

Words that Father Buh had spoken the week before went through Dante's mind. *"The Bible tells us that if a man will not forgive, neither will he be forgiven. We make for ourselves the choice of how God will deal with us."*

Dante moved across an unstable bit of ground near the center of the caving. Without warning, the rock and ore shifted, and Dante found himself sucked into the debris. Like water pouring out of a funnel, the debris swirled around him and pulled him deeper. Dante called out for help, but the nearest miner was some twenty feet away.

I'm going to die. I'm going to be buried alive.
The rock continued pulling him down—ripping at his flesh—crushing the life out of him.
God, save me!

Chantel was glad the mine captain had sent Papa and Alfredo home. She knew there was little they could do but sit and contemplate all that had happened, but it comforted her to have them at home.

"I sent a wire to Isabella and Orlando. I let them know about Marco, but told them not to try to come back for the funeral, as it would no doubt occur before they could reach us."

Papa nodded. "I think that's best."

She kissed his wrinkled forehead. "More coffee?"

He held up his cup without answering. Chantel poured the coffee for him, then looked at Alfredo. "More?"

Alfredo shook his head. "No. I think I'll go to where it happened and look for clues. I know that Leo was behind it, even if he didn't do the deed himself." He stood and looked at Chantel and Papa. "I'll find a way to even the score."

"You could have ten more deaths, and it wouldn't even out our loss," Papa said. He contemplated his cup of coffee. "Marco is gone. I'll not lose you, as well."

Alfredo started to speak, but his gaze met Chantel's and he stopped. She gave him the slightest smile and nod. It would be pointless to carry on this conversation—especially now. There was simply too much pain. Too much anger. Alfredo sank back into the chair.

"I'll go check on Mama." Chantel returned the coffeepot to the stove, then went to peek in on her mother.

Mama had awakened shortly after Papa and Alfredo had left for the mine. But she had refused to talk, and only called for Chantel to ask for more medicine. It was heartbreaking to see her mother's grief.

I've never lost a child, so I cannot know how great that pain must be. But he was my brother, and that void can never be filled. Chantel saw that her mother was sound asleep. Perhaps it was for the best.

Chantel had just closed the bedroom door when a loud whistle blast filled the air. It wasn't yet time for lunch or the end of the shift. The blast continued, signaling trouble. She hurried into the kitchen, relieved once more to see her father and brother safe and sound.

The whistle continued, and Papa and Alfredo

got to their feet. "We'd better go see what's happened," Papa declared.

"They may well need our help," Alfredo said, pulling on his boots at the back door.

Chantel didn't want them to go but knew this was how it worked in their community. The miners would help each other in these life-and-death matters. It was a brotherhood not easily ignored. Unfortunately, those who went to help were often killed in the effort.

"Please be careful," she said. "I love you both so much." She tried not to sound as frightened as she felt.

"We will be fine," Papa said, seeming to understand her feelings. "I'll try to get word back to you as soon as we know something. But don't fret so. I'm sure nothing has happened to Dante."

Her hand went to her mouth. Dante! She hadn't even considered that he might be in the middle of this. Her stomach churned. What if Dante had been hurt? She wanted to go with her father and brother, but knew that someone had to remain at the house for Mama.

The minutes seemed to drag by. No one came to the house to bring news—not even the neighbor women. Maybe the accident hadn't been that bad. Chantel could only pray that whatever had taken place had resulted in no injuries to the men. Not long after her father and brother's departure, Nonna Barbato arrived at the house to offer her assistance. Chantel had never been so happy to see anyone in her life.

"Do you know what's happened at the mine?" Chantel asked, ushering the old woman into the kitchen.

"No. We heard the whistle at the boardinghouse, but no one had news. Do you know anything?"

Chantel shook her head. "Papa and Alfredo went to see. Marco . . . he's . . ."

"I heard about Marco," Nonna said, patting Chantel's hand. "I know your mama will need consolation, and that is why I have come. I want to help. I know what it is to lose a son."

Chantel nodded. "He was badly beaten, Nonna. Dante said he was barely recognizable."

"I know. He told me the same." The old woman pulled off her shawl and head scarf and placed them over the back of a chair. "How is your mama doing?"

"She's been sleeping. The doctor gave her medicine to help her rest. That's all she wants to do."

Nonna considered this for a moment. "That won't be healthy for her to do for long. She will need to face what has happened. We will pray for her, sí?"

"Sí, Nonna. And for Dante and his father, and all the other men working at the mine."

"I have been praying for the men," Nonna admitted. "I am always concerned for Vittorio and the boys. I'm glad my Orlando is gone from there. I wish they could all leave the mines and work elsewhere."

Chantel twisted her hands together. "I can't stand not knowing. Would you . . . could you wait here with Mama while I go to the mine?"

Nonna smiled and it lit up her face. "Of course. Your heart is so full of love for my Dante, you must know what has happened."

"Did he tell you that he proposed to me?" Chantel asked.

"He did. I was so glad to hear the news. You two are perfect for each other. You go now and see what you can learn. Then you come back and let me know."

Chantel quickly agreed and made her way from the house. A sense of urgency caused her to break into a most unladylike run as she hurried through the town streets to the west side and the mines.

She rounded the depot, not at all concerned with the large number of men who had gathered on the roadway to the mine. She had to find her father and brother and learn what had happened. She had to see Dante and know that he was unharmed.

No one seemed to even be aware of her presence, and for that Chantel was grateful. She searched the faces for someone she recognized. There were a few of the men her father and brothers had worked with, but she couldn't find Papa or Alfredo. Where could they be?

Chantel slowed her pace as she approached the shaft tower. What could she do? Who could she speak with? She gave a frantic search once more and spied her father. He had his back to her, but Chantel felt a great sense of relief in recognizing those stooped shoulders. She made her way to his side.

"Papa?" She looked at him for reassurance. "Papa?"

He met her eyes with a look of utter distress, and she knew in that instant that Dante was in trouble.

Chapter 26

"He's stuck in a sinkhole," Papa explained. "I'm going to help get him out."

Chantel looked at her father in disbelief. "What happened? Is he . . . was he . . ." The words wouldn't come. Her emotions ran wild. *He can't be dead. He just can't be dead.*

"We don't know how bad it is. I've spoken with his father, and he told me that Dante is unconscious and barely visible above the debris. Dante's father has an idea and I'm going to be the one to try it." He took hold of Chantel's shoulders and smiled. "I don't want you to worry. Pray instead."

Just then Dante's father appeared. He had a long coil of rope over one shoulder and a canvas bag in his hand. He looked to Papa and nodded. Papa patted Chantel's arm. "Don't worry your mama with this. Let's just wait and see . . . what happens."

"What are you going to do?"

Her father shook his head. "There's no time to explain. Just pray."

Chantel watched him climb into the shaft elevator and disappear. *"Just pray,"* he had said. Why did that seem so insignificant? *I know prayer works. I know it as well as I know my own name.*

God, I'm not trying to sound doubtful, but I feel so helpless. Please save Dante and keep my father from harm. Please keep all the men safe as they work to help free Dante. She bit her lip and forced back tears.

"I thought maybe you could use a shoulder to lean on."

She turned to find Alfredo. Falling against him, Chantel hugged him tight. "What are they going to do? How bad is it . . . really?" She pulled back and looked at her brother. "Tell me the truth."

"It's bad. Dante stepped into an unstable area of debris—a sinkhole. It collapsed beneath him, and rock tumbled down on him and knocked him out. When the shifting stopped, it set in almost like concrete. It's going to be hard to get him out of there without . . ."

"Without what?" The turmoil on Alfredo's face made it clear that he didn't want to continue. *He doesn't think I can handle the truth. He knows I will only worry more.* Chantel reached out to take hold of his arm. "I need to know."

Alfredo nodded. "They'll have to set a small charge so that hopefully the debris will continue to drain down into the tram cars and open stope. Papa is going to go into the sinkhole to secure a rope around Dante so that when the charge is blown and the debris begins to loosen again, Papa can pull Dante free."

"Why can't they just dig him out? I mean, couldn't they secure themselves with ropes and just pull the debris from the sinkhole?" Chantel questioned.

"Like I said, the rock and ore is stuck around Dante and holding him fast. It's like the kind of hold quicksand might have. It's pulling downward and packing tighter and tighter. Gravity, in this case, is working against us."

"But if they set another explosion, isn't there a chance it will pull them both in deeper?"

Alfredo's expression was quite grave. "Not only that, but if the charge isn't set in just the right location and with the exact amount needed, it could prove fatal to them and blow debris upward and into their bodies."

Chantel could understand why her father had been unwilling to discuss the matter with her. "But why Papa? Why not a younger man?"

"Can't you guess?" He looked at her and shook his head. "He told Mr. Calarco that he was willing to risk his life for Dante to prove to him that the feud needed to end."

"Blood for blood," she murmured. Only

this time instead of a mule, it was her beloved father's blood they were risking.

"Besides that, with the risk so great," Alfredo continued, "no one else was overly eager to volunteer."

Chantel nodded and looked to her brother for affirmation. "This will work—won't it?"

He looked away. "I don't know. It's unlike anything we've ever tried before. I just don't know."

Chantel looked at the shaft tower and then back to her brother. "How long will this take?"

"They'll have to move quickly, but they will also have to be very precise. I really don't know."

"I need to run home and tell Nonna Barbato. She came to help with Mama, but she needs to know that Dante's life is in the balance." She bit her lip momentarily and added, "Papa's too. I must tell her what's happened, and then I'll return."

"Why don't you just stay at the house? I'll come tell you when . . . I know something."

She shook her head. "No. I need to be here. If the worst happens, I want to be here."

Chantel left Alfredo and hurried through the crowd of men. She saw several other women gathered—friends she knew who would also pray. "My father and Dante Calarco's father are working to free Dante from a sinkhole. You must pray," she told them. "They will need to set off an explosion."

Mrs. Nardozzi nodded. "We will pray, Chantel. Tell your mama we will pray."

"Mama doesn't know anything about this. Marco was . . . killed last night." Several of the women gasped and covered their mouths with their hands. Anna Nardozzi reached out to grasp Chantel's hand. "He was beaten to death, but we don't know who did it. The doctor gave Mama laudanum to help her sleep. She doesn't need to know about this until it's over and done with. I was just heading home to let Mrs. Barbato know what's happened. She's there now with Mama."

"We will pray for your mama, as well," Anna replied. "Won't we?" She looked to the other women. They nodded and closed in around Chantel.

"We will," one of the women said, patting Chantel on the back.

"I have to hurry. They'll soon be setting the charge, and I want to be here . . . no matter the outcome." Chantel broke away from the group of women and continued her race against the clock.

At the house, Nonna Barbato sat knitting in the front room. She looked up with a smile when Chantel burst through the door. Chantel flew to the older woman and knelt at her side.

Breathless, she related what had happened as best she could.

"I knew you would want to be praying."

Nonna paled at the news. "I have been praying. I didn't need to know who the men involved were. I only knew that prayer would be the only thing I could offer."

"I'm so afraid," Chantel admitted. "I do believe in God's power to make this right—to save them from further harm . . . from death. But Nonna, what if . . . what if . . ." She couldn't say the words.

"What if it is God's will that they die?"

Chantel met the older woman's eyes and nodded slowly. "What if it is?"

"Then God will also make provision for our loss and grief. We cannot know when a man's appointed time might come. Your brother Marco could not realize that when he walked home he would be killed. We live in a world full of evil, Chantel, and bad things will happen. Jesus said there would be many trials and troubles. We must have faith, however."

"I don't think I could bear it if Papa and Dante were taken from us." Tears began to drip onto her cheeks. "Oh, Nonna, I can't lose them. I just can't."

"There, there." Nonna touched Chantel's damp cheek. "We mustn't speak as foolish women. We will ask God for His help with confidence and trust in Him. No matter what happens, Chantel, God is still in control. He won't abandon us."

"No," Chantel acknowledged, "but bad things still happen, Nonna. You and I know that. Marco died, though I prayed for him. Bad things happen all the time."

She gave a sympathetic smile. "Yes, they do. Do you remember Job in the Bible? He had bad times come to him. He lost everything he had, with exception to a wife who told him to curse God and die. But Job trusted God and knew that God had given him all that he had, and that God had the power and right to take it away. But through it all, the Bible says that Job did not sin, nor did he charge God foolishly."

She had known the story of Job since she was a little girl, but Chantel couldn't say she truly understood it. After all, God could have prevented all of the bad from happening to Job, and yet He hadn't.

"Job perplexes me," Chantel admitted. Realizing the time was getting away from her, Chantel decided the conversation could wait. "Nonna, I need to get back. I want to be there when they bring Dante out."

The older woman nodded. "I will be praying. Just remember, Chantel: God is still God even when all hope seems lost and nothing in the world is going our way. He may not always do things as we think He should, but He is perfect and holy and His ways are, as well. As Job said, 'The Lord gave and the Lord hath taken away.'"

"Blessed be the name of the Lord," Chantel murmured.

Giovanni Panetta was uncertain this rescue could work, but he felt it necessary to try. He knew his daughter dearly loved this man. He knew as well that Dante Calarco loved his daughter. A man could not want for more than a successful marriage for his children and God's blessing on their future. Now as he studied the depth of the sinkhole and Dante's barely visible head and shoulders, Giovanni pushed aside a wave of doubt. He could fear that this might never work, or he could remain positive and trust God to intercede on their behalf.

"Are you ready?" the mine foreman asked his men.

"We've got the rope tied fast to Panetta," one man declared. "We've secured it to the winch. He won't get away from us."

Giovanni nodded and answered in heavily accented English. "Has Calarco set the charge?"

"It's set, and he's awaiting our go-ahead. The boys and I will lower you down. You secure the rope around Dante, and when you're ready, let me know, and we'll pull you back up."

"No," Giovanni declared. "That boy may need my help. I will stay with him. When the charge goes off, pull us both up. There's only gonna be one chance."

The foreman frowned. "Are you sure that's the best way to go about this?"

"I'm sure. He's unconscious and cannot help himself."

The foreman considered the matter a moment, then turned to the other miners. "All right, this is how we're going to do it."

With everyone duly instructed, Giovanni was lowered into the sinkhole. He was careful to avoid disturbing the sides, but rock still came loose, tumbling below and hitting Dante. Giovanni cringed with each release of debris. The poor man. If he hadn't been killed already, he could still be mortally wounded by the falling rock before they could pull him from the pit.

When Panetta finally reached Dante, he realized that the man was still alive, but barely able to breathe. Giovanni hurried to secure the rope, but it was impossible to get the coil around Dante. Part of his shoulder was exposed, but his arms were buried.

"This won't work," he called up. "I cannot get the rope around him. I'll have to pull him out myself and hold on to him. When the blast comes, just pull me with all of your might."

"Panetta, we could lose you both that way. Are you sure this is how you want it to be?" the foreman called down.

"Just do what I say."

Giovanni moved several larger pieces of rock and was able to get a better hold on Dante's shirt. "Go ahead and tell Vittorio we're ready."

They gave the signal and waited for the men to call up that the fuse had been lit. Giovanni prayed silently and thought of his wife and children.

"The fuse is set, it'll take about ten seconds," the foreman called.

Giovanni tightened his hold and counted backward. "Nine . . . eight . . . seven . . . six . . ." He closed his eyes, tucked his head closer to Dante's, and held fast.

The charge went off seconds later, and in a flash the rock moved all around Giovanni. He pulled hard against the sucking force crushing Dante's body. His right hand slipped and Giovanni fought to regain a hold. He buried his hand in the younger man's hair and held fast as the miners above him worked to pull both men upward.

It wasn't until he felt someone's hand on his ankle that Giovanni opened his eyes. Dante's body was free and hung limply from where Panetta held him fast. The miners worked quickly to take Dante from Giovanni.

"You're bleeding," the foreman told him.

Giovanni reached up and felt the warm wetness. "I'm fine. See to the boy."

"We'll see to you both," the foreman insisted. "Take Panetta on the other stretcher."

"No, I'll walk. I'm not gonna scare my daughter that way. She's already beside herself." Giovanni pushed away from the foreman and looked to where they were securing Dante on a stretcher.

By the time they moved out of the drift to a larger area of the shaft, Vittorio Calarco had joined them. He stood beside the still body of his son, watching and waiting. Giovanni put his hand on the man's shoulder.

Vittorio met his gaze, but said nothing. He didn't need to. Giovanni could see the anguish and gratitude in the other man's expression.

Chantel heard someone exclaim that the men were coming up from the shaft. She held all the tighter to Alfredo's arm, praying that

God would keep any real harm from befalling the men she loved.

By the time the first of the miners appeared, she was very nearly beside herself. Of all the things in life that she wished she could fix, this one eluded her in every way. There was nothing she could do to right this situation. Prayer was all that she had to offer.

Father, I know I'm a weak woman when it comes to trust. I want to be steadfast, but sometimes I am not. Please help me. Let me keep my trust in you, no matter what this day delivers.

"There's the stretcher," someone in the crowd called. "They must have got him free."

Chantel let go of Alfredo and pushed through the gathering of men. She saw Dante's bloodied face and forced herself to be strong. The caked-on dirt and blood against the grayish pallor of his skin made her wonder only momentarily if he might already be dead.

They cover the faces of the dead, don't they? He must be alive, or they would have hidden him from view.

She reached his side and touched his cheek as the men maneuvered the stretcher onto the back of a buckboard. His face was icy cold. Fighting back tears, Chantel looked to one of the miners who'd carried him out.

"I'm going with him," she told him.

He didn't argue, but lifted her into the wagon beside the stretcher.

Chantel saw her father and Mr. Calarco approach. She could see that her father was bleeding. "Papa?"

He smiled and whispered in Italian, "I'm not hurt all that bad. Don't be worried."

"We've room for you both," the driver called. "Climb aboard, and we'll head over to Dr. Shipman's."

She lifted the edge of her skirt and spit on the hem, dampening the material just enough to wipe some of the blood from Dante's face. It didn't help all that much, but doing something rather than nothing made Chantel feel as though she had helped.

When Chantel glanced up, she found Mr. Calarco watching her quite intently. She had no way of knowing if Dante had managed to tell his father of their engagement. She had no way of knowing if her father's gesture of sacrifice had softened the man's heart. She could only pray it had, and pray that Calarco would find her worthy of loving his son.

Chapter 27

Chantel waited impatiently while Dr. Shipman and one of his nurses took charge of
Dante's still-unconscious form. They allowed
Vittorio Calarco to accompany them, but
no one else. Though this grieved Chantel,
she understood. *I'd only be in the way.* She
twisted her hands together and tried to calm
her nerves.

With her father's minor wounds treated,
Chantel thanked him for what he had done.
"Papa, there are no words for what I want
to say. I love you so much, and to know that
you would risk your life for the man I hope
to marry . . . well . . . I just don't know what
to say."

He hugged her close. "I understand. No
words are needed." He held her tight. "I
know you love him dearly. I can see it in
your eyes, just as I could see his love for you
in his. It is the same kind of love I hold for
your mama."

"Oh," Chantel put her hand to her mouth.
"Someone should go to Nonna Barbato and

let her know what has happened. She'll want to be here."

Papa nodded. "Will you be all right if I go?"

She nodded and withdrew from his arms. "I will be fine. It's better that you get Dante's grandmother. If he doesn't . . . if it's really bad . . ." She still couldn't bring herself to say it. Not long ago she'd stood in this very room only to hear that her brother was dead. Chantel knew full well she couldn't bear to hear similar news regarding Dante.

"I will go, then. I will bring her back." He kissed her on the forehead and left without further ado. Chantel began to pace the room, feeling terribly alone.

Glancing toward the ceiling, Chantel sought God's comfort. "I need you, Lord. I cannot bear this by myself. Please, Father . . . please save Dante. Let him be all right."

The waiting seemed to drag on and on, and after nearly twenty minutes there was still no word from the doctor. Nonna Barbato arrived with Papa, but he had quickly returned to the house so that Mama wouldn't be alone.

"We will bear this together," Nonna told Chantel. "Together with our precious Savior." She took hold of Chantel's hand, and together they sat and waited for news.

The mine captain showed up some ten minutes later to get a report on the situation. He was sympathetic and kind, but his words felt hollow, giving little comfort to Chantel.

"He's a good, strong man," the captain said. "I'm sure he'll pull through this." He smiled at Chantel. "Your father was quite heroic to go in after him. You should be proud."

"Of course I'm proud," Chantel replied. "I've always been proud of my father . . . my brothers, too."

The captain nodded. "I was sure sorry to hear about Marco. He was one of my best workers. Have they found out who killed him?"

Chantel shook her head. "My brother Alfredo intends to learn the truth . . . but I fear it may cost him his life, as well."

The captain frowned. "I hope he won't do anything foolish to further grieve your folks."

"He's determined to find the men responsible," Chantel replied. "I can only imagine the harm that might befall him in doing so."

"But our heavenly Father, He can protect," Nonna interjected in English, then switched to native Italian. "Just as He has protected my Dante. You'll see. Our Father will provide all that we have need of—including answers."

The captain shrugged in confusion. Chantel could see he hadn't been able to follow Nonna's Italian. She quickly translated for the man.

He shook his head. "I've not known God to worry overmuch about giving me answers, but I do know how the determination of a man can work to his benefit. Alfredo will want a reckoning for what's happened to his brother. That will be enough to get the answers."

Nonna waggled her finger at the mining captain and again rattled off a rebuke in Italian. Chantel turned to the man and repeated the older woman's words. "God alone will reveal the hidden things. You might not have answers from Him because you do not think to ask. I have put Dante and all that has happened into God's hands. He will provide for our needs."

Dante opened his eyes, and a white-hot stab of pain flashed through his head. He couldn't keep from moaning aloud and tried to raise his hand to his head. Dante's arm refused to obey as weakness washed over his entire body.

"Don't try to move, son," a voice commanded gently.

Dante fought against his blurry vision to make out the features of Dr. Shipman.

"What . . . happened?"

"There was an accident at the mine." This time the voice came from his father. Dante turned his head slightly to the left and located the older man. He blinked hard to clear his vision.

"You stepped into a sinkhole," his father explained. "You were pulled down. Very nearly killed."

Dante tried to remember the accident, but he had no memory of it. The last thing he remembered was trying to speak to his father. He had wanted to tell him something, but for the life of him, Dante didn't know what it was.

"Giovanni Panetta saved your life," Papa continued. "He pulled you out after I set another charge to dislodge the rock."

"A Panetta helped a Calarco?" he asked, barely able to voice the question.

His father shrugged. "Miracles do happen."

Dante smiled and attempted to nod. The pain in his head stilled his actions. He closed his eyes, and when he reopened them, the doctor was standing directly over him.

"I believe you have several broken ribs, but it doesn't appear they've punctured your lungs as I originally feared. Other than that, you have a broken collarbone and a concussion with multiple contusions and lacerations. It will be best for you to remain completely still."

"I believe you," Dante whispered. "Does Chantel know?"

His father spoke up. "She's waiting in the other room."

"Let her know . . . I'm alive." He closed his eyes and grimaced from the pain.

"I will, but first you need to know something, son." He touched Dante's hand.

Dante opened his eyes again. "What is it?"

His father frowned. "I was a fool. I treated you wrong."

Was Papa truly repenting or was this all a dream?

"I was wrong to hold on to my grudge. You were right about ending the feud, and Giovanni . . . well . . . he made me see what a stubborn fool I'd been. Almost losing you made me realize . . . well . . . I love you, son. I was wrong to send you from me. I was wrong to disown your brother. I guess I've been wrong about a great many things."

Dante could see the sincerity in his father's eyes and hear it in his voice. His father had never been a man of apologies, and Dante knew the words hadn't come easy. He risked complicating the situation. "I'm in love with Chantel Panetta."

His father nodded. "It's just as well, because that little girl loves you dearly. She's not been willing to leave your side until the doctor forced her to wait outside."

"I didn't intend to fall in love."

The older man chuckled. "I didn't intend to fall in love with your mama, but she wrapped me around her little finger with a single look. I was never the same after that."

"She's a good woman, Papa."

He chuckled again. "For a Panetta?"

Dante felt his strength fade even more. He was so tired. "I hope you won't mind another Panetta in the family."

His father's expression became serious. "I prayed while you were trapped. I haven't prayed in years, but I prayed then. I told God that I would give anything for your protection and recovery. The one thing He wanted from me was to end the feud and forgive the past wrongs. I intend to hold up my end and bury the past, rather than a son."

Dante let out a pain-filled breath and smiled. "Thank you, Papa. I don't think you'll ever be sorry."

"I need to clean and stitch this gash in your head now," Dr. Shipman interrupted. Dante saw a blurred image of the doctor holding up something. "It won't be pleasant, so I want you to drink this. It will ease the pain."

"I'll go speak to your Chantel," his father declared. He gave Dante's hand a squeeze and was gone.

Dante fought back waves of pain and nausea as the doctor helped to lift his head. He drank the bitter liquid, feeling it burn slightly as it trickled down the back of his throat. The doctor lowered Dante back to the table. "That should take effect rather quickly."

"Was anyone else hurt?" Dante asked as the doctor began scrubbing the wound. The pain was blinding, but Dante did his best to focus on other things.

"Mr. Panetta was banged up a bit, but nothing all that bad. You're lucky to be alive. You know that, don't you?"

Dante tried to smile. "My nonna would say that luck had nothing to do with it."

"In this case, I believe she would be correct," the doctor replied. "You were clearly in greater hands. Your father told me you were mere inches from being buried alive. Obviously God has another purpose for you."

"Chantel," Dante whispered the name.

"As soon as I finish up with you here, I'll allow her to see you, but right now we have work to do."

When Mr. Calarco appeared in the waiting room, Chantel felt the wind go out from her. She gripped the back of the nearest chair to keep from collapsing to the ground. Nonna Barbato got to her feet and went to her son-in-law.

"How is our Dante?"

"He'll survive," Calarco declared.

Chantel forced herself to take in a deep breath. He was alive. He would live. She looked up to find Calarco and Nonna watching her.

"You aren't gonna faint, are you?" Dante's father asked.

She shook her head, but took a seat nevertheless. "Is he conscious?"

"Sí, and the doctor, he is stitching up his head." Mr. Calarco came to where Chantel sat and squatted down beside her. "Dante asked me to let you know that he's all right. He told me, too, that you plan to marry him."

Chantel nodded and could see by the look in the older man's eyes that a miracle had taken place. Not only was Dante going to live, but Mr. Calarco had obviously come to terms with the Panettas being a part of his life.

"I love him so very much," she said in a near-whisper.

Mr. Calarco nodded. "Brothers married to

sisters. It will make for a very close family, no?"

"That is my hope," Chantel replied. "There's nothing quite so important as family."

He smiled. "I agree. Of course, there's a good number of Calarcos who won't agree with this blend of families."

Chantel shrugged. "Then they'll just miss out on the best of what each family has to offer, because I intend to have a great many children with Dante, and I'm sure Isabella feels the same way about Orlando. We will bring the Panettas and Calarcos together in such a blessed way that no one will ever again feud over mules or women or anything else."

Nonna laughed. "Ah, you paint such a pretty picture, but you forget one thing."

Chantel frowned. "What? What did I forget?"

"We are Italian," Nonna reminded and laughed all the more. Chantel joined in, a sense of relief flooding over her.

Nearly an hour later, the doctor honored his word and allowed Chantel to visit Dante's bedside. "You can only stay a few minutes," he instructed. "Mr. Calarco is weak and needs to rest."

Dante looked up into Chantel's face and saw her worried expression. "Don't look at me like that. I'm not going to die."

"I thought I might have already lost you," she murmured.

"You promised to marry me—you aren't getting off that easy."

She smiled for the first time since entering the room. "I thought perhaps now you would have changed your mind."

Dante gave the slightest shake of his head. "Nope. I'm gonna marry you, Chantel Panetta. There's no changing that."

"And when do you plan to do this thing?"

"Well, I have to buy a ring," he said, feeling groggy from the medication he'd been given. "And you'll need to talk to Father Buh."

"And you'll need to fully recover," the doctor interjected.

Chantel nodded. "I'll see to that, Dr. Shipman. Calarcos are known for their stubbornness, but I'll see to it that he obeys. He won't be allowed to do anything unless you approve."

Dante looked at her in amusement. "Calarcos aren't the only stubborn ones, Doc. Don't even try to come up against a Panetta. They are fixed in their ways and quite unyielding. There's no end to what they'll do to get their own way."

Dr. Shipman chuckled. "Well, for once I'm

glad for someone's obstinate ways. It will only serve to aid in your healing."

Four weeks later, Dante was still being pampered and looked after as if he were an invalid. His ribs felt completely healed, but his collarbone still caused him some discomfort. The head wound ached for nearly two weeks, but now even that had subsided and bothered him only occasionally. Being unable to work at the mine had helped Dante to realize that he was ready to find another means of supporting himself. While speaking with his father, he realized Papa was also tired of mining work.

"There are other ways to use explosives," his father suggested. "Perhaps we can explore those methods and move away from this particular line of work."

"I agree," Dante replied. "I know Chantel would be happy for that."

"And a warmer climate would help your nonna."

"That's also true." Dante flexed his arm and felt a dull ache in his neck and upper arm.

A knock at the open front door drew their attention. Nonna got up and admitted Chantel to their company. "Come, come. We were just speaking about the future."

Chantel met Dante's gaze and smiled. He felt a longing to hold her in his arms—to kiss her lips. They were to marry in two weeks, and it couldn't come soon enough as far as he was concerned.

"There's good news," Chantel declared. "One of the men responsible for beating up Marco has confessed. He made a deal of sorts so that he wouldn't be hanged. He's going to testify against Leo Fortino. Leo was the one who set up the entire thing. He wanted Marco not only beaten, but dead. Leo has been arrested, and the constable said it seems almost certain he will be found guilty and hanged instead of jailed."

"That is good news," Dante said, patting the sofa seat next to him.

Chantel strode toward him, her lightweight green gown rustling in a most alluring fashion as she crossed the room. She sat down carefully and adjusted her skirt. "It won't bring Marco back," she said, looking at the trio, "but Mama said she will be able to rest now, knowing that his killer has been called to pay for his crimes."

"She's right, it won't bring him back," Nonna said, nodding. "Very little can fill the void of losing a child, but in time the Lord will ease that emptiness and fill it with good memories of the love between a mother and her son."

Dante took hold of Chantel's hand and pressed a kiss on her fingers. "Enough sad talk. Tell me, have you finished making your wedding gown?"

Chantel's expression changed from solemnity to pure delight. "We are putting on the last pieces of Chantilly lace tonight."

"But I thought Chantilly lace was usually black. Surely you aren't having black lace on a wedding gown, are you?" Dante asked.

"Of course not, silly. Mama made some beautiful ivory lace years ago. She made some for each of us girls, but of course Isabella eloped—though she did use just a little of her lace for her wedding gown. She's saving the rest for a baby gown."

"They're going to have a baby?" Dante asked in surprise.

"Well, not just yet," Chantel replied. "But when the time comes, that's what she plans for her lace."

Dante grinned. "Maybe we can still beat them in starting a family."

Chantel felt her cheeks grow hot as Dante's father chuckled. Even Nonna was fighting to suppress her amusement. "I didn't know we were having a race," she replied, feeling rather awkward.

Dante hugged her close. "Orlando and I have always been in competition. He married first and it grieved me. I'm the elder brother, and I should have been the first to wed."

"Well, in two weeks you will wed me." Chantel lifted her face to his. The joy in her expression melted his heart. "And if God so wills it, I will give you a child before Isabella can do so for your brother."

"But even if you don't," Dante said, cupping her chin in his hand, "I will have you, and that's more than I could have ever hoped for."

Chapter 28

Italian custom held that a Sunday in June was the best possible day to marry, and so Dante and Chantel set their wedding for the twenty-first of June. Although Chantel had decided the wedding would be a simple affair, there were still many traditions to uphold.

With her veil carefully in place and the beautifully crafted wedding gown displaying her figure to perfection, Chantel met Dante on the street just outside their house. He looked quite regal in his dark suit. Chantel met his gaze with a smile.

"Are you sure that's you in there, Chantel?" he asked, trying to peek through the lacy veil.

"You'll just have to wait and see," she teased.

He took hold of her hand. "Are you ready for our walk to church?"

"I am." She glanced behind her to make sure that Isabella and Orlando were following. "Issy has my bouquet, and I presume Orlando has the rings."

"Rings? Were we supposed to have rings?" Dante asked, sounding surprised.

Chantel had grown used to his teasing. She shrugged. "I suppose we don't have to have them. In fact, I suppose we can call this whole thing off."

"Ha!" Dante tightened his hold on her. "I've waited too long as it is. Besides . . ." He paused and held up a piece of iron ore. "I have my lucky piece of iron, so you cannot run away. My father assured me that this tradition held strong merit, because if you try to leave me, I can simply throw it at you."

"I would never try to leave you," she assured.

He put the piece back in his pocket. "See, the luck works."

She smiled behind the veil, knowing she was going to have a life of laughter and happiness in the company of this man. They moved off down the street to face the customary obstacles laid in their path by friends.

The first thing they came to was a broom. Chantel picked it up and gave a little sweep. "Ah, she'll be a good housekeeper," one of the women lining the street called out.

"She'll have to be," Dante replied. "I'm quite a pig." This elicited laughter from the crowd.

Chantel was unconcerned. "Nonna Barbato

told me that you're already trained to leave your boots off at the door. We'll continue that tradition in our own home."

"Of course, my little wife."

He led her on down the road toward the church, only to find someone had placed a perambulator in their way. Inside, a very unhappy infant cried. Chantel stepped forward and lifted the infant into her arms. The baby reached for her veil, but Chantel managed to keep the child from pulling it from her head. As the infant continued to cry in her arms, Chantel produced a sugar cube she'd hidden in her sleeve for just such an occasion. She touched the sugar to the baby's lips and the crying ceased.

The crowd howled with cheers and delighted laughter. "What a good mama she'll be," an old woman declared.

The baby's mother came to relieve Chantel of the child and gave Dante a wink. "May you have a dozen."

He laughed and thanked the woman before leaning over to whisper in Chantel's ear, "Do you think a dozen will be enough?"

"To start us off," Chantel replied, unfazed.

Dante roared and apparently the viewers understood the situation, for they joined heartily in the laughter.

The next obstacle was one for Dante. There

were coins strewn on the dirt road, and he bent to retrieve each one. Once collected, he handed them to Chantel, who placed them in a little white silk bag.

"He will be a good provider," several men said in unison. Again cheers went up.

There were several other impediments that suggested Chantel would be a good cook and seamstress, and that Dante would remain strong. Just before they reached the church, they were required to saw a log in two using a double-handled saw. This would prove their ability to work together.

Having met all of the requirements, Chantel took her bouquet from Isabella and allowed Dante to lead her into the church. A stream of friends and family followed behind the happy couple. While the congregation took their places, Dante escorted his bride to the altar, where the ceremony began with Father Buh's prayers.

Chantel thought she might well burst from joy, and she reveled in the moment. She had never thought it possible to love anyone as much as she loved this man. *This man who was my enemy not so long ago.*

They recited their vows, pledging before God and man that they would remain faithful through adversity. And Chantel knew adversity would come. Just as Nonna Barbato had reminded her of in Job, life was full of problems and trials. It would be her duty to keep her eyes on God.

With Dante at my side, there is nothing I cannot face.

Father Buh motioned them forward, urging Dante and Chantel to each hold a lighted candle. "These candles represent two families—the Panettas and the Calarcos," the priest declared. "And now they become one family in the eyes of man—one flesh in the eyes of God."

Chantel and Dante lifted their candles and together lit a third candle. Chantel couldn't halt the tears that spilled onto her cheeks. She remembered how the longstanding feud had separated Nonna from her dear friend and prayed that somehow the two women might be rejoined in more than secret letters.

Father Buh called for the wedding rings and blessed them before handing them to Dante and Chantel. Chantel smiled at the simple gold band Dante held. This would be her only jewelry today—most days. It symbolized their eternal love for one another, and inside the ring Chantel knew Dante had the engraver mark her ring with his name and the date of the wedding, while her name was engraved inside of his.

Dante's voice was strong and unfaltering as

he slipped the ring on her finger. "With this ring, I thee wed." He lifted her hand to his lips and sealed the ring with a kiss.

Chantel bit her lower lip to keep from crying even more at the happiness of it all. She barely managed to speak her vows and place Dante's ring on his finger. Following his gesture, she kissed his band and finger.

Father Buh had more to say, but Chantel barely heard the words. She could think of nothing but Dante's hold on her hand. *He's my husband now. I am my beloved's and he is mine.*

When Dante lifted her wedding veil and gazed upon her face for the first time that day, his dark eyes seemed to drink her in before he covered her lips with his own and sealed their marriage with a kiss.

The priest offered a final blessing, and before Chantel even knew what was happening, Dante quickly whisked her down the aisle and out of the church, where a small carriage and driver awaited them.

At their small house just off of Central and Harvey Streets, the carriage driver brought the horse to a stop and waited while Dante lifted Chantel from the carriage. He barely let her feet touch the ground before he whisked

her into his arms and carried her up the walkway. At the door, he held her with one arm
and turned the handle with his free hand.

"Welcome home, Mrs. Calarco," he said,
gazing deep into her eyes. It was all he could
do to believe this wasn't a dream. When she
touched his cheek, Dante felt the warmth of
her hand and smiled. It was all very real.

"May it be a place of love and godly wisdom," she whispered.

He kissed her ever so briefly once they were
across the threshold and gently lowered her to
the ground. Chantel wrapped her arms around
him and hugged him close. Dante felt flush
with a desire that he had been most careful to
put aside until this day. Waiting to be alone
with her—to hold her, to touch her—had been
almost painful to him.

Without another word, he lifted her into his
arms once again. Their waiting had come to
an end.

Hours later, Chantel and Dante arrived at
the traditional wedding feast. In the hours of
celebration that followed, Chantel laughed
and shared dances with her father, brother,
and many other men before Dante finally
reclaimed her and announced it was time to

put an end to the festivities. After fourteen courses of food, dozens of offered toasts and blessings, and hours of dancing, Chantel was more than ready to agree. Her feet ached, and weariness threatened to leave her sleeping in her husband's arms.

"Come, my lovely lady," he said, reaching for her hand.

The well-wishers gave the couple one last set of cheers before Dante once again helped Chantel into the waiting carriage for the drive back to their little house. With the night stars shining down upon them and a full moon overhead, she thought it the most beautiful night of her life.

"I'll always remember this moment—this feeling," she told Dante, laying her head upon his shoulder.

"And what feeling is that, my love?"

"Safety. Joy. Peace. Wonder. And the assurance of a blessed future."

He laughed. "That's a great many feelings."

She raised her head to meet his gaze. "No. It's really just one. It's the love we share. The love I hold for you—the love you hold for me."

He smiled and cupped her chin with his warm fingers. "And the love we have in God."

Tracie Peterson is the author of more than ninety novels, both historical and contemporary. Her avid research resonates in her stories, as seen in her bestselling HEIRS OF MONTANA and STRIKING A MATCH series. Tracie and her family make their home in Montana.

Visit Tracie's Web site at *www.traciepeterson.com*.

More Adventures in the LAND OF SHINING WATER Series!

For more on Tracie Peterson and her books, visit traciepeterson.com.

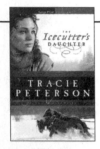

Merrill Krause promised her dying mother she would take care of her father and brothers, but she longs to start a family of her own. Could newcomer Rurik Jorgenson be the man she's been waiting for—or will the arrival of Rurik's former fiancée shatter their chance at love?

The Icecutter's Daughter

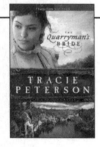

Emmalyne Knox has always loved Tavin MacLachlan, but she gave up her plans to marry Tavin when her father revoked his blessing. Years later Emmalyne and Tavin cross paths once again and find the feelings between them are as strong as ever. Can Emmalyne dare to dream that God could heal a decade-long wound and change the hearts of those keeping them apart?

The Quarryman's Bride

More From Bestselling Author Tracie Peterson

In the years following the Civil War, loyalties in the Lone Star State remain divided. Amidst the bitter prejudices and harsh landscape of the Texan plains, is there any hope that the first blush of love can survive?

LAND OF THE LONE STAR: *Chasing the Sun, Touching the Sky, Taming the Wind*

As the lives of three women are shaped by the untamed Alaskan frontier, they find it's a land of heartbreak and healing—and romance and adventure.

SONG OF ALASKA: *Dawn's Prelude, Morning's Refrain, Twilight's Serenade*